# A LABYRINTH OF SECRETS

GLYNNIS HAYWARD

**CONSTANTIA PRESS**
Los Gatos, California

For further information, write Constantia Press
constantiapress@gmail.com

Library of Congress Control Number: 2023950665

# A LABYRINTH OF SECRETS

GLYNNIS HAYWARD

# PART 1

# JOANNA

*The cruelest lies are*
*often told in silence.*

—R L STEVENSON

# CHAPTER 1

"It's just hormones and lust, that's all—doomed to fail. Hormones and lust," he insisted. "I'm telling you, romantic love is nonsense. It doesn't make a marriage work."

My father almost spat out these words, forcing me to listen as he described the marriage he'd planned for me—and no matter how much I tried to ignore him, his words echoed in my head, making me shiver: *Romantic love is just hormones and lust.*

He hardly drew breath as he continued his lecture. "In the old days, parents guided their children to make important decisions. But now kids get married for this thing they call love—and before long, they get divorced."

God, I wanted to vomit. He expected me to accept a proposal of marriage from Marius Abrahams, his best friend's son. Marius is forty and I'm twenty-one. The guy's a dried-out piece of old biltong who happens to have lots of money. Well, I don't care. I don't want to talk to him let alone marry him, but my dad is desperate for a son to carry on his business. It's not worth arguing with my father though; he just flies into a rage. Best to keep quiet and let him drone on about the virtues of arranged marriages, without any intention of complying with his demands.

"Love can develop afterwards if that's what you want, but marriage is a working arrangement. Look at your sisters, Esther and Emma; they're good examples of what

I'm telling you. They're both happily married and I was the one who found husbands for them. Don't worry, you don't have to give an immediate answer. Finish your exams first. Marius understands that you're busy and he's impressed that you're getting a degree. He's happy to wait a few weeks." He paused, waiting for me to say something. When I remained frozen, he added another factor for me to consider. "Look at your mother and me; our marriage was also arranged—and here we are, still together."

I turned my head and rolled my eyes. If ever there was an example of an unhappy marriage, theirs was it. I'd seen my mother with many a black eye—no love had ever developed there. In that instant, I decided that I would leave as soon as I'd finished my exams in three weeks' time, or before that if necessary. With a degree, I could get a job and be financially independent. I'd leave Cape Town if I had to.

My mom said nothing while all this went on, but later she came to my room and whispered something about a vague plan to get me away. Her voice was so soft I could hardly hear her when she took my hands in hers and said, "He's wrong, liefling. Romantic love is the most important ingredient in marriage. If you don't have it, there'll always be something missing. It's the foundation you need to build on. Love doesn't always grow if it isn't there to start with. Sometimes the opposite happens."

For the remaining weeks I had left at UCT, my mother reassured me every day that things were falling into place and I had nothing to worry about. I wanted to believe her, but as she wouldn't elaborate, I had my own plan in place. With very little money, I arranged to stay with a friend until I found a job. So, the moment I handed in my last test paper, I grabbed my backpack, shot out of the exam room, and headed home to grab my stuff. With no plan yet revealed by my mom, I needed to be in and out of the house before my father returned from work. I wasn't taking any chances.

I didn't make it home. My mother was waiting at the bus stop at 3 o'clock. She grabbed me as soon as I climbed off the bus and tugged my arm. "Hurry, Joanna. You must come with me." When I resisted, she said again with more urgency, "Come on. Hurry up."

"What are you doing? What's going on?"

"I'll tell you in the car. It's parked around the corner. Hurry. There's no time to waste."

"Wait. I need to grab my things from the house."

"No. There's no time. Come…"

"Mom, I want to get my stuff."

"I'm telling you, there's no time. Trust me, please. Don't argue. Just come…"

My mother was acting like a crazy woman as she pushed me into the passenger seat and slammed the door shut. She took off at speed, saying, "I'll explain soon, but we need to get away before he gets home; he's invited Marius and his father, Hendrik, to dinner tonight. Sorry, I can't tell you more now, I need to concentrate on where I'm going; I haven't been there before."

I was fuming. What the hell was she up to? I wanted my stuff, dammit, but when I complained, she ignored me and sped up. Neither of us said a word after that for the next thirty minutes until we passed through some iron gates—the entrance to a residential complex. As soon as she'd parked the car and switched off the engine, she turned to look at me and took a deep breath. It wasn't a hot day, yet I could see she was sweating copiously as she started to speak.

"I have a lot of explaining to do and not much time to do it."

"Yes, you bloody well do. What the heck is going on? Where are we? What's happening?"

"My liefling," she began, "things are not what they've seemed all these years. What I'm about to tell you has been a terrible secret I've kept from you—from everyone."

"What are you talking about?"

She closed her eyes and kept them tightly shut. I could see that she was trembling as she spoke. "August Nel is my husband." Then she swallowed hard before blurting out, "He is Esther and Emma's father—but he's not yours."

"What?"

Her eyes shot open with a look of panic as she grabbed my hands. "August doesn't know that. He mustn't know it. He's a dangerous man. Who knows what he would do if he found out?" She swallowed hard again and I could feel her hands shaking. "Your birth father lives here, in this house. That's why I've brought you here." Her words were coming out in short, nervous bursts. "His name is Tom Montgomery. We worked together once upon a time. We were both married, but we fell in love...we couldn't help ourselves. It's no excuse, I know; what we did was wrong. I really loved him and he loved me. I know he did. He was kind and gentle, so different from..." Her voice trailed off.

Feeling as if I'd been punched in the chest, I stared at her in disbelief and pulled my hands away from her. When I was able to find words, all I could say was, "My God, I'm twenty-one years old and you're telling me this now for the first time. Why didn't you tell me before?"

"I couldn't. I'm sorry, Joanna. August would've killed me."

"Sorry? That's all you can say? What the hell are you talking about? This is insane." My hearted pounded as I pulled away from her with my hands clenched in tight fists.

"Let me try and explain, Joanna," she said. "I was in a terrible predicament when I discovered I was pregnant with you. Apartheid had come to an end, so Tom and I didn't have to worry about breaking segregation laws any longer—your father is white, you see—but we had spouses to worry about. We'd hidden our affair successfully, but everything changed when I got pregnant. I couldn't hide that."

My anger continued to grow as I absorbed what she was saying. By now, tears were pouring down her face.

"I was terrified. You know how violent August is. You've seen what he's like. I had two little girls I needed to protect, and not only that, he supported my mother financially as well. There was too much to lose if he found out. I had no choice but to end the affair and pretend August was your father. There was nothing else I could do."

It felt like I was listening to somebody else, not my mother. She'd made me live with August Nel, suffering his abuse, when he wasn't even my dad. "So, what did you tell this man, Tom Montgomery?" I muttered.

"Nothing. I couldn't tell him the truth; I couldn't tell him anything. Nobody knew my secret. I broke it off without telling him that I was expecting his baby, and I never saw him again. He never knew I was pregnant. It was only three weeks ago that he discovered he had a daughter—that you are his child. That day when August said he wanted you to marry Marius, I knew I had to get help from your real father even though I was terrified of telling him after all this time. I couldn't let you be forced into a marriage you didn't want."

I continued staring at her in shock, trying to digest this information, realizing that my entire life had been a lie. She'd deceived me—as well as her lover and her husband. Who was this woman I called my mother? Who was I? It was too much to take in. All I could utter was, "My God..."

Her face was drawn when she added, "You see, when August refused to pay your university tuition, I paid for it with my savings. He only agreed because he didn't have to pay anything—but now I don't have any money left to help you. You have to get away and you need money to do that, Joanna; that's why I reached out to Tom. I explained everything to him. Oh, my God, he's so angry with me; I knew he would be. But he didn't hesitate to offer assistance to you. He immediately wanted to know all about you. I doubt he'll ever forgive me—and I can't blame him for that—but he wants to meet you and help you. This is a way out for you, my liefling; it's an escape route." She tried to hold my face between her hands as she spoke. "You have his sparkling brown eyes and his brains. You got very good genes from him. Now he wants to give you his love and support as well."

I pulled away from her, not wanting her to touch me. She quickly withdrew her hands—maybe because she saw my expression change. "I'm so sorry," she said, gulping. "You have no idea how sorry I am. I hope you can forgive me, even though Tom might not. He's not to blame for any of this, he'll try to help you in any way he can. He's waiting to meet you. That's why I've brought you here."

I began to shiver. Anger and resentment welled up inside me as I reached for my backpack; all I wanted was to escape from this nightmare of lies. When I tried to open the door, however, my mother put out a hand to stop me. "Please, Joanna," she pleaded, "I know this is a lot for you to take in, but give your father a chance. Allow him to meet you and let him help you. He wants to do that. Don't let anger cloud your judgment."

"My judgment, did you say? My judgment is very clear. I'm done with all this deceit. I don't care about any of this. I'm out of here."

My mom grabbed my arm and wouldn't let go. "Just give him a chance," she persisted. "None of this is his doing. It's entirely my fault." She wiped her eyes and added, "Listen, my liefling, I packed some of your belongings in a suitcase; they're in the back of the car. Please, go to him. Give him a chance to be a father."

"What are you saying? I hate that man you married and never want to see him again, but do you expect me to just walk away from my sisters? I don't believe this."

She nodded. "Just for now. I'll let your sisters know that you're safe. I can't tell them everything yet, in case August questions them. You know what he's like; he's very forceful."

Despite my anger, I was choking up. "What about you? Will I see you again?"

She tried to smile. "Of course. You'll see me—and your sisters—when it's safe to do so, but we'll have to be careful. He'll be looking for you. You've finished all your classes and exams, so now you can lie low. Don't let him find you."

She continued to hold onto me and I was surprised

by the strength of her grip. I stared at her, feeling myself start to relent as curiosity kicked in. Who was my biological father? What did he look like? What did he do? I think my mom could sense I was weakening when she said, "Liefling, here's the plan I've been making these past three weeks; I bought us each a new phone. Toss out your old one so that August can't trace you, and take this new one. You can transfer all your contacts to it quickly, but don't call any of them until it's safe to do so. He'll be asking questions everywhere, for sure. Maybe it's better still if I take the old one and chuck it out for you. Here, you see, I'll only use this new phone of mine to reach you and that way he'll never know we're in contact with one another, because I'll keep it hidden. He'll check the other phone, my old one, but he won't be able to find anything regarding you.

"And there's something else I'd like you to do, please. I know he'll suspect I have something to do with your disappearance, so I brought this too." She produced a notecard and envelope from her handbag. "Write something, telling us both that you're leaving. It'll be better for me if he thinks I don't know anything about it."

I shouldn't have doubted that she was making a plan. She'd worked it all out and she was right; August Nel would take it out on her if he was suspicious—and although I was angry with her, I didn't want her getting beaten up. I'd seen that happen too many times.

"I can't believe this," I said, snatching the notecard from her and scribbling a message: I won't marry Marius. Don't bother looking for me. Goodbye, Joanna. I addressed it to Mr. and Mrs. August Nel and handed the envelope to her, aware that in just ten minutes my whole world had changed. I wasn't who I thought I was, and my mom wasn't the woman I thought she was.

She interrupted my thoughts. "Before I take your old phone away, is there anyone you need to contact? Did you make any arrangements you need to cancel?" she asked.

"I was going to my friend Shazza's place tonight."

"Text her and say that you're going away for a bit so she doesn't get worried about you." Once again, she had it all worked out. "It's better she knows nothing about any of this. If August tracks her down—or any of your friends—nobody will have to lie."

"Oh, I see. Just me—I have to lie. And you, of course; but everything has been a lie with you." I was glad when I saw her reaction—she gulped and wiped tears from her eyes. I continued to inflict more pain, adding, "Anyway, my friends would never tell your husband anything about me; they know I hate him—and they know why. They know he's a brute. Besides, he doesn't know any of my friends because I never invited any of them home. Why would I? I was embarrassed. What would they think of me? I never wanted any of them to meet that man you live with. What would they think of you?"

My mom flinched, but pointed her hand at my phone, urging me to do as she'd asked. She remained silent while I sent a text and then transferred all my contacts, and as I handed her my old phone, I made a decision—I would meet this man who was my father for interest's sake, and then I would head off. I was not committed to anything, or anyone. I would trust no one but myself and I'd leave behind this lie that had been my life.

# CHAPTER 2

I felt numb as my mother knocked on the imposing front door of a three-story house. The door was opened almost immediately by a tall, silver-haired man who smiled at me—and there I was, standing in front of a complete stranger, my father.

Our eyes met and we stared at each other without saying a word. Embarrassed, I dropped my gaze and looked instead at his hands, noting that he had long fingers that were a bit like mine. It was a strange thing to observe and I'd never felt more awkward in my life. I think he realized this and was trying to put me at ease when he finally spoke. He had a deep voice and said quietly, "Joanna, it's lovely to meet you. Please, come inside."

His eyes strayed from me to my mother and a look passed between them that was hard to interpret—I wouldn't say it was friendly—but despite his invitation, nobody moved. After another awkward silence, it was my mom who spoke next. "I can't stay. I must get back before I'm found out. He has a tracker on my phone. I didn't bring it with me for obvious reasons, but he'll go ballistic if he gets home first and discovers my phone there without me." With that, she attempted to give me a hug, and then she was gone—while I stood alone with my real father for the first time in my life, feeling as if I'd been hit by a bus. I watched my mom drive away and just like that, it was done. A chapter in my life was closed.

My head was spinning as I stepped inside. Tom Montgomery looked as shell-shocked as I felt when he took my suitcase and laid it on a bench in the entrance hall, before ushering me into a spacious sitting room. I followed in silence, thankful that he hadn't rushed to embrace me or anything. I'd only known of his existence for ten minutes, while he'd had at least had three weeks to get used to the idea, since my mom had called him with the news of my existence. I could see he was tense and neither of us seemed to know what to say. Finally, he asked, "Can I offer you some tea or coffee, or maybe something stronger to help you get over the shock?"

"Tea would be nice, thank you."

He laughed. "Ah…she speaks."

His eyes sparkled, just as my mom said they did, and I relaxed a little. Still feeling uncomfortable, though, I said nothing more.

As I followed him into the kitchen, I looked around thinking how my mother would love something like this. It was a huge room. The counter tops were white marble and the cupboards had glass fronts, displaying an array of beautiful china behind them. It had a woman's touch to it. He disappeared into a pantry, emerging with tea bags and biscuits, and I finally found my voice again. "Is your wife here? I presume you're still married."

He cleared his throat and said nothing for a few minutes. I noticed his hand shaking as he poured the tea, but his gaze was steady as he looked at me and replied, "Yes, I'm married, and no, she's not here. She's an antiques dealer. Cynthia is English. She's on a buying trip to the UK at the moment; she'll be away for ten more days. I wasn't sure what would happen, whether you'd want to meet me or not, so I've told her nothing about any of this until we figure out what to do."

I nodded. "Will you tell her then?"

"Of course. It'll be a shock, and I'm sure she won't be happy about my infidelity, but I hope she'll accept that it was in the past. We don't have any children, sadly; I'm hoping she'll accept you as a stepdaughter." I could see him hesitate a moment before he added, "I want you to know that I really loved your mother, Joanna; it wasn't just a one-night stand or anything. But it was complicated and I had to respect her wishes when she ended it, even though she..."

He paused and didn't finish that thought, but took a deep breath before adding, "We've had no contact for nearly twenty-two years, until she called me three weeks ago and we met for coffee. That's when I found out about you." His eyes lost their sparkle for a moment and he looked away, but then he took a gulp of tea and said, "Although Cynthia will understandably be disappointed in me, I'm sure she'll be happy to meet you. I hope you'll consider this your home, if you choose to do so."

We sat on stools in the kitchen drinking our tea, without saying anything more. I relished the silence, but I ached for the comfort of my mom's presence—until my longing was replaced by anger again. To think that the person I'd trusted most in the world had kept this enormous secret from me. By not telling me the truth, she'd lied. In fact, she'd turned my whole life into a lie. As I fought back tears, I could feel Tom Montgomery watching me—I glanced at him and saw the pain in his face too.

"I'm sorry, Joanna," he murmured. "I hate to see your anguish. This has come as a huge shock for both of us. I deeply regret that I've missed out on twenty-one years of your life, but I'm trying to reassure myself that it's not too late to be a father to you. Please give me that opportunity. Tell me what you want to do and I'll try to help."

His concern prompted tears to stream down my face and I looked away. He was so different from August Nel who never gave a damn how I felt. I had no respect for the man who had supposedly been my father, and loathed him even more every time he hit my mother. Now, at least I didn't have to feel guilty about my feelings.

As if he read my thoughts, Tom said, "If I'd known she was pregnant with my child, I would never have let her go. I would've moved heaven and earth to keep both of you. She hid the truth from me and, my God, I resent that deeply. I understand she was protecting your sisters, but I would have taken them too. She knew that. She also knew how much I wanted a child. It was a great sadness to me that I wasn't a father—and now it turns out that all this time, I was one after all." I saw him clench his jaw before adding, "So many lost years… that's something for which I can't forgive her. I've thought about it a lot these past three weeks and it pains me to think of you being raised by that terrible man. I can't believe he was trying to coerce you into marriage."

"Oh, don't worry, there's no way I would've agreed. It wasn't going to happen." There was an awkward silence after that. I watched the undisguised emotion in his face as he nursed his anger. Finally, I said, "What about your wife? What about your marriage?"

He closed his eyes and looked away. "I loved your mother, Joanna," he said simply. "I would've asked for a divorce from Cynthia and married your mom if she'd agreed to it. We could've been happy—a happy family. She denied us that."

I believed him. We had both been cheated.

After a second cup of tea, he carried my suitcase and led me up to the bedroom I would be using on the top floor. It had a bathroom en suite that was bigger than the one we'd all shared at home—at the place that used to be my home.

"You've had a rough day. Relax and make yourself comfortable," he said. "I'm going to do something about dinner. What do you fancy?"

"Just a sandwich would be great, thanks."

"Oh no, we can do better than that on an occasion like this. Not only have you finished your exams, this is our first meal together."

"My exams feel like a lifetime ago already and I've escaped from purgatory. That's a celebration, for sure."

He smiled. "So, what kind of food do you like? I know nothing about you. Maybe we should go out for dinner."

The idea was appealing, but what if someone who knew August saw me? I shook my head and said, "I'm exhausted. Not tonight. Why don't you surprise me? I eat just about anything; the only thing I don't like is broccoli."

"Then you're definitely my daughter. I eat anything you put in front of me except broccoli—and tripe. I don't eat that."

"Oh, I forgot about that. Me neither!"

We both laughed and he said, "I'm looking forward to learning more about you, Joanna. I'm so happy to have you in my life."

The bedroom door closed behind him and I stood alone for the first time that day, with my life packed into one small suitcase. My mother had considered my needs and packed carefully for me. She'd also written a note saying,

"Sleep tight, liefling," and included a photo of the two of us together. On the back she'd written, "Love you."

That did it for me. I sat on the edge of the bed and sobbed.

# CHAPTER 3

After a while, I managed to regain my composure, but I didn't feel ready to face Tom yet. The reality that a chapter of my life had closed and there was no going back was still settling in. Trust had been broken and I felt betrayed. Needing time to think, I stretched out in a warm bath where I could admire the view of Table Mountain through the window. As I did so, I felt myself begin to relax.

*This must be what they call luxury*, I thought. When I pressed a button, bubbles burst out of jets around me; I pressed another button and the jets became pulsating vibrations moving up and down my spine. I could add more hot water by pushing the tap with my toe; this I did when the water cooled. I lay soaking in the bath for at least twenty minutes—that in itself was luxury, not having someone pounding on the door for me to hurry up.

As I watched the cloud—the Table Cloth as my mother called it—drift off Table Mountain, and I saw its familiar flat top reappear, my mind began to clear as well. What became apparent was that I really did need to get away from Cape Town—the danger of being discovered by August was too great if I stayed and who knows what he would do if he found me. I lay there thinking of ways to kill him without being caught, and my forehead grew clammy as my imagination went into overdrive. Poison or a bullet? God, how I wished he were dead. However, my hatred of him was tempered by a couple of things: relief that I didn't share his DNA, and the knowledge that I was out of his clutches at last.

I relished the thought of his fury when he discovered I'd bolted, recognizing that my mom had been wise to cover her tracks—suspicion of her involvement in my escape would have dire consequences for her. Although I was still seething, I admired her cunning.

It was scary to think about leaving Cape Town, yet it was exciting at the same time and when I emerged from the bath, I felt better. With a change of clothes, I made my way downstairs, taking in the details of the house—and as I did so, something else became clear. This place belonged to Cynthia. I was a visitor here. This was not my home. I would never belong here and I didn't want to. I wanted to get away—though I no longer felt a need to rush out the door immediately. This man, my father, seemed worthwhile getting to know. I liked him. I'd stay a while.

When I walked into the kitchen, Tom looked at me and smiled—his eyes were sparkling once more. "You look so much like your mother," he said.

"She said I have your eyes."

"Well, let's see if she's right," he replied, leading me to a mirror in the hallway.

We stood staring at ourselves for a while—I looked at him, and he at me. My mom was right. We agreed that our eyes were exactly the same, but otherwise, not much else—except that we both had square jaws, while my mom's jaw was pointed. She had an oval face. "What color was your hair before you went grey?" I inquired.

"Blonde. My mom was Danish and my dad was

Scottish; they came to South Africa just after I was born. That's your heritage from my side of the family." He laughed and added, "You're a healthy mix, but frankly, I think you're lucky to have inherited your mother's good looks, Joanna."

Dinner was a lot more than I'd expected: grilled chicken peri-peri, fried rice and a green salad, accompanied by a bottle of chenin blanc. As I sipped the wine, I tried to imagine the scene back home with August, Hendrik and Marius—a thought that made me feel even more comfortable being right here.

"I don't really know what to call you," I said.

He shrugged. "Oh, you'll figure it out, along with everything else that needs figuring out. Tom is fine... I'm touched that you were called Joanna, by the way. It was my mother's name. Your mother knew that—we often talked about our parents and our childhoods. I suppose I should be grateful that she had the decency to acknowledge me in some way."

His anger was obvious. My anger was eating at me as well, but to talk about it was uncomfortable. I hesitated a moment before asking, "Wasn't it strange for a White man and a Coloured woman to get together in those days? Nobody cares about it much now, but back then..."

He laughed. "I know we seem old to you, but it wasn't that long ago, Joanna. You know, we never stopped to think about it. And nobody knew about us anyway."

"Well, did you know my mom was a Cape Coloured?"

"I don't recall whether I knew that when I first met her, but it wouldn't have mattered. Skin color is no different than the color of someone's eyes or hair, as far as I'm concerned. I'm sure she told me at some point, but it wasn't an issue for us."

This gave me an opening for another question I wanted to ask. "How did you meet each another?"

He took a sip of wine and smiled. "Where do I begin? Let's see... I'd just started working at Sudar and Green—I'm still there, actually. It's a big clothing company here in Cape Town. I was in sales and marketing, but I'd secretly always wanted to be a photographer. That was a hard road to follow though, with little opportunity or money in it; I needed to do something more lucrative to survive. Part of my job was working with agencies, trying to find models for our new clothing lines. It was frustrating because everyone any agency sent as a photographic model seemed so wooden. Then one day I saw your mother walking past my office and I was gob-smacked. She was just what we were looking for. I couldn't take my eyes off her. I followed her back to her desk to ask whether she would try out at a photo shoot. She was hesitant at first, but she finally agreed and oh man, she was an absolute natural. Her shy demeanor belied the personality that came alive in front of a camera. Everything she put on looked one hundred times better because she was so graceful.

"There were professional photographers doing the shoots, of course, but I made a point of attending as many sessions as I could—partly because I wanted to learn from them, but mainly because I wanted to see more of Petra Nel. She seemed to enjoy me being there—and I loved watching her. I kind of fell in love with her from a distance, I must confess."

I was intrigued to hear this. More than intrigued, I was stunned. It didn't sound at all like my mother. "So, who made the first move?" I asked.

He laughed. "You're full of questions, aren't you? I suppose you have a right to ask them. Let me put it in perspective for you, Joanna. It was 1994, a momentous year in South Africa as you know, when apartheid finally came to an end. The country was full of hope and a competition was offered by the Arts Council to acknowledge the momentous event—the theme of the competition was liberation. Contestants could choose any genre they liked for their entry.

"I'd been mulling over it, wanting to enter a photograph, but not sure quite what to do—until I got inspiration watching this beautiful, quiet woman exploding with life in front of the camera. By now we'd been talking every day; she would give me her ideas about what clothes to put together and how they should be worn. She was right every time and I relied on her judgment, so I felt comfortable asking if she would model for me. It was a big ask and I wasn't sure she'd agree, but she did."

Eager to know what happened next, I felt impatient when he went silent, staring into his glass of wine. After a while he cleared his throat and said, "I rented studio space in an old warehouse where we could work. My God, the photograph we came up with was absolutely brilliant. It was a masterpiece. And it wasn't just me who thought so; it won first prize. It was quite something."

"Wow, Mom never mentioned anything about that!" I exclaimed. "Geez, how many more secrets does she have?"

"Oh, I think I can understand why she said nothing about it," he said, slowly nodding. "I've never produced anything like that again, unfortunately." His jaw tightened and he paused, staring into his glass before he added, "As I told you, I wanted to get a divorce to marry your mother. A few years earlier it wouldn't have been possible, but by then the law forbidding marriage between the races was a thing of the past. We would've been free to live our lives together, openly. She wouldn't do it though, because of her mother and your sisters—at least, that's what she said. And then out of the blue, she came to my office one day and told me she was quitting her job. She broke off our relationship—said her husband had found out about us—and walked out the door. I couldn't stop her. I knew he mistreated her because I'd seen bruises, and I was afraid for her, but she was gone, just like that. There was nothing I could do. She made it very clear that I was to stay away from her. I was devastated, but there was nothing for it. The affair was over—and I stayed in a marriage that was neither happy nor unhappy, but comfortable; Cynthia and I were good friends. I'd lost the woman I loved and stayed with the woman I'd married, trying to forget about the love I'd once known." I could see him grinding his teeth. "But it was all a lie, wasn't it? Petra was pregnant with my child. My child. And because of her deceit, she cheated me out of twenty-one years of your life, Joanna. I can't forgive her for that. She did us both a great wrong."

I hesitated a moment before asking, but finally plucked up the courage and said, "Why didn't you go after her?"

I didn't know whether I'd overstepped the mark—I wouldn't have dared question August Nel—but Tom replied in a calm voice. "It's a fair question and I've sometimes thought the same thing, Joanna. Why didn't I? Just because she told me not to? Well, I suppose it came as such a shock that I was stunned—and before I realized it, she was gone. And I have to admit, my pride took a battering; it was hard to accept that she would walk away from me and stay with that man."

"Things could've been so different if you'd gone after her," I murmured.

I'm not sure whether he heard me or not, but he didn't respond. His face was unhappy as he reached across to refill our glasses—I grabbed his hand before he could do so and he looked at me, surprised by this physical contact. We stared at one another for a moment, before I asked, "Do you still have the photograph?"

He nodded.

"May I see it?"

Holding onto my hand a few seconds longer, he said, "Come, let's take our wine with us and I'll show you."

I followed him into his study. There were no antiques in this room. The white desk and book shelves looked Scandinavian, and the wooden floor had an African rug on it. One wall was covered with team photographs from school and university—he'd been a rugby player and cricketer by the looks of it. He also had a surround sound system for his TV with a comfortable couch in front of it. It was only when I turned around that I saw the photograph hanging on the wall—and I was transfixed.

In the background was a woman with her back to the camera, hunched over, clutching her arms around herself as if she were shivering. There was no face visible because her head was lowered and her knees were bent. Dark, wavy hair fell around her, like a blanket. The image was fuzzy and indistinct, taken from a distance, looking down, making the shape smaller than the one in the foreground.

By contrast, the larger image in front was sharp and crisp. This one had been shot from a different angle, looking up at the same woman. The shape of her body formed an X as she stood upright, bold and strong, her legs planted firmly apart with her arms stretched high. Her hands reached upwards, grasping at something, while her head was tilted back so that once again her face was not visible—only her pointed chin could be seen as her long, dark hair cascaded behind her shoulders. It was a work of art and undoubtedly my mom.

In both photographs, my mother was completely naked.

I stared in silence for a long time, thankful that Tom said nothing. The situation could have been weird, but it wasn't. It wasn't personal, or sexual; it was an expression of freedom which they had created together—and the longer I studied it, the more I understood something about my mother. It wasn't the camera that had made her come alive, it was Tom. She'd been liberated by his love—until she went back to being hunched over, clutching her middle, keeping her head down.

I had tears in my eyes when I eventually turned to him and murmured, "I wish she had married you."

# CHAPTER 4

Despite being exhausted, I lay in bed that night, tossing and turning. My brain wouldn't let me sleep as it jumped from one thought to another. I couldn't fathom why my mother would've given up the happiness she had enjoyed with Tom, to live a miserable life with August Nel, a man who abused her. And how could she let me believe that such an ogre was my father? How different my life might've been living with my real dad, a thought that made my anger bubble up once more. Everything could've been so different—and I couldn't stop thinking about that photograph. I wanted to see it again, but did I dare? Eventually I gave in to the urge and crept downstairs, using the flashlight on my phone to light the way.

Tom's study was in darkness. Closing the door behind me, I shone light onto the picture and stood in awe, gazing at my mother standing tall and proud, like an Amazon warrior in Greek mythology. It was hard to equate this figure with the submissive woman I knew, so intimidated by her husband. Yet as I stood staring at the photo, it dawned on me how brave she'd been getting me away from him, despite her fear. And not only that, she'd gone to bat for me so that I could go to university. She must've used all the money she'd saved over the years in order to help me when August refused to pay. She'd given me the freedom that she herself didn't have. She was still an Amazon warrior—and even though I couldn't understand her actions twenty-two years ago, I was thankful for what she'd done now. I felt compelled to take a photo of the masterpiece, and turned on the light to do so; a better camera would've been useful, but my phone had to suffice. I had to move way back behind the desk to get it all in the frame and as I did so, I realized why Tom had positioned things the way he had. Whenever he looked up from his desk, he could see my mother—which made me wonder whether he still loved her. I kind of hoped so.

Back in bed, as I looked at the picture on my new phone, it made me think about my photography class at UCT. I'd loved that course, but the beauty of this photograph surpassed anything I'd seen in those studies. It reaffirmed something that I'd considered before—perhaps I should pursue photography as a career, especially now that I knew the aptitude for it was in my genes. I thought about Tom saying it was a difficult way to make a living, though, and that made me a little less sure of the idea. But still, maybe it was worth a shot; I wouldn't know unless I tried and I had nothing to lose.

I must have finally drifted off to sleep because I awoke with a start when I heard a knock on the door. Opening my eyes, I saw Tom with a tray in his hand. "Here you are, sleepy head," he said. "It's 10 o'clock, time to get up. I thought you could have breakfast in bed first, though; I've brought you some tea, fruit and cereal. Hope it meets with your approval, ma'am."

"Oh, my gosh!" I exclaimed. "I've never had breakfast in bed in my life. What a treat!"

"Well, it's high time you tried it." Over his arm, he had a white dressing gown which he dropped on the bed for me. "And this comes to you, courtesy of Sudar and Green; I wasn't sure if you had one or not. Your suitcase seems very small—it can't have too much in it. We might have to go shopping." He smiled and added, "Take your time. I'll be downstairs when you're ready. We've got things to do today, young lady."

I smiled, waiting until he closed the door, before I sat up. That first cup of tea in the morning was always the best; my mom sometimes brought me tea in bed, but breakfast...never. It was like telepathy, because as I thought about her, I heard my phone buzz. There was only one person who would be calling me on it and I leapt to grab the phone, my anger pushed aside by my longing to hear my mother's voice. "Mom," I gasped. "Are you OK?"

"Yes, liefling, I'm fine. But, more importantly, how are you?"

It was such a relief to hear her, knowing she was there at the end of the line, that the angry thoughts I'd been harboring during the night evaporated. "I'm fine. But what happened last night? Tell me. What happened when you got home?"

She giggled. "Oh, I couldn't wait for him to leave this morning so I could phone and tell you. I rushed back after leaving you yesterday, fighting the traffic, and made it home just before he got back; I left your note in the post box on my way in. You know how he always collects the post."

I held my breath for a moment. "And?"

"Well, I heard him opening the door and going into the front room like he usually does, to make sure I'd cleaned it. Then I heard him dropping the post on the table before he came to see what I was preparing for the all-important dinner. You know he never comes into the kitchen normally, but he was in a cheerful mood and said,

'It smells good. What are we having?' Before I could answer, he looked around and his mood changed. He shouted, 'Where's Joanna? Why isn't she helping you?' I felt a bit nervous, I can tell you, but I just shrugged and kept my back to him so that he wouldn't see my face. I'm not a very good liar."

I wanted to say, "That's not true, you've perfected the art of lying,"—but I kept the thought to myself and waited to hear what happened next.

"He asked again where you were and I could hear that tone in his voice that comes when he's getting mad. I tried to sound calm, so I just said, 'I don't know. She hasn't come home yet. Maybe she's celebrating. She finished her exams today.' He grabbed my phone and said, 'Have you called her to find out? Doesn't she know Marius is coming to dinner? Haven't you told her?' I said, 'No. I thought you would do that.' Well, he stormed off and bellowed, 'I'm going to call her right now and tell her to hurry up. What the hell does she think this is? A boarding house where she can come and go as she pleases, without telling us?'

"I heard him trying to call you and that's when he heard your phone ringing in your bedroom. I'd put it there when I got home. Geez, Joanna. He was mad. And when he found your note, he went wild."

"Mom, promise me you're OK," I said. My heart was racing. I know what he's like when he's like that. My mother has had many a black eye to show for it.

"I'm OK, I promise. Thank heavens for that note; just as well you wrote it to both of us—but he's suspicious. He immediately checked my phone to see whether there were any calls from you, and it put him off the scent because he couldn't find anything there. Be careful, liefling. He's out looking for you. He's got your old phone, going through all your contacts, trying to track you down. He hasn't stopped to wonder why you left your phone behind—he's just gone off on the warpath. And he's taken my car keys away. He doesn't want me to go out."

"Oh Mom, why do you stay with him? He's a brute. Just leave him."

"Where would I go, Joanna? I've got no money of my own and nowhere else to go, other than to my brother. But August owns that house; he bought it for Granny to live in when we got married. He'd find me there. Uncle Willie would be thrown out, for sure. It's fine, don't worry about me. The main thing is that you're OK and you're safe. Have you made any plans yet?"

"I've got just one plan. I'm getting you away from that man," I replied.

"No. Don't waste your time thinking about it. I can't leave. It's not him; I don't care about him. But if I leave, not only will it be tough for my brother, but I'll be walking away from Esther, Emma and my grandchildren. I can't do that. He'll poison their minds and make it impossible for me to see them. He's told me that—and I know he would do it. I can breathe easy because you're safe from his clutches. I miss you, but we'll stay in touch and one of these days..."

"My sisters will understand, Mom. They've seen how he treats you. And you won't be walking away from them. That's rubbish. I'll come and fetch you; I'll hop in a taxi right now. Just pack your bags and come with me. We'll go somewhere together, please. I'm sure Tom will help us."

"Liefling, I love your optimism, but I hurt Tom very much. I didn't mind asking him to help you, but I would never ask anything for myself. I made my choice and I have to live with it."

"Listen to me. I saw that fantastic photograph of you—the one that won a competition way back when. It's the most beautiful thing I've ever seen. I'm so proud of you, both of you."

I heard her gasp. After a few seconds, she said so softly that I could hardly hear her, "He shouldn't have shown that to you."

"Why not? I asked him to," I replied. "Anyway, I would've seen it sooner or later. He has it hanging in front of his desk. He looks at it every day." She was silent for such a long time that I wondered whether the call had been cut off. "Mom, are you still there?"

"Yes, I am."

"He'll help you, Mom."

"My answer is no, Joanna, absolutely not. Please don't waste time discussing it and I wish he hadn't shown that photograph to you. Listen, I can't talk long, but let me explain something. I've hidden this phone of mine in a plastic bag in my flour canister. He'll never find it here in the kitchen; he doesn't come here much. Please don't call me on it, though. I've got the sound off, but I don't want to risk him hearing a buzz or anything. You can text me, that's fine, and I can call you when he's out. Let me know how things are going with you, please. Has Tom been kind? Have you met his wife?"

"He's a nice man. I like him a lot. And no, I haven't met his wife. She isn't here—she's in England on a business trip. We're going to chat this morning about plans for the future, but I've decided I don't want to stay in his house. He invited me to do so, but it won't work. I really don't want to meet her—I don't want her to know anything about me and you."

"Why ever not?"

"This is not my home. It's hers." I took a deep breath and said what had been bugging me all night. "This could've—should've—been your home. It makes me really sad that it isn't. That's why. It's a monument to what might have been."

I heard her choke on a sob as she whispered, "I have to go," and the call ended abruptly.

Maybe what I did next was cruel, but it was done with love. I texted her the photo and added a message: *It's time for your liberation, Mom. My real father loved you very much, he told me so. It's not too late. He's a good man, unlike that awful creature you're married to. Leave August Nel, I beg you. That man is toxic. He's a monster.*

When I carried the tray downstairs, I found Tom reading the paper, waiting patiently for me to appear. "Sorry I took so long," I said. "My mom called."

His expression changed immediately and I saw him swallow hard. "Oh yes. Did she make it home in time?"

"Yes, she did, and I want to tell you something," I said, sitting down opposite him. "My mom's life is miserable. When I looked at that photo last night, I saw something I've never known in her. She looked exuberant, full of joy and life. But her husband is a cruel man. He's a control freak, and when he gets angry, he hits her, he beats her up. He's violent. She's an abused woman. I wish she would leave him, but she won't—because of my sisters and their children, and her brother." I shook my head and added, "She looked so strong and brave in that photo—what happened to all of that?"

He stared at me for a long time before replying. His deep voice sounded strained. "I would say that she's still strong and brave; it was courageous to bring you here. She knows how angry I am that she kept you a secret from me, and yet she did the only thing she could think of to help you. That took guts. So, although I despise her lies and deceit, I have to admit she has courage. Bravery doesn't always look the same, Joanna."

# CHAPTER 5

When I told him that I'd decided not to remain under his roof, he stared at me intently, his eyebrows slightly arched, and said nothing. The ensuing silence made me feel awkward, ungrateful even, so I tried to give some sort of explanation about how I felt—the same thing I'd expressed to my mom. He listened without interrupting, nodding his head slightly every now and again. When I'd finished my attempt at an explanation, I was relieved when he said, "I understand what you're saying, Joanna, and I respect your wishes." Rubbing his forehead, he added, "Having you come into my life is a gift and I am so thankful, but I have to remind myself that you aren't a child; you're an adult. I'll have to be satisfied to watch you take off and fly."

I smiled at him, filled with gratitude. It was a new experience, having a man—my father—who saw me as a person in my own right, not a pawn to do his bidding. I gave an involuntary shudder, remembering August Nel and his plans for my future. Any thought of that man gave me chills down my spine. Fortunately, I didn't think of him for long as Tom began to speak. "Now that you've finished your degree, have you any ideas about what you want to do? What sort of job do you want to find?" he asked.

"Actually, yes, I do have some thoughts."

I described the photography class I'd taken and explained how, although it had been short, it had been my favorite course at UCT. I told him about part-time photography jobs I'd had, and that I wanted to try pursuing that path.

He began to laugh and his eyes were sparkling once again. "Well, well, well," he said. "The apple doesn't fall far from the tree, does it?" Then he grew silent. He stared at me, biting his bottom lip and frowning, until suddenly he smacked the table with his palms. His face cleared and he said, "I think I can help you. Tell me, how would you feel about moving to Durban?"

My mouth opened, but no words came out.

"Sometimes you have to make a leap, Joanna. It takes courage."

I remained silent. What was he talking about?

"I'm originally from KwaZulu-Natal, you see," Tom began to explain. "I grew up just outside Durban in a town called Westville. I still have close friends there, and lots of connections—and the Old Boys' network is strong. Just last month, one of my buddies contacted me to say he was starting a new job with an advertising agency. It's a newish venture and it's going gangbusters, apparently. They've got plenty of clients and they're hiring entry level people with photography experience. I can't promise anything, but what do you say? Would you like to give it a go?"

I was stunned. How could this all be happening to me? My response was to stammer, "Um, yes. Yes, I would."

"Great. I'll call him immediately." With that, he left and went to his study to make the call.

I'd just finished packing the dishwasher with our breakfast things when Tom returned to the kitchen. "Right, young lady, you have an interview in three days."

My hands shot to my face. "What?"

"Yup, my friend is keen to meet you. Have you got any work you can show him?"

I pulled a face. "I've got lots, but it's all back at—you know, the place where my mother lives. It's there with my camera and computer. I didn't have time to get any of my stuff before she brought me here."

"Not a problem. Tell your mom where it all is and we'll make a plan to meet."

"That won't be possible. Her husband's taken away her car keys. She can't get out."

His eyebrows shot up and then he frowned. "Hell's teeth, what sort of man is he? Well, never mind, I've got my keys! We'll just go and get your things. He can't stop you."

I shook my head. Tom had no idea what August was like. "No, I don't want to go anywhere near there. My mom told me he's looking for me. I'm really afraid of him."

Tom clenched his jaw. "I'll go alone then. I'll get them for you. Why don't you make a plan with your mother? She can text when the coast is clear. I'm sure you'll want to let her know what's happening, that you're going to Durban. I suspect she'll be relieved. Everything will be fine now, Joanna. You've got nothing to worry about anymore. You're safe with me."

# CHAPTER 6

It was a busy day, my last day in Cape Town. After I'd spoken to my mom, it was tempting to call my sisters and friends to say goodbye, but I dared not. It was too dangerous. There would be time to connect later, but for now I needed to keep out of sight. August would probably be questioning them all and I didn't want to ask them to lie for me. There'd been enough lies already. Tom managed to get my camera and work folder, as well as my computer. He said my mom was looking over her shoulder the whole time when they met for a drop-off outside Pick 'n Pay. The store was just down the road from her house, so the cover story, if needed, was that she'd made a trip to the supermarket. My laptop was small and all my things were easily concealed in her shopping bags.

Tom rushed back to make our flight reservations for the following day and book us into a hotel in Durban. When that was done, he said, "Right, now I've got a surprise for you. Jump in the car."

I must have looked apprehensive, because he reassured me I would be safe; we were simply driving to Sudar and Green where he needed to pick up some work papers and make a few changes to his calendar. The building was deserted because it was a Saturday afternoon, so I was able to look around. I noted that he'd climbed the corporate ladder to the top; he was now the managing director of the company. I was waiting for him on a plush sofa in the lobby, wondering if much had changed in two decades since my mother had worked here, when I felt a pat on my shoulder. "Ready for your surprise?" Tom asked.

He led me down a corridor and unlocked the door to a huge store room filled with women's clothing—row upon row of garments. "Here you are. Take your pick," he said.

I gawked at him. "What?"

"It's one of the perks you get for being my daughter, Joanna. You get to choose whatever you want and we'll charge it to my account. Start over here with the summer collection; you won't need much in the way of winter clothing in Durban, just a sweater or two. It's sub-tropical there. But you might need some smart work clothes for your new life—and anything else that takes your fancy. I brought a big duffel bag with me; I'll just go and get it from the car. You can take your time selecting what you want." Seeing my hesitation, he smiled and added, "Come on, go for it. Knock yourself out."

It was overwhelming. Everything was beautiful and I badly wanted to share it with my sisters. I especially wished I had Esther with me. She has such a good eye for clothing and style. Obviously, they were talents she got from our mother—something we never knew before. We were always trying to get Mom into new clothes; Esther would make new dresses for her that were the latest fashion, but Mom never seemed interested. God, I wanted Esther to see all this; she'd be in heaven. I had to restrain myself from texting her a photo—my fingers were really itching to do so.

By the time Tom returned, I'd selected two outfits that seemed suitable for work. I didn't really know what would be required, so I chose two skirts and blouses, and a linen jacket that would go with everything. "That's a good start. I like those," he said, inspecting my choice and promptly adding eight more outfits. "There's a fitting room in the corner. Why don't you try them on? I'll wait here, but I'd like to see how they all look."

He beamed his approval as I showed him each garment. "I like them all. Just one more thing, though. Your mother looked great in black, you know. You have her dark hair and olive complexion; I think black would suit you as well." He handed me a dress he'd found as he said this. It was stunning. I was starting my new life with a new image, feeling like Cinderella, hoping that things wouldn't fall apart at midnight.

They didn't—but that night, I had the first of many recurring nightmares in which I was being chased by August. I kept tripping, and while I struggled to get up, he got closer and closer, sneering at me and shouting abuse. In a panic, I woke up shaking and sweating, hastily turning on the light to reassure myself it had only been a dream.

Flying was a new experience for me and the excitement made me forget that I was leaving Cape Town. It wasn't until I saw Table Mountain and the Twelve Apostles through the plane window that I realized the enormity of what I was doing. As I watched the mountain range disappearing, a shiver crept down my spine and I turned my head to watch it as long as possible. Tom reached over and squeezed my hand. "Nothing's forever. You'll be back someday. It will all still be there," he reassured me. I said nothing, but swallowed hard and closed my eyes, keeping the imprint of those mountains firmly in my mind.

The two-hour flight was smooth and seemed to pass

quickly. We followed the eastern coastline of Africa and soon were getting ready to land at King Shaka Airport, just outside Durban. As Tom and I exited the air-conditioned terminal, the outside heat hit us with a blast—but it felt like a warm embrace to me. The humidity was quite different from Cape Town, and although it took only fifteen minutes to reach the rental car, I was dripping with sweat by the time we got there. People often complain about Durban's heat, but I loved the moisture in the air—and I was soon enamored with the lush foliage all around us. Banana trees grew wild by the side of the highway, and paw-paw trees—dripping with yellow fruit—popped up everywhere. Orange flowers on coral trees dotted the landscape, while green sugar cane fields stretched far into the distance—and I fell in love with the vibrancy.

From our sixth-floor rooms at the Elangeni Hotel, the sea looked so inviting that we decided to go for a swim in the Indian Ocean to cool off. The water temperature was almost as warm as bath water and I could have swum for hours, but it was getting late. As we dried ourselves, Tom's face became serious. "We've got quite a bit to do in the next few days," he said. "Tomorrow we start by getting you a car."

"Don't be ridiculous."

"I presume you can drive," he said, ignoring my response.

"Yes, of course. My mom taught me, but that's crazy. You've done so much already. A car is too much. I'm sure there are buses and taxis in this city. That's what I'm used to."

"Oh no, definitely not. I don't want my daughter riding taxis here. Please don't think about doing that, Joanna. I know I'm late to the party and I can't tell you what to do, but please humor me. Let me buy you a car, nothing fancy. Consider it in lieu of all the birthday presents I've missed." He didn't wait for me to argue anymore, before adding, "Then we can return the rental and check out a flat for you. I'll pay the first two months' rent, and after that, if you agree, I'd like to share the rent with you. You see, I come to Durban on business at least once a month and, if you'll have me, I could stay with you instead of going to a hotel. It's only a couple of nights each time. What do you think? If you don't feel it's appropriate and would rather I didn't do that, that's fine. It's just a thought I had."

"Oh yes, that's great. I would love you to stay with me. Why wouldn't it be appropriate? You're my father."

His smile made me realize how much my response meant to him and it mirrored my feelings. I had no hesitation agreeing. It was actually a relief. There was so much unknown about the future that the idea of having Tom visit regularly seemed like a lifeline. And more than that, it would provide an opportunity for me to get to know him better. He seemed kind and understanding; I wanted him to be in my life, not disappear so soon after arriving in it.

By lunchtime the next day, I was the proud owner of a small, white Fiat—and by 4 o'clock, we'd found a furnished flat in Musgrave Road. I felt anxious about signing the lease when it wasn't certain I had a job, but Tom said it was too good a deal to let slip. "If you don't get this job, I'd be very surprised. I'm sure they'll take one look at your work and snap you up double quick. If I'm wrong, we'll find another job for you and I'll cover the rent in the meantime." By 4:30 p.m., I was no longer homeless. "We should get you some basics now, like bedding and kitchenware. There's a Woolworths right around the corner; we've just got time before they close. After your interview tomorrow, we'll stock up the kitchen."

It had been such a whirlwind of changes that when I lay down to sleep that night, I was overcome with weariness. Maybe it was exhaustion that was the catalyst, or maybe it was because I'd missed a call from my mom, but I began to sob. I thought of her miserable existence, kowtowing to August—and my sisters who worked so hard to help provide for their families. They'd scrimped and saved to buy second-hand cars that were always breaking down; they lived in tiny rented flats and they'd had to rely on our mother to help with child care before their kids started school. Suddenly I felt embarrassed that I'd been showered with so much, and embarrassment quickly turned to guilt. I missed them all so much, but everything that had happened in the last few days made me feel distanced from them—more than just physically. I'd been uprooted and was suddenly living in a different world. Would it always be like this now, because I had a different father from them? Would they resent me?

# CHAPTER 7

I tried to steady my trembling hands as I was shown into Mr. Gibson's office for my first proper job interview, but his greeting was so warm that it put me at ease. After a few pleasantries, he asked to see my work—and once again, I suddenly felt unsure of myself. The silence was unnerving as he looked through my photographs, giving no indication of whether or not he liked what he saw. I watched him biting his lips and frowning, and I felt exposed, like he was looking into my soul. Suddenly he whistled and exhaled, pointing to an image of a quarry on Robben Island. Bright light blanched the limestone and the effect was blinding and desolate. He said nothing as his eyes ran over other photos in my portfolio, resting on a black and white one of my mother and sisters. They were seated with their backs to the camera, deep in conversation.

Finally, he spoke. "You do a lot of black and white photography. Why is that?"

I thought quickly and replied, "It has a crispness that appeals to me; it makes the viewer concentrate on the subject, not the color. But obviously, it depends on the subject matter. Some things cry out for color."

"I agree," he replied. "Of course, in advertising, images are almost 100% color, but sometimes black and white is a must. For example, when I think of our mutual friend Tom Montgomery's masterpiece, *Liberation*—well, that couldn't have been anything but black and white. Have you seen it?"

I nodded and looked away quickly, feeling myself blushing. "Yes, I have. It's beautiful," I replied.

He laughed and said, "I was so proud of my mate when he won that prize. It was a quite a surprise, too, I might tell you. At school, he played first team rugby and cricket; he was a good sportsman, but he never showed any artistic inclination whatsoever. You just never know, do you?" He walked back to his desk and motioned for me to sit opposite him. "So, Joanna. What draws you to photography?"

This was an easier question to answer. "Well, I can speak without words; my lens does the talking for me. I can capture a moment in time, or a certain mood—and it's there forever."

He smiled at me and nodded, but said nothing further as he shuffled some papers around and pulled a folder from a drawer. When he'd found what he was looking for, he looked across at me and said, "I think I've seen enough. We'd love to have you on board, Joanna. How soon can you begin?"

The relief was enormous. I tried to contain my excitement but I couldn't keep the smile off my face, even as I tried to look professional. After signing a few papers and filling in some forms, it was agreed that I would start work in two days' time. I couldn't quite believe it when he said that I'd be provided with a new camera, one that I'd always dreamed about, and my salary was going to be much more than I would've expected. I was blown away—I knew approximately how much my sisters earned after years of hard work; I would immediately be making considerably more than either of them.

This made me feel uncomfortable. When I expressed my surprise about it to Tom, he said, "Well, you have a degree, Joanna. Your sisters don't. From what I understand, that's because you were determined to do so. Now you're reaping rewards for your ambition and hard work."

"But they're hard-working too. You can't imagine all they do. And they're so talented. Esther designs and makes wedding dresses—God, I can hardly sew on a button. And Emma is a sous chef at a Michelin-starred restaurant in Constantia. You wouldn't believe how creative she is."

He shrugged. There was nothing he could do about it, I knew that, and it wasn't his responsibility. I didn't want to sound ungrateful, so I kept quiet, but the guilt I felt was unsettling.

I appreciated how much time Tom took getting me acquainted with Durban; it had a very different feel from Cape Town. Table Mountain dominates the landscape there, but in Durban, there's no mountain—just lots and lots of hills. And while Table Mountain makes the weather so changeable that you can have four seasons in one day, in Durban it's balmy all the time. I loved it.

My flat was close enough to the office in Musgrave Centre that I could walk to work. I was pleased that I would not have to battle traffic or find parking—from what I could see, both of those could be major problems in this city. All too quickly, though, it was time for Tom to head back to Cape Town and I drove him to the airport with a mixture of dread and excitement—because once he left, I would know nobody here. Before he climbed out of the car, he wished me well for my first day at work. He looked so anxious that suddenly I was the one reassuring him. "Don't worry. I'm going to be fine. I can't thank you enough for all you've done, Tom. I won't let you down."

"I know that. We've only been together a short time, but it's enough for me to realize how resilient you are. I used to say that your mother reminded me of a Protea flower. There was nothing of the delicate rosebud in her—and the same goes for you. You're strong, and I bet there's nothing you can't do if you put your mind to it. You go get 'em. That's my girl." The look on his face showed such concern that I felt a lump in my throat.

It was a touching thing to say, so different from anything August might have said, that it seemed natural to lean across and kiss him lightly on the cheek. "Thank you," I whispered. "That means a lot."

His eyes were sparkling again. "Thank you, Joanna. Off you go now, on your way; I'll see you in a month's time."

I felt sad as I watched him leave, but pleased to be sad. It was such a contrast to how I felt whenever I would walk away from August. That had always been a relief. I'd had a hard time with the commandment that I should honor my mother and father; I loved my mother (despite the big secret she'd kept from me), but the man I'd thought to be my father—well, I hated him. I loathed him. However, I didn't want my thoughts straying to him now because whenever they did, I felt years of grievances bubble up and this was no time for such negativity. My new life was about to begin in earnest and, thank God, my real father seemed to be a man I could honor and trust.

# CHAPTER 8

Mr. Gibson gave me a quick introduction to the other staff members. They were Myra Pillay in the accounts department, Promise Khumalo and Andile Gumede in sales, Lucy Watkins and Bob Dube whose field was graphic and digital art, and Gabby Strydom. Gabby was a designer and photographer and I would be working with her.

"We're small and informal around here, Joanna, so please feel free to call me Walter. This is how we work; Myra is solely responsible for our accounts and does a very good job of it, but for the rest of you, although you're assigned to different departments, there's plenty of room for overlap. What I'm saying is this—if you see an opening for a sale, go for it. And if you need help, ask anybody. We're doing a lot of magazine and newspaper adverts right now, and that keeps us busy, but we're trying to break into TV and online advertising. Bob is working on that specifically. Now, follow me," he said, walking me over to a cubicle. "Here you are; this is your desk. As I mentioned, you'll be working with Gabby. She's had lots of experience and you'll learn a lot from her. She'll get you started."

Gabby had been trailing us. Her cubicle was adjacent to mine and as Walter walked away, she turned to me. "We'll head out into the field in a few minutes and I'll work with you on your first assignment. We've got an order from Tropicola, a new fruit drink on the market. It tastes disgusting, but we have to convince the public that their lives will be more enjoyable if they drink it." She said this without smiling.

That was how my first day started—right in at the deep end, and I loved it. Gabby was a cynic and appeared aloof at first, but I soon realized it was a façade. She was considerate and Walter was right, I learned a lot from her. It was all about work with her; no time for chit-chat. It was exciting to see how things took shape and by the time the whole team had finished with the project a few weeks later, I felt some ownership of the result— which featured cans of fruit juice playing ukuleles on the beach. Lucy and Bob's work with Photoshop was impressive, making me realize I had a lot to learn from them, too.

# CHAPTER 9

I'd been in Durban a month and Christmas was just around the corner. That gave me a sinking feeling; I was going to be on my own, far away from everyone I cared about. Tom was married and his wife knew nothing about me; my mother needed to keep up the pretense that she didn't know where I was; and I couldn't speak to my sisters who were still in the dark about my whereabouts. I hated that. Apparently, my mom had reassured them that they needn't worry about me, without giving details—she'd told them the less they knew, the better. I longed to talk to them, though I understood it was better this way—they wouldn't have to lie if August questioned them, and he wouldn't be able to extract information from them about my whereabouts. I was sure he would try to check their phone calls.

This brought on a fresh round of loathing on my part, thinking about that man. Apparently, he'd been ready to report me a missing person; he wanted the police to search for me and bring me back in disgrace. My mom had convinced him it would be futile because I was an adult and I'd left a note saying I was leaving, so the police would do nothing. All it would do would create a scandal. That was enough to stop him. I said that I hoped he wouldn't hire a private detective, which made my mom laugh; she replied he wouldn't spend that much money when Marius had withdrawn his marriage offer. That made me laugh too.

My mom managed to call me briefly on Christmas Day when August went out—as did Tom when he had a moment to himself. Both of them had sent me gifts; it felt even lonelier opening them on my own in an empty flat, but I appreciated the lengths they'd gone to on my behalf. Being lonely on Christmas Day was a small price to pay and I had much to be thankful for. My mom would be telling me to count my blessings if she were here, and that's what I did.

But homesickness hit me full force the following week when I thought about the Tweede Nuwe Jaar Carnival in Cape Town. I knew my sisters' husbands would be dressed up as minstrels, playing their banjos with fellow band members and parading the city streets on this holiday. I always loved the festivities and I watched TV, hoping to see familiar faces in the crowds—maybe even my sisters and brothers-in-law. There were too many people though, and the cameras moved too quickly. I saw nobody I knew, but the familiar sights and sounds were enough to make me feel very far from home. After a while, I had to force myself to stop watching the carnival and go outside for a walk in the Botanical Gardens to take my mind off things.

I worked on a few more assignments with Gabby until she felt I was ready to start working on my own. For two more months, the projects I was given were small, creating something to promote dreary household products—mayonnaise and shampoo. They were so mundane that I was growing disheartened, but when Tom visited Durban each month, he encouraged me to stay the course. He came for a couple of nights each time and showed interest in my work. Sensing how downhearted I was feeling, he gave me advice: "You can't expect to be the star at the top of the tree immediately. Everything you do is a lesson. One of these days you'll find it all comes together and you'll get your break. Trust me. But you have to persevere."

My break came with the next assignment I was given, which was helping produce a catalog for a clothing factory. I had a good feeling as I set out on the hour's drive up the North Coast on the N2, much more confident with three months' experience under my belt. When I arrived at Zinkwazi, I was bowled over by the beauty of the long, unspoiled beach and the milkwood forest surrounding it. I really wanted to go for a walk, but that wasn't an option; my new project was beckoning and I had to get started.

As I perused the clothing that afternoon, I was reminded of the afternoon I'd been to Sudar and Green with Tom, and an idea began to grow; Walter had said that if we saw an opportunity for a sale, we should go for it. Well, maybe we could get Sudar and Green as a client. That night I texted Tom. He was quick to call me back, laughing. "It seems like you've got your break; you've taken to this job like a duck to water," he said. "And I'll let you into a secret—Sudar and Green is buying that factory in Zinkwazi. That's why I travel to Durban so often. I'll be up there again in a month's time."

I looked forward to that and arranged to pick Tom up at the airport, eager to spend time with him again, but the day before his arrival, he texted me: *Change of plans. Cynthia's coming with me. We'll grab a taxi from the airport and stay at the Elangeni. Can you have dinner with us tomorrow night? I'll call you later to make plans.*

My hands began to shake. That word "us" screamed at me. "Us" was him and me, not her and him. Besides, I'd arranged my schedule so that I could meet him. I wanted him to see the work I was doing at the clothing factory and I wanted his input. Now everything would be different. He wouldn't be staying in my flat and she would be there in the hotel with him. Did she know about me? How was I to act when I met her? I didn't want to meet her. I didn't want her coming to Durban.

My indignation increased as I waited for the phone to ring and when it did, my voice sounded strained—even to me.

"What's the matter? You sound different. Are you alright?" Tom asked.

"I'm fine," I replied abruptly.

"Look, I'm sorry about the sudden change of plans, but Cynthia wants to attend an estate sale in Durban, day after tomorrow. I think it'll be a good opportunity for you two to meet."

I hesitated before asking, "Does she know about me, then?"

There was a long silence before he said, "Not yet."

"So how are you going to explain having dinner with me?"

"Not a problem. You're the daughter of someone I once worked with and you've recently moved to Durban. Don't worry about it. I have a meeting in the afternoon, but can you come to the Elangeni at 6 o'clock? Meet us in the lobby, if that works for you."

My heart was pounding as I approached the hotel and I hid behind a palm tree to secretly observe Tom and Cynthia for a few moments. He was dressed in a light suit and tie, she was in a flowing, coral skirt with an ivory blouse and a broad, gold belt. Although she was wearing high-heeled gold sandals, she stood only chest-high next to him. Her hair was short and spiky blonde. I figured she must be in her mid-fifties, like my mom and Tom, but she didn't look it. They didn't appear to be talking; she was checking her phone and he had his eyes on the door, looking tense. Finally, I took a deep breath and stepped out of the shadows. When he spotted me, his expression changed; he seemed happy to see me. I was pleased to be wearing the black dress, especially when he gave me an approving nod.

She smiled and put out a hand to greet me, her gold bracelets jangling as she did so. "Joanna, I'm pleased you could join us. Tom didn't tell me how beautiful you are," she said, and added conspiratorially, "It's always nice to have young people around, otherwise Tom and I run out of things to talk about. That's what happens when you've been married forever. You've said it all already—there's nothing new to say."

She laughed, but her remarks made me uncomfortable. I could feel myself blushing, unable to imagine running out of conversation with Tom and wondering how she would react when she realized there were many things he hadn't told her. He had plenty of secrets. I glanced at my father to see his reaction to her words; he was frowning, but he said nothing.

We went to a nearby bistro and as soon as we were seated, Cynthia told the server that she had called ahead with her dietary restrictions. He looked at her blankly and she grew agitated. The maître d' was summoned and placated her. "Yes madam," he said. "I have a note here; gluten free, dairy free, low sodium. Is that correct? We have a special selection for you on the menu." She smiled and nodded. Turning to me, she whispered, "It's not easy getting older. All sorts of changes start to happen when you least expect them, and I hate change. I used to be able to eat anything when I was younger, but now I constantly find things that don't agree with me and they can make life miserable. Best just to avoid them. If I feel in the slightest bit concerned about something, I simply won't have it. Better safe than sorry. I don't try anything new in case it doesn't agree with me. It probably sounds dull to you, but you're young. You might understand one day."

I smiled at her, but felt slightly embarrassed. Tom paid no attention; this situation was clearly nothing new to him. Although I'd been prepared to dislike her, I didn't actually. I think I'd subconsciously built an image of a stuffy woman wearing a twin set and pearls, but she didn't seem like that at all. Apart from being fussy about food, she seemed friendly and pleasant.

Tom was very quiet. Although he asked about my work, he seemed to know quite a bit about it already. When I raved about Zinkwazi, Cynthia remarked, "Maybe we should get a beach house there, Tom. It'll be perfect to get away from the Cape in winter. We should look into it."

I swallowed hard and thought how amazing it was to buy a second home. There were so many people, including my sisters, who couldn't afford their first. But I said nothing.

After dinner, Tom walked me to my car and remarked, "I think she likes you."

"I hope so. I like *her*."

He stopped suddenly and looked at me intently. "Joanna, it's time to tell her. I should've done it before; I've been a bloody fool—a coward, really. I don't like living with secrets; I can't do it anymore. The longer I go on concealing the truth, the harder it's getting. It's been almost five months now that I've known about you, and four months since we met. Sitting at dinner tonight, I kept thinking how much nicer it would've been if I'd been honest and we were dining together as a family. Instead of that, we have this charade." He punched his right fist into his left palm with a resounding smack. "I know she's going to be furious with me for the deceit, but still, I'd rather risk her wrath than lead a double life any longer. I did that before when I was seeing your mother and I didn't like myself then. I can't do it again. Anyway, this is different; you're her stepdaughter, whether she likes it or not. You're my daughter, my flesh and blood. She needs to know about you."

# CHAPTER 10

I tossed and turned all night, wondering how Tom's news would be received by Cynthia. I kind of liked her and hoped she would be reasonable. Although I wouldn't want to live in their house, maybe it would be possible to have a relationship with her as a stepdaughter. But then I immediately wondered how my mother would feel. Would she accept me being part of Tom's family? It would be awkward to tell her and I dreaded doing so if it all worked out.

But things did not look good when Tom walked into Walter's office next morning. He was solemn as he closed the door, remaining in the room for some time. When he emerged, he left without looking my way. Shortly afterwards, I received a call from Walter, summoning me.

"Well, Joanna, you're creating a stir. Tom Montgomery likes the work you're doing and wants you on a project for Sudar and Green. He's waiting for you now to go with him to Zinkwazi," he announced. "He wants to see your work there."

"Oh, I was just finishing up…" I replied.

"Don't keep him waiting. Stop whatever you're doing. Grab your things and go. He had to take a call, but he's waiting for you outside. He'll be at the main entrance of the Musgrave Centre."

It was a shock to see Tom's face close-up; he had a bruise developing next to his left ear and a cut above his left eye. I opened my mouth to say something, but the set of his jaw made me hold my words until we got to my car. As we closed our doors, I said, "What's going on? What happened?" I knew I couldn't drive and have this conversation at the same time, so I didn't switch on the ignition.

He shook his head. "It didn't work out so well. I told Cynthia the whole story—about the affair with your mother, that you're my daughter. I explained that I knew nothing about you until the end of last year, that I hadn't seen your mother in over twenty years. She wouldn't accept it. She freaked out and expressed her feelings quite physically. She's going back to Cape Town after the estate sale today and doesn't want me back in the house."

I gasped. "Oh, my God. I don't believe it." I wanted to reach out and comfort him, but I held back. "Maybe she'll relent once she's had time to digest the news. I mean, remember what a shock it was for you and me? Maybe it was a reflex reaction and she'll change her mind. I heard her saying last night that she doesn't do well with change; maybe she just needs time to get used to the idea."

"I doubt it," he replied. "She was pretty clear about her feelings—said I would have to choose between you and her. I told her that was ridiculous—you don't hold the same places in my life; she's my wife and you're my daughter. But she wouldn't hear it. 'Her or me,' was all she kept saying, after hitting me with a book and throwing whatever she could lay her hands on. It was ugly."

My heart began to pound loudly and I held my breath, unable to speak as I waited for him to continue.

"She didn't like my answer, as you can see." He rubbed his cheek and shrugged. "I said if she was going to force me to make a choice, she would regret it. She didn't give me a chance to say anything more. She knew what my answer was going to be." He turned and looked at me, "I will never give you up, Joanna. I've lost too much of your life already."

The relief was enormous. I flung my arms around him and cried, and as he stroked the back of my head, I heard him stifle a sob too.

We drove out of Durban in silence, heading to the toll road. Although I was concentrating on the traffic, I was aware of the tension in him. He looked lost in thought. Eventually he said, "Do you have a passport, Joanna?"

"Good grief, no. I've never been outside of Cape Town until I came here."

I glanced at him and saw that he was beginning to look more relaxed; he'd stopped gritting his teeth and was no longer drumming his fingers on his knees. "Well, please get onto that immediately and apply for one. Get it expedited if you can," he said.

"As far as I'm aware, you don't need a passport for Zinkwazi."

"No, but you do need one—and a visa as well—for the United States. It might take a few months."

"What on earth are you talking about?"

"I want to take you with me to San Francisco on a business trip. That's what I was speaking to Walter about. A large clothing company called GREEN has its headquarters there, and that's where I'm going. I'm trying to get a manufacturing contract from them, and I want you there to show some of the work you're doing here at Zinkwazi. What do you say? Nothing is too immediate; I can wait until you get a passport and visa. It'll help if you expedite the process, whatever the cost, and I'll pay for it."

I just about drove off the road I was so taken aback.

Then I started to laugh and couldn't stop. Tom grew concerned at this point and suggested I pull over so that he could drive. That sounded like a good idea and as I collapsed onto the passenger seat, I wanted to pinch myself to make sure I wasn't dreaming. How could all this be falling into my lap? Not only a job, a flat, and a car, but a trip to San Francisco as well. The recollection of my sisters' struggles jumped up to stab my conscience again, but I didn't want to dwell on those thoughts; they were too uncomfortable. Instead I reflected on how, just a few months ago, August had been trying to coerce me into marrying some creep. That started me laughing all over again.

"Tom, you're the best," I said.

# CHAPTER 11

When I missed my mom's regular lunchtime call, I wondered if she'd phoned while Tom and I had been in a restaurant. I'd silenced my phone there—but no missed calls were showing. I texted her immediately: *Some amazing news. Call me as soon as you can. Love you.* Lunchtime came the following day and still no call from her. I texted again: *Are you OK?* There was no reply once again.

My thoughts were running wild. Had August found her phone and beaten her up? I wanted to call but I couldn't; I could only communicate by texting. What if something awful had happened? My nerves were on edge and so when my phone finally rang in the middle of the afternoon, I grabbed it so fast I almost dropped it. It wasn't a number I was familiar with and my hand was shaking when I answered. Immediately I recognized the voice on the other end—it was Uncle Willy.

"Joanna," he said, "Don't be alarmed."

"What's going on? Where's Mom? Why isn't she responding to my texts?"

"Calm down. It's OK. I'm with her. She's in the hospital, but she's alright. Don't worry. I'll put her on the line. You can speak to her yourself."

I heard her say, "Joanna," and my heart almost stopped.

"Mom," I gasped. "What's happened? Why are you in the hospital?"

I feared the worst, sure that August had beaten her and gone too far.

My heart was pounding when she spoke again. "There was a bit of an accident, but I'm OK."

"My God, Mom. What happened?"

"It's OK my liefling, don't worry. I'm fine. I was careless. It was my stupidity that caused it. I was frying onions and forgot about them because I wanted to reply to your text. But the onions started to burn and there were flames jumping up—I think I used too much oil. I was trying to find the lid so I could stop the flames and I forgot about my phone. And then August arrived home and came in to see what was happening because he could smell the burning." She stopped to draw breath, before adding, "Unfortunately, he found my phone before I could hide it."

"Oh geez, Mom."

"I tried to get it away from him, but I couldn't. I couldn't stop him. He started looking at all our texts. I was pleading with him to give it back..."

My heart was in my mouth. "Did he hit you, Mom?"

She hesitated before answering me, and I heard a sigh. "He found the picture you sent, that photograph your father took. He read the message you sent with it—and he went berserk."

"Mom..." I couldn't find words to express my horror. He had discovered I wasn't his child. He knew my mom had been unfaithful.

"That's why I'm in the hospital, liefling. He picked up a carving knife and..."

My heart seemed to stop beating and I closed my eyes, trying to shut out the scene I could imagine that took place. Stifling a sob, she described what had happened.

"I grabbed the nearest thing to me, the frying pan, and hit him with it. I hit him over the head as hard as I could, but—as he fell—the knife in his hand sliced my arm open."

I held my breath, picturing his fury—and my mother's fear. It was a terrible prospect and I choked on my words. "Oh God, Mom…"

"It's OK, I managed to get away from him. I left him lying on the kitchen floor and ran as fast as I could—before he could get up and come after me. I ran all the way to Uncle Willy's place. But some of the hot oil spilled down my arm."

"Oh geez, no. How bad is it?"

"Not too bad. The burn's OK, and they've stitched up the cut and given me a tetanus shot. Now they've put me on some antibiotics. I'll be fine. They've taken care of everything here in the hospital."

"Thank God you hit him back for once in your life. I can't bear to think what would've happened if you hadn't. I hope it was that heavy, cast iron frying pan."

"Yes, it was. I fought like crazy because I thought he would kill me if I didn't defend myself. He was wild, worse than I've ever seen him. But don't worry, all's well now. I'll probably go home later today."

"No, no. You can't go back there. No. You have to leave him, Mom. He's violent. He's dangerous. And now that he knows about all of this…"

"He can't hurt me anymore, liefling. He's in the ICU at Groote Schuur Hospital; he's in a coma."

"Thank God," I said. "I hope he never comes out of it. I hope he dies."

My mom totally ignored my comment. "You see," she continued, "because there was a knife wound, the police came and questioned me. They took my statement.

There's no need to worry, though. It's an open and closed case of domestic violence. They saw my wounds so they understood that I'd acted in self-defense. And they told me something interesting, that the government is trying to stop all the gender violence that's happening in the country. Shame, it turns out there's a lot of it going on—and I thought it only happened to me."

My mom was unstoppable, a bit like a tap that had been turned on. She didn't stop talking and I suspect she'd been given something for the pain that made her a bit high. "A social worker came with the police; she was very kind to me, liefling, such a nice lady. I really liked her. She gave me information about a group that offers support to women like me, women who've been abused. That's the word she used. It's funny, I never thought of myself as an abused woman; I'm not sure I like the sound of that. I never really thought about it at all—it's just the way it was with August. He had a bad temper and I kind of lived with it as best I could; I kept out of his way as much as possible. It's horrible to think it's happening so much, but it's good to know there's help—although I won't be needing help now, thank God. Is it bad to be pleased that my husband is in a coma? I suppose I shouldn't say so, but I am.

"Honestly, I didn't realize so many women get beaten up—killed, even. That's what the social worker told me. It's terrible. But I'll tell you something, liefling, it's all very well to say that the government is trying to stop it, I don't know how they can though. It's the men who have to stop it, don't you think?"

I held my tongue. I wanted to say that women could stop it if they would only leave the men who were doing this to them—but now wasn't a good time to bring that up again.

When I explained to him that there was a family emergency, Walter said, "If you want to, you should go home immediately. Maybe you could fly back with Tom Montgomery tonight. Stay as long as you need to." I wasn't sure whether my boss knew the whole story about my parents or not, but he said, "I believe your mom is a talented, beautiful woman—like her daughter, it would seem. Go to her." The look he gave suggested he knew more than he was letting on about my mom and dad.

Tom refused to come in when he dropped me off. "No, it wouldn't be appropriate," he said. "She'll be waiting for you. I'd be a distraction." My sisters were there, as well as Uncle Willy, and I was overjoyed to be back with them all. My mom looked pretty good, considering what she'd been through, and I raced to her while carefully avoiding her injured arm. As we hugged, I could feel her sobbing against my chest. "I'm so happy to see you, my liefling," she whispered, "I thought my last day had come."

When I turned to greet my sisters, however, my heart sank. I was met with icy glares. Esther was the first to speak. "What the hell have you been up to, Joanna?"

Emma chimed in. "You should be ashamed of yourself, breezing in all smiles like the prodigal daughter. Are you expecting us to bring out the fatted calf for you? I gather you've got some fancy job in Durban, living a life of privilege, with a car and your own flat. We're not good enough for you anymore, is that it? You don't want anyone to know where you come from. Best keep us a secret, hey?"

They had never spoken to me like this before. It was a shock to hear a torrent of anger and resentment come pouring from them and I struggled to restrain myself. Their words hurt. How could they say these things? If only they knew how guilty I'd felt—exactly because I'd been given so much by my father while knowing how much they struggled. I chose not to offer any apologies, however, and my voice was calm when I replied. "Mom knew where I was all the time but she didn't want me to tell you, for your own protection. Maybe she didn't explain to you, but the reason I left was because your father was trying to make me marry that creep Marius Abrahams, that's why. August Nel would've whipped my backside if he'd been able to find me. And for your information, he's not my father. He's yours, but he's not mine." I let that sink in for a moment before adding, "Frankly, he deserved everything that happened to him; it's been a long time coming. He was a brute. I'm glad Mom fought back at last—she should've done it years ago."

I wasn't able to observe their reaction because my mom collapsed in my arms, sobbing, and when I looked up, they had disappeared.

I spent two days with my mother before heading back to work, during which time we talked about our future plans. "Maybe I'll sell this house," she said. "It has so many unhappy memories. August will never completely recover, apparently. He can go to a convalescent home and I don't need anything more than a small flat. As soon as I'm stronger, I'll start looking for one."

She was happy to hear about my work and the upcoming trip to San Francisco. I could see that she was grateful to Tom for all he had done for me, and when I said, "I can see why you fell in love with him, Mom. He's a good man," she nodded and looked away. She blushed when I added, "I bet he was a stud back in the day. He's still pretty hot now."

I didn't see my sisters again until right before I returned to Durban. Although I'd been eager to see them when I'd arrived in Cape Town, after their outbursts I was relieved that they'd kept their distance. Their words stung. Being much older than me, they'd always been motherly towards me in the past, but now I felt under attack.

Although Uncle Willy had been speaking to them and was confident that things would smooth over, I wasn't so sure. I held my breath when they walked in the door. Their body language looked awkward and we all stood staring at one another. The first to speak was Emma. "Joanna, we had no idea about any of this. I'm so sorry, baby."

Esther spoke next and her words came out in a rush. "Mom kept telling us you were OK and that we didn't have to worry, but it was all so mysterious and she refused to explain. We were really anxious and confused. We tried calling you but everything went straight to your voice mail and you never replied. I'm so sorry...I hope you understand why we reacted like we did."

I swallowed hard and nodded. "And I'm sorry I caused so much worry. You've no idea how much I wanted to speak to you and explain; I missed you so much. I hated not talking to you, but Mom insisted I say nothing to anyone. She was afraid. She didn't want there to be any chance August could track me down—for her sake as well as mine. But I hated keeping a secret from you." Choking on my words, I added, "I can't stand secrets. I detest them. Things that are held together with secrets, always come apart in the end—and spell disaster for everyone concerned."

I think we were all feeling emotional; I know I was and I could see they were both holding back tears. I wanted them to understand that I had never stopped loving them and so I tried to explain further. "Mom had a new phone and she used it only to call me; she kept it hidden from your father. I also have a new phone, so that's why I never received your calls. I left my old phone behind here so that he couldn't track me." I could see understanding dawning on them and took the opportunity to repeat an important fact. "Mom helped me escape. She knew where I was all the time and we were in contact almost daily. She was trying to protect you by not telling you any details. I bet he tried to check your phones to see if we'd spoken."

"Yes, he did," Emma said. "I remember him examining my phone because he said he wanted to get a new one for himself, and then he just stuck with that old flip phone of his."

"He did the same with me," Esther added. "I suppose he was checking to see who we called, and who called us. We didn't realize it at the time."

"You see, Mom was right. She worried that he would've pried things out of you, and then come after me."

"I suppose he would've tried, but we would never have given him any information. We love you so much. We were afraid for you. We wanted to report you missing, but Mom wouldn't let us. She insisted you were OK and we were not to worry, but we were worried. It was all so weird. Mom was jittery, especially around Dad; she wouldn't talk about you in front of him and he was always in a foul mood, worse than usual," Emma said. "Truthfully, I was beginning to wonder if he'd done something terrible to you and Mom was trying to cover up for him."

Esther nodded in agreement. "I didn't dare say it, but I thought the same thing. I was terrified he'd gone too far and killed you." She took my hands in hers and added,

"We could never understand why you got such rough treatment from him. It made us feel guilty, but we get it now."

Mom spoke up very quietly. "I'm sorry for all the anguish this has caused, really I am. We all know how much he wanted a boy and he'd convinced himself he was getting one when I got pregnant again after such a long time. And then, you see, apart from the disappointment of getting another girl, I think he suspected that Joanna wasn't his child. He'd say things like, 'She doesn't look like her sisters. She's not like them at all.' He even said, 'Are you sure you brought the right baby home?' Joanna's father is white, you see—so she was a bit different.

"August always remained suspicious, but I suppose he didn't want to believe it. And then, after more than twenty years, he found something that confirmed his suspicions on the phone that I'd kept hidden. Well, all hell was let loose after that." She began to tremble and murmured, "I deserved the treatment I got; I wronged him. It was a terrible thing that I did. I made some big mistakes, but Joanna didn't. You can't blame her. None of it was her fault."

I immediately turned to my mother. "You didn't deserve that treatment, Mom. Stop thinking things like that. Nobody ever deserves to be treated that way. Your biggest mistake was not leaving him. You could've taken my sisters with you and oh my goodness, how much better all our lives would've been."

My mom shook her head and sighed. "It wasn't that easy. He held the purse strings, liefling. I had a little bit of money of my own that I'd saved, but it wasn't very much—and I wouldn't allow myself to sink back into poverty, dragging everyone down with me. I just couldn't do that. So, there was nothing else I could do. He owned my mother's house, the one that Uncle Willy lives in now. He threatened to throw Mom and Willy onto the street if I left him—he would have done that. And what's more, he threatened I would never see my children again. I knew very well what he was capable of, so my hands were tied. I had to stay. There was no other option."

I heard footsteps as they came towards us—and then I felt the warmth of Esther and Emma's arms encircling us both.

# CHAPTER 12

If anyone was annoyed that I was going on a business trip to San Francisco when I'd only been working at the agency for less than a year, nobody said anything—except for Gabby. "Talk about luck and timing," she remarked. "I wish I'd taken that Zinkwazi project instead of passing it onto you. It serves me right; I didn't feel like driving up there so often—I've got too much stuff going on here. My husband, oh hell…what can I say? These men in the Strydom family are a difficult bunch. He's just like his father and brother. They're all the same. Sometimes I don't know why I married him, honestly. He used to be so different when we were first married, but now…" She shrugged it off and gave a weak smile. "Enough about that. You deserve this, Joanna. You've worked hard and put in long hours. Your work is really impressive. Well done. I'm happy for you."

I appreciated the praise, but I shuddered inwardly as she bemoaned her husband. August Nel's words rang in my ears: *Romantic love is nothing but lust and hormones.* I didn't want to believe him, nor to think about that awful man.

Tom and I met at Oliver Tambo Airport in Johannesburg for our flight to New York, with a connection on to San Francisco. There would be lots of time for us to talk. I was looking forward to that, although not to all the hours sitting on a plane. It had been a difficult time for Tom on the home front and I wasn't sure how, or if, it had been resolved.

Shortly after take-off from Johannesburg, we were served dinner. As we sipped wine, he described what had happened when he returned home after dropping me off at my mother's. "I opened the door to find four large boxes, with all my clothes in them, sitting on the hall floor. There was a note on top of one: *It's over. Sleep in the guest room until you've found somewhere else to stay.*

"I suppose I'd hoped she hadn't meant it when she said she wanted me to move out. Those boxes made it clear that she did. The house was very quiet; in fact, the silence was oppressive, so I went into my office to put on some music—and that's when I saw what she'd done." He shook his head and muttered, "I'll never forgive her."

I felt myself go cold. He asked the flight attendant for a whisky and I waited to hear what Cynthia had done; I almost didn't want to know, though.

He gulped down some of his drink before telling me what had happened. "She'd slashed the photograph of your mother to shreds, Joanna. They say hell hath no fury like a woman scorned—well, I can attest to that. There was such frenzy in those cuts; I would never have expected it from Cynthia. She's always been very much in control of her emotions. Not anymore." I turned away, embarrassed to see him in such distress, but he wanted to talk and needed my attention. "I suppose I was happy enough living with her. It wasn't like it had been with your mom—but Cynthia and I made it work. We were companions, more than anything. She got on with her life and I got on with mine, and we were respectful of each other." He grunted and shook his head. "Respect!

Well, there's no more of that now—absolutely no respect. That's dead and buried. I wish I'd divorced her years ago. I should've done it when I fell in love with your mother, and then maybe Petra would've divorced that monster she married. Maybe she wasn't sure of my commitment because I didn't leave my wife. Maybe that's why she wouldn't leave him. Goddammit, I should've divorced Cynthia then. Maybe that would've convinced Petra to marry me." I could see that the whisky was loosening his tongue and he was getting things off his chest as he continued to rant. "My God, I didn't know Cynthia was capable of such passion; it's a pity she didn't display some of it in other ways. Living with her was like living with one of her goddam antique clocks—a beautiful object ticking away the hours, something I had to treat carefully in case it broke. Well, there's no going back. It was a prized piece of art that she destroyed. She can't forgive me, and I can't forgive her either. It's over."

"But don't you have the negative?" I asked.

He shook his head. "She went through my desk and found it. She did a good job of destroying the negative too. I suppose I can see if the Arts' Council has any images of it still, but it's been such a long time, I doubt they will."

"Wow," I said, trying to imagine such behavior—and then a smile spread across my face. Reaching into my bag, I grabbed my phone and found the photograph I'd taken in his study. "Does this help?"

He took the phone from me and as he stared at the picture, his hand began to tremble. His expression started to change as he looked at it. After a while he started to smile and said, "Oh, Joanna. Thank you, thank you. You have no idea what this means to me." He gulped his whisky down, still holding my phone, still staring at the photograph.

I couldn't believe how long the flight was. We both managed to sleep a fair bit on the overnight section to New York, but we still had another six hours to go after landing at JFK. Tom seemed in a much better mood when he awoke; the whisky had worn off and his prized photograph was not lost after all. I recognized some landmarks as we flew over the Rocky Mountains and the Grand Canyon, and then I must've dozed off, waking in time to see the snow-capped Sierras. It wasn't too long afterwards that the pilot announced we'd soon be arriving in San Francisco where it seemed like we were going to land on the bay itself as we approached the runway, flying lower and lower over the water. I held my breath and gripped the armrests until we'd touched down safely, at which point I breathed a sigh of relief that we were on dry land. It all seemed unreal. Reaching across to Tom, I took his hand and said, "Never in my wildest dreams did I imagine this could happen to me. Thank you."

"And I never imagined I'd have a daughter to travel with. Thank *you*," he replied.

Despite exhaustion and jet lag, adrenalin had me wide awake. I knew it was a business trip, but it felt like a vacation. Fortunately, we didn't have any appointments or meetings until the next day, so we had an afternoon and evening to explore. Our hotel was situated near Union Square, a famous landmark in the city, and we caught the cable car from there down the hill to Fisherman's Wharf. I'd seen movies set here before, and listening to the sounds the trolley made—the wheels on the tracks, the cables turning below the road, the occasional clanging of the bell—made me feel like I was in a movie. I half-expected to see a car chase down the steep hills, but when we reached the wharf, it looked familiar for another reason. I turned to Tom and said, "Look at all the seagulls swooping around, checking for anything dropped by fishermen. It reminds me of Cape Town. It could be Hout Bay."

"Funny you should say that," he replied. "I've always thought the same thing—maybe that's why I feel so at home here. Every time I come, I love the place more. It's not just the beauty of the city—although it *is* spectacular—but the people are so diverse and cosmopolitan. I think you'll love it too."

"I do already," I replied.

He laughed and said, "And I love your enthusiasm, Joanna. Please don't ever become blasé and lose that quality. I remember how you loved Durban when you first arrived there; now you're reacting the same way to San Francisco."

I thought it would be impossible for me to become blasé. I came from nothing and he had given me the world. I felt enormous gratitude. I would never take it for granted.

Back at the hotel, we checked emails and I airdropped the photograph to Tom; I saw him staring at it again for quite some time, with a smile on his face. I wasn't sure whether his pleasure came from seeing his masterpiece, seeing my mother, or outwitting Cynthia—but I was pleased that I could help him. In fact, while we had a quick bite to eat—local clam chowder that he recommended—I noticed him looking at the picture surreptitiously. But despite the excitement, by 8:30 I could hardly keep my eyes open, and although I didn't want to waste a minute, I had to give in to exhaustion.

I awoke early the next morning and headed out for a walk before breakfast. It was chilly, but I loved the crisp autumn freshness with the smell of coffee emanating from cafés. People were grabbing their early morning to-go fixes before hurrying on their way—with beverages in hand, they all smiled at me as they passed by, making me marvel at the friendliness of the city.

I walked all the way around Union Square, peering at store fronts already decorated for Christmas, feasting my eyes on the wealth of merchandise, and gawking at a Christmas tree through the windows of a department store—the tree stood three stories high. I wondered how on earth they got it in there? It was mind-boggling—and frustrating that the stores didn't open until 10 o'clock, by which time I would be in a meeting. Remembering that, I looked at my watch and hurried back to the hotel so that I could prepare for the day ahead. Christmas shopping would have to wait.

Tom did almost all the talking when we met the clients at GREEN headquarters. He called on me to show various garments we'd brought as samples, and I was able to explain details about the styling. We also had samples of fabric to show them, all of which were woven in South Africa. The team scrutinized everything and questioned me extensively, and although I was nervous, they appeared satisfied with my answers. To my delight, I was then free to go, leaving Tom to negotiate the deal with the client.

With a day and a half to see the sights of San Francisco, I hardly stopped for breath and my camera worked overtime. The concierge at the hotel suggested I take a bus tour, but that sounded lame. I wanted to do things on my own, so he gave me suggestions about where to go. My first stop was nearby Chinatown. The street signs were all in Mandarin and as people around me were speaking a foreign language, it made me feel like I was actually in China. Next up, I visited an art museum, the Legion of Honor, where I wished I could have spent a whole day—but time was too short for that; a quick whip around was all I could manage. I was able to see the small Holocaust memorial close by, and when I saw the Golden Gate Bridge in the distance, it felt like I was in a dream. I'd seen so many photographs of the iconic bridge, and there it actually was. I could hardly contain my excitement and ran across the road to take my own photos of the structure, wishing it was close enough for me to walk there. When I jumped in a taxi and asked to be taken to it, the cab driver informed me that the road was temporarily closed because of a major accident and oil spill; there would be a lengthy delay until it was cleared. This was very frustrating. There was so much I wanted to see with so little time, and I was running out of steam. Exhaustion was getting the better of me and I regretted that I hadn't elected to go on a tourist bus instead of trying to do it all myself. What was I thinking? I hadn't even got to the Golden Gate Bridge and now I wouldn't be able to do so.

Seeing how disappointed I was, the taxi driver suggested a ride through Golden Gate Park instead, and a drive-by to see the mansions in Pacific Heights before he dropped me off on Fillmore Street. This he described as a fun residential area of San Francisco—it seemed like a poor substitute, but I did it anyway and later would be glad that I had done so.

Needing to sit down, I stopped for a bite to eat at one of the restaurants lining the street and texted a photo of my food to Emma. She was always keen to see what other chefs were preparing. I found enough energy after that to explore some of the nearby boutiques where the clothes on display were stunning; I took copious pictures and texted them to my sisters. It was a relief that I could communicate with them again; I wanted Esther and Emma to see everything here and wished they were with me. It was a shock though when I looked at the price tags in the boutiques; my South African rands could afford nothing. All I could do was take photographs and hope that talented Esther would be able to replicate the designs someday.

I loved everything about San Francisco; it was alive with beauty and excitement. I knew I wanted to return and determined to start saving so that I could make that happen as soon as possible.

# CHAPTER 13

It was a long way to go for a week. Despite the fact that I slept for hours on the way home, I was still exhausted when I arrived back in Durban. Fortunately, I had all of Sunday to recuperate from jet lag and was able to head into the office somewhat refreshed the next day. Everyone was eager to hear about my trip—there were a few comments about it being a boondoggle. I didn't mind their teasing until Promise took it a step further. She laughed and said, "Just admit you've found yourself a sugar daddy, girl. It's not enough that he wines and dines you here in Durban. Oh, don't try and play the innocent; I've seen you out together. I've also seen him going to your flat when I'm on my way to catch a taxi. And now he flies you to America on a business trip! Hey, what sort of business was that? He's twice your age but I reckon he's still got what it takes. He could put his shoes under my bed any day!"

There was an immediate hush in the room; everyone knew she'd gone too far. I was incensed. Without thinking, I spun around and said, "How dare you say that? He's not anybody's sugar daddy. He's my father."

There was silence in the room as everyone stared at me. I glared at Promise, who murmured, "I'm sorry. I had no idea." She looked confused as she hurried back to her desk, and I was fuming as I headed to my cubicle. When I picked up a pen, my hand was shaking. As I tried to steady it, it dawned on me that this was the first time I had acknowledged publicly that Tom was my dad. It felt good—and I felt proud.

I became aware of someone behind me and when I looked up, Gabby was standing there. She put a hand on my shoulder and patted me gently. "How much longer will you be working at Zinkwazi?" she asked.

"I'll probably finish up by the end of January."

"You've done great work there and Walter tells me that the meeting at GREEN went well. Good job."

I blushed, appreciative of the praise. It proved to her, and me, that I'd earned the trip because of my work, not because of my father. This was confirmed when she added, "I want you to work with me on a big project that's come up with the KZN Tourist Board. It involves a lot of travel for me, unfortunately, but it's too good to refuse. Here's my plan. I'll start work here in Durban as soon as I can, then I'll head down the South Coast to cover that area. After Christmas, I'll go to the Drakensberg and the Midlands, and then in February, it's off to Mkuze Game Reserve, the iSimangaliso Wetlands, and the Saint Lucia Estuary. That's where I'd like you to help me—if you're done with the clothing factory by then. You've got a good eye for capturing unique angles and I've told Walter that's just the help I need; another set of eyes—and a traveling companion."

I was touched by her words, and relieved not to be returning to advertise household products again. This new project sounded even better than the Zinkwazi one and I couldn't wait to get started in February. First, though, the office would close for a week between Christmas and New Year.

The previous Christmas I'd spent on my own and it had been miserable, so I suggested to my mom that she join me in Durban. I really wanted her to see where I was living and, now that she was unencumbered by August, she was delighted with the idea. Two days before Christmas, we visited a day spa—me to have a pedicure, and my mom to have a hair appointment. She emerged with a new look. Gone was the long hair, streaked with grey, tied up in a boring twist; instead she sported a short bob, cut to just below her ears, with not a grey hair to be seen. More importantly though, gone was the anxious frown.

Tom had invited me to spend Christmas with him, joining some friends in Westville who'd taken pity on him after the break up with Cynthia. I declined the invitation. Because the relationship between my parents was strained, I didn't tell him what my plans were; I let him presume that I was going back to Cape Town for the holidays. He looked astonished when he facetimed me on Christmas morning and saw me in my flat in Durban. There was a note of exasperation in his voice when he said, "Joanna, you can't be on your own for Christmas. Let me come and fetch you. Please come and join us here; my friends would love to meet you—and I want to see you."

"It's OK. I'm not on my own," I replied.

There was a moment's silence before he said, "I see. Are you dating someone? Is there something I should know?"

I started to laugh. "Perhaps you'd like to say Happy Christmas?" I turned the phone so that he could see my mom, who waved at him before looking away. I could tell that she felt uncomfortable as I saw her back stiffen and her smile disappear.

"Oh, I see. Your mother is with you." His tone was sharp.

There was an awkward silence and I wanted to scream,

"Get over it." I said nothing, however, and Tom muttered something to the effect that he hoped we had a happy time together. On an impulse, I replied, "Why don't you come over and join us?"

"I can't just walk out on my hosts here. I wish you'd asked me beforehand. We could've made a plan."

The injured expression on his face prompted me to blurt out, "Well if you and my mother were on better terms, I would've done so." I heard my mom gasp and saw Tom frown, so I added, "I'm sorry if your feelings are hurt, but I don't know how to deal with the situation between the two of you. I feel like I have to tread so carefully around you both."

A few hours later, Tom knocked on the door. He held a bunch of flowers, looking flushed and slightly unsteady on his feet as he handed me the bouquet. "I hoped this would be our first Christmas together, Joanna. For twenty-two years, I've not had that pleasure." Turning to my mother, he muttered under his breath, "You denied me even that, Petra."

She flinched and I felt indignation rising in me. "It had nothing to do with her. She didn't even know you were in Durban. It's the goddam awful way you two act that forced me to choose between you for Christmas. It's awful. I wish you would get over it, both of you." There was a stunned silence as I looked from one of them to the other. Finally, I turned to Tom and said, "Seeing that you're here now, why don't you come in? Don't just stand in the doorway."

He hesitated, but when I handed him a glass of champagne, he stepped inside and I raised my glass to say, "Happy Christmas, Mom and Dad."

"So, Mom," I said to her, a few days later, "explain to me why you married August."

We were together in Ramsgate, a small beach town on the South Coast of KwaZulu-Natal, where I'd booked us into a bed and breakfast for a few days. There was a coastal path in front of the house and as we sat on the rocks, listening to waves crashing around us, it seemed a good place to ask some of the questions that had been puzzling me. She tilted her head backwards, breathing in the salty spray, and I thought for a moment that my voice had been drowned out by the sound of the sea—but she inhaled deeply and turned to me. "It's probably hard for you to understand and I'm pleased about that. It means I brought you up to be an independent woman," she said. "I wasn't so fortunate, you see. I'm not saying my mother didn't try her best; she did. But her circumstances were different. She was a single mother and the sole provider for her family."

"What happened to your father?" I asked. "You've never talked about him."

She frowned and sighed. "I didn't know him. He was French. His name was Marcel Thibault and he was white—so he and my mother broke the law. This was back in the days of segregation, you see, and Willie and I were living proof of their relationship. Apartheid forbade them from, you know...having relations, even though they were in love with one another."

I wanted to ask many more questions, but she looked away and I realized that she needed to compose herself first. I could tell that it was going to take a while before she answered my original question as to why she'd married August Nel.

She took her time before starting to tell me the story.

"My father was a winemaker from Bordeaux who came to South Africa frequently on business. Mom was working at an old wine estate in Stellenbosch at the time. One of her duties was to arrange fresh flowers in the tasting room and the restaurant. That's where they met and fell in love. They had to be very careful about their affair—and because of the apartheid laws, it was impossible for them to marry unless they moved to France. Mom was trying to get a passport so that they could do that, but the authorities were suspicious. She felt she was being watched, and when she discovered she was pregnant, she and my father were really afraid. He decided it was best to get her away from Stellenbosch. They found a place in Salt River, a small flat that she rented for years—where I grew up. They were lucky to escape detection because if they'd been caught, Mom would have gone to prison. He might have been imprisoned too, or deported.

"It was a big shock when they had twins. Of course, he supported her financially after Willie and I were born, and things were on track for her passport, but then she had to get passports for us kids as well. Questions were asked about our father. She'd put 'unknown' on our birth certificates to protect Marcel—they planned to change that when they got to France. This didn't fly with the passport office; they stalled endlessly, wanting to know where Mom was planning to go and why. And then, while they took their sweet time, Mom got terrible news from Marcel's parents—he'd been killed in a car accident. Willie and I were just two years old."

"My God, that's awful," I said. "Poor Gran..."

"It's hard for us to imagine how difficult it was for her. Marcel had left her with a little bit of money," she continued, "and his parents sent more. They really wanted to come and see their grandchildren, but they were afraid to get Mom into trouble if it was discovered that she'd had children by a white man. She told them not to come; it was too dangerous. She never did get the passports, so we never met our grandparents—and she never told others who the father was, for the same reason. She used the money to start a florist shop; Willie and I worked there, helping her, from when we were young. Later on, when I finished high school, I went to night school and studied bookkeeping so that I could do the accounting. Willie did the deliveries."

"But it still doesn't explain why you married August."

"I'm coming to that. You see, we struggled financially, but we survived; we squeaked by from month to month. It was especially tough in winter though, because flowers were so expensive at the market. Rent for the shop and flat combined sometimes chewed up all we earned and then we eked by on bread and water for weeks. But August's family were well-off; his dad had a shop..."

"Don't tell me; I know all about it. If I heard it once, I heard it a million times. He had a shop in District Six that was bulldozed, along with their house," I said, groaning.

"I know how often you've heard it, but it was very traumatic. Don't downplay it. They were tough times we all had to live through—everybody in the country who wasn't white lived through the same miserable time. The government was cruel. There were so many injustices, even for those who had money, but it was much, much worse for those of us who were poor—which was most of us." She sighed and stared at the ocean for a while. I was eager to hear more, but I couldn't hurry her with the story.

"It was winter and times were particularly tough that year," she eventually continued. "There was a heck of a storm going on when August came into the shop with

Hendrik one day, to escape the rain. They were sharing an umbrella and laughing as they came in the door. I was busy preparing some flowers for an arrangement and I remember him watching me. He wasn't bad looking in those days. Nor was Hendrik, believe it or not. After that, August came again often—not to buy anything, just to stand and stare. He never said anything."

"I'm not surprised. He came because you're so beautiful," I said.

She swallowed hard and said, "It became uncomfortable, so whenever I saw him coming, I used to duck out the back door. He got wise to that and followed to ask why I was avoiding him. I didn't answer, but honestly, it made me nervous—he was like a predator. It really put me off when he started asking all sorts of personal questions, like how old I was, and where did I live. He even asked if I had a boyfriend. He seemed very sure of himself, entitled to ask all those things, yet he never invited me out or anything. He just watched and asked questions. Every now and again he would buy flowers, so I couldn't ignore him because he was actually a customer. Then one day he arrived with his father, who also stood watching me. That was really creepy, and it was even worse when they came back a few days later with an offer—they would give us quite a sum of money if I would marry August.

"I just about choked; it was an outrageous proposition. Your grandmother gave them short shrift, I can tell you. 'Gentlemen, I'd like you to leave. I sell flowers. My daughter is not for sale,' she shouted at them. They left immediately and I burst out laughing.

"Months went by and oh my goodness, it was a terrible winter. The storms were unrelenting; it rained nonstop and it was bitterly cold. We had one little bar heater to try and stay warm in our flat, but our place kept flooding every time a northwester blew. The shop was also freezing. Flowers were expensive and scarce—and so were customers. When your grandmother developed a cough that wouldn't go away, there was no money to take her to the doctor. She was in such a bad way that I thought she was going to die, for sure. She was shaking and delirious; she didn't even know I was there. She probably had pneumonia. I was really frightened and I didn't know how we were going to pay the rent. I thought we'd have to give up the shop and become flower sellers at the side of the road. That's when I began to think about August Nel's offer.

As luck would have it, he didn't give up on his idea. He came back with his father one day and offered to sweeten the deal. Not only would they give us a large sum of money, they would also pay for Mom to get medical attention. She could stop working immediately and furthermore, they would buy her a house—if I accepted the proposal to marry August. When I looked at the offer coldly, it seemed the only way out. What else could I do? I was no longer laughing when I made inquiries to find out more about him and his family. Everything they'd described about their finances was true and there didn't seem to be any scandal linked to the family, so—as there wasn't anybody else in my life—I agreed."

I shuddered, but tried not to show my reaction. "I've never seen pictures of your wedding," I said.

"Well, it was a simple affair. No wedding photographer. We got married in a registry office with my mom and Willie standing up with me; August had his parents and Hendrik with him. Hendrik was his best man. It was very small; that was the entire wedding party. I wasn't exactly a radiant bride, but I wasn't unhappy. It was a bit of an adventure in a dreary existence that seemed to offer me and my mom a better life—it was an escape from drudgery. And actually, August wasn't all that bad in those early days; as I said, he really was quite good-looking."

"He looks like a walrus now," I grunted.

I think my mom wanted to laugh, but she looked away quickly and continued to talk. "I don't know why he hadn't found a wife before because he had a lot to offer—but when I met him, he was over forty years old already and still unmarried. When I told my mother that I'd agreed to marry him, she wasn't convinced I was doing the right thing. I didn't want her to worry so I persuaded her that I loved him. What a joke! I hardly knew him."

"How could you, Mom?"

"Don't stand in judgment, liefling. You haven't walked in my shoes; you have no idea what it was like. It was a way out of poverty for all of us—Mom, Willie and me. Willie moved in with Mom and they were able to live comfortably together; I was grateful to August for that." She sighed before adding, "Hendrik got married at about the same time; he married a distant cousin. I liked his wife and was happy for them when she produced a son."

"I never met his wife. What happened to her?" I asked.

"The marriage didn't last long. She ran away and left him with baby Marius; the little chap was only one year old at the time. The poor boy was brought up by his grandparents and a nanny. He had an unhappy childhood. I don't know where his mother went—I worried about her; a woman must be unwell to leave her child like that. I thought she might be suffering from post-partum depression and in need of help. But people didn't pay much attention to mental health in those days and August wouldn't speak about it at all; he said she didn't deserve my concern.

"I really had no idea what a bad temper August had until a few years into our marriage when I hadn't produced the son he wanted, only two daughters. He got steadily worse the older he got—and Hendrik seemed to make things more unbearable, making derogatory remarks about me. It was upsetting that August always laughed, rather than defending me."

"He might be out of the coma now, but I'm glad he can't speak. August Nel got what he deserves," I said.

My mom shook her head and frowned. "I don't like to hear you say things like that," she replied.

"Oh please. I'm being honest."

"Stop it, Joanna. Don't talk like that. I'm told that he's able to communicate with Hendrik somehow, but he hasn't spoken to me or your sisters at all. I'm not sure I believe Hendrik; I think it's wishful thinking on his part. Whenever I've been to the hospital, August is just lying there, staring into space with his mouth open. He might be able to make sounds, but I don't think he can speak. I was worried about affording long term care for him, but thank goodness Hendrik is paying to transfer him to a convalescent home and keep him there for rehab. He told Emma he doesn't want August coming back to live with me."

"Thank goodness. That's a plus for you. It's generous of Hendrik; maybe he's got a guilty conscience for all the digs he's had at your expense. But no matter what you say, I think August deserves everything that's happened to him. It's karma. It's divine justice."

She didn't bother to deny it and I put an arm around her as we sat silently, staring at the waves. When I closed my eyes, I listened to the never-ending ebb and flow of the sea, punctuated with mournful cries from gulls; it was restful. After a while, Mom leaned her head against my shoulder and whispered, "I'm thankful I saved you from a similar fate, liefling. Esther and Emma didn't mind marrying men of their father's choosing—they seemed eager to get away. Fortunately, they married good men and their lives are happy. But you were not his. I couldn't let him trap you into a marriage you didn't want. And Marius...well, he's not exactly an appealing man. I was not going to let that happen."

"I would never have agreed to it, Mom."

She sighed. "My poor mother, she found her love but she couldn't marry him because he was a white man. And I found my love, but I found him too late; he was married and so was I. My prayer for you is that when you find love, you recognize it, nurture it, hold on to it, and live happily ever after. The women in our family need a story like that for a change. History must stop repeating itself."

I had tears in my eyes as I hugged her. "You know, you still have a chance to be happy, Mom," I whispered. "It's not too late."

She shook her head. "It's a sad thing when love turns to hate, liefling. There's no going back. What I did to your father can't be undone. He despises me for it."

# CHAPTER 14

Much as I'd enjoyed the project, it was a relief when I signed off at Zinkwazi and was free to accompany Gabby to Mkuze. I'd grown to enjoy her company and accept her abruptness. She'd avoided questioning me about my family, just as I avoided asking about hers—although she'd mentioned she was having issues with her husband. He disliked the long hours she was working and he especially didn't like her going away on business trips. I was happy to keep our private lives just that—private.

It took us just under four hours getting to Mkuze, and my excitement was growing. I'd never been to a game reserve before and my world was expanding with new experiences I never dreamed might happen to me. Once we passed Richard's Bay, we saw signs to the World Heritage Site, iSimangaliso Wetlands Park, and Gabby announced that we were almost at our destination. "We won't be far from Mozambique, you know. We should've brought our passports so that we could hop over the border and have some peri-peri prawns. They're cheap and delicious, especially if you wash them down with Portuguese white wine."

"That sounds good. For someone who'd never been out of Cape Town until a year ago, my horizons have exploded, but maybe it wouldn't be quite kosher seeing we're working for the KZN Tourist Board."

"That's true..." After a moment she added, "So, what

made you move to Durban?"

It was a question I didn't much feel like answering, so I gave an abbreviated version. "I needed a change of scene. That's all."

"Boyfriend issues?" she asked. I was surprised that she was asking questions; it was unlike her.

"Kind of," I replied, "but not really. I haven't had many boyfriends. Actually, none at all. Lots of friends, but no romances."

"I find that hard to believe," she said, glancing at me for a moment. "You look like you could have any man you want. Come on, be honest."

"I'm telling you, it's true. It was difficult—my family life wasn't really conducive to having a boyfriend. I had a very strict upbringing. And I've never really met anyone who… you know… made my heart beat faster. So, what was the point? Just to say I had a boyfriend? I don't think so…"

She said nothing at first, but after a few moments she commented, "But your dad seems so mellow."

I smiled. "Yeah, he is. I didn't grow up with him, though."

"Oh, I see."

That stopped the questioning.

I could hardly wait to get going the following morning, my camera at the ready. The sun was just rising as we set out and I begged Gabby to stop so that I could capture images of trees, darkly silhouetted against the orange sky. "Don't be ridiculous. You're in a game reserve. You can't get out here," she said. "We have to stay in the car until we get to the hide. It's not safe otherwise; you don't know what's lurking in the bushes." She was clearly annoyed and sounded very grumpy, but I ignored her sharpness. Nothing was going to dampen my excitement and I'd already taken many photos by the time we got to the hide, ready to watch for game at Nsumo Pan.

"Animals come to drink at the water hole here, so it's a great viewing spot. It's fed by the Mkuze River and I'm told it's a breeding ground for pelicans—there are plenty of hippos and crocs here, too. We might even get lucky and see other stuff as well."

"You've done your research, but hey, it looks like we've got company," I said, pointing to a vehicle parked nearby.

"That's an official jeep. Hopefully they're not in the hide. I like to work without spectators," she muttered.

Perhaps Gabby had slept badly, or else she was still fuming over an argument with her husband, but I hoped her attitude would improve soon. The next few days could be unpleasant if her bad mood prevailed.

We climbed a steep ramp into the hide and discovered two guys there ahead of us. We nodded silently at the men and quickly positioned ourselves to watch impala drinking at the pan. Pelicans swooped amongst them while hippos were rising, snorting, and submerging again—and a croc drifted by with just his eyes visible. Another crocodile lay on the bank with his mouth wide open. It was unlike anything I'd ever experienced, and although I was enthralled by the wildness of it all, I grew apprehensive. Voicing my concern, I whispered, "I hope those hippos won't walk up the ramp into the hide. Aren't they supposed to be the most dangerous animals in Africa? There doesn't seem to be much separating us from them."

The Zulu man smiled at me reassuringly. "Oh no, you don't have to worry here. They stay in the water during the day to stay cool. They only come out to eat at night." He then introduced himself as Mpilo; his friend was Ryan.

"Yup, no worries. And they're mostly herbivores. You're totally safe here," Ryan added.

I'd hardly noticed either of the men, but I did a double take when I heard Ryan talk. "Are you American?" I asked, louder than I'd meant to speak.

"I sure am," he replied.

I couldn't help smiling. "Wow. Where are you from in the States?"

"San Francisco," he replied.

"Oh, my gosh, I don't believe it. That's insane. I've just come back from there a couple of months ago. What a coincidence. Oh man, I loved San Francisco. So, what are you doing here?"

"Same as you—birdwatching and game viewing."

"You know what I mean... Why are you in South Africa?"

"It's a long story," he began, but was cut off sharply by Gabby.

"Can you keep your voices down?" Her tone was brusque as she settled her elbows on a ledge, trying to steady her camera. "The idea is to be quiet so that wildlife doesn't know we're in these hides."

I rolled my eyes and mouthed, "I'm sorry," to Ryan.

He seemed unperturbed and whispered, "If you're at the lodge tonight, I'll tell you then. We could talk some more."

I wouldn't normally have agreed to make a date with a strange man; in fact, it was the last thing in the world I would've done. August had made me distrustful of men, although Tom Montgomery was beginning to prove to me that August Nel was not every man. But, the fact that this guy was from San Francisco was intriguing—and Gabby was being a pain, so it would be a relief to escape her company. I nodded and Ryan gave me a thumbs-up before lowering his voice and pointing out the pelican breeding grounds on the other side of the pan. I noticed Mpilo give him an amused look and punch him as he did so. They appeared to be good friends.

I couldn't help but be impressed by Ryan's looks. He was tall and unshaven. His skin showed evidence of spending a lot of time in the sun—he was kind of rugged. Although I was trying to concentrate on the pan, I kept peeping at him. It was almost unbelievable that I should meet someone from San Francisco here in the wilderness of Africa. He caught me glancing at him once and smiled at me. His face lit up when he did so; there was an ease about him that was warm and engaging. I wanted to see him again and when Gabby and I left after half an hour, I surprised myself by whispering, "See you later."

I wasn't sure why Gabby was being so unpleasant and I tackled her when we got back to the car. "Why did you want to leave there so quickly? I thought it was such a good place to watch animals coming to drink. We hardly gave it any time."

She grunted. "It was long enough for you to hit on some American guy. Anyway, it's a big reserve and we've got more to see. You can't sit around chatting up some stranger all day; you're supposed to be working." Her face was frosty as she turned on me and said, "I thought you had such a strict upbringing; you've certainly shaken that off without any problem."

"That's unfair," I replied. "I was hardly chatting him up—or hitting on him."

"Stop playing the innocent, Joanna. I can see through

the façade."

I was furious. We barely spoke for the rest of the day as we made our way through the park. Nothing we saw was as good as what we'd seen at the hide, and it became apparent that we needed to return there the following day. I wanted to say, "I told you so," but held my tongue. Gabby's issues with her husband were spilling over into other areas of her life and I resented her comments—it took all my willpower to keep quiet. Years growing up with August Nel had taught me the futility of arguing with an angry person.

It was a relief when Gabby chose to stop work early, pleading that she had a headache and wouldn't be eating dinner. I took the opportunity to take a shower and wash my dust-coated hair, thankful not to be with Gabby while she was acting so strangely. I didn't care whether she was disapproving or not; in fact, it made me more determined to meet this American man again. She might be in charge of my work, but she was not in charge of my private life. With that in mind, I took extra care selecting what I would wear just to prove my point; I chose white jeans and a body-hugging red shirt. When I was ready to go, I struck a pose in front of her and said, "See you later. Hope you feel better soon."

She was lying on her bed in our shared room, talking on the phone, a wet cloth over her forehead. She lifted it and stared at me through half-opened eyes, grunted, shook her head, and replaced the cloth without saying anything.

I got to the lodge before Ryan and ordered a glass of wine while I waited. But five minutes began to feel like fifteen, and ten minutes later I began to think I was making a fool of myself. Well, I wouldn't give Gabby the satisfaction of seeing me return; I'd have dinner in the lodge by myself and she wouldn't be any the wiser. I was still sipping my wine when I saw him arriving in a rush. He was apologetic about keeping me waiting as he ordered a beer and took a sip. Smacking his lips and smiling as his eyes strayed over me, he said, "Ah, that's pretty good." It made my heart beat a little faster. I wasn't used to receiving such appreciative looks and I liked it. Was it the beer that was pretty good, or was it me? The look on his face made me think it might be the latter. If Gabby saw me now, she would definitely have something to say.

I was curious to know more about where he'd lived in San Francisco and what he was doing in Africa. He explained where he'd grown up—it was close to Fillmore Street, he said—and I instantly felt prickles down my arms. Suddenly I was glad that I'd gone there instead of to the Golden Gate Bridge.

"That's so amazing. I've been there," I said. "I had a bite to eat in one of those restaurants that line the street."

He smiled and said, "I hope it was good."

"It was—and it was expensive too."

He laughed, and then continued to explain that he'd been teaching for two years in a remote Namibian village, working for the Peace Corps.

"And now you're heading back to the States?" I asked.

He screwed up his face and shook his head. "Not just yet. I've got a few months left here still, exploring, and then I'm supposed to be starting a job in New York. I've fallen in love with Africa though, it'll be hard to leave the place. What about you? You've heard my story. Where are you from?"

"I'm originally from Cape Town, but now I live in Durban," I replied. I didn't want to get into discussions about family, so I said, "Nothing as exciting as San Francisco. I'd like to be a freelance photographer but that's tough going, so I work for an advertising firm to pay the bills until I can establish myself. We have a gig with the KZN Tourist Board, which got me a few days working here at Mkuze and the estuary."

"Nice," Ryan said. "What about Gabby?"

"She's also a photographer."

"She seems an in-charge kind of woman. I'm glad you could get away from her for a bit."

"She's not so bad really. I get on well with her most of the time, but her life is a bit tough at the moment. I left her arguing on the phone with her husband."

He shrugged and said, "She doesn't have to take it out on everyone else. Bossy people are a pain in the ass—must be difficult working with her." It was a surprise to discover how perceptive he was and I appreciated his candor. He smiled and added, "Come on, let's go and sit in front of the campfire outside the lodge. We can have our drinks there. It's a beautiful place in the evening; you can get lost in your thoughts." He stood up and gestured towards the door—and when I arose, he placed a hand on my back to guide me. It felt good. And he was right, it was beautiful outside, and peaceful too. "I've heard they call this bush TV. You can sit here, staring into the flames, and forget about everything else. It's mesmerizing."

It seemed like sacrilege to speak and spoil the silence of the bush, except it wasn't silent. I could hear a chorus of frogs, with crickets adding to the concert. A lion gave a solo performance with a roar that sounded very close by. It startled me, but Ryan assured me it was miles away. "Sound travels a long way at night," he said. It was magical, sitting there warm and safe, with the wildness of an

African night surrounding us. As I sat listening to the crackling logs, I was aware that Ryan was watching me. I looked up at him and said, "A penny for your thoughts."

"They're not worth that much," he laughed, quickly looking away, seemingly a bit embarrassed. "My mind was a blank," he replied. "I was just listening to the night sounds. What were you thinking?"

I could feel myself blushing and was thankful for the dim light which made that less noticeable. I didn't want to admit exactly what my thoughts were, because they were about him. So, it was only partly true when I replied, "I was thinking how strange it is to meet someone from San Francisco when I've just been there."

"Yeah, that's quite a coincidence. Were you working there, or was it a vacation?"

"A bit of both," I replied. "I had the best time. I'm already saving to go again."

"I tell you what, I'll make a deal with you. How about you show me around Durban, and next time you come to San Francisco, I'll show you around my city?" he suggested.

"Sounds good. I'd love to show you around Durban, but aren't you going to be in New York when you go back?"

He grimaced and sighed. "I'm not so sure. Africa has got into my soul—I'd rather stay here."

"That's crazy. So many South Africans are wanting to leave, but you want to come here to live. Is that what you're saying?"

"I don't really know what I want to do," he said and shrugged.

He suddenly lost his macho appearance and I felt sorry for him. On an impulse, I reached out and touched his hand. "Sometimes things we dread turn out to be different from what we expected," I said. "You can always come back to Africa; it's not going away."

It felt quite natural when he rolled his hand around mine and held it firmly. He smiled at me and said, "I already have a trip planned next year. Mpilo and I are climbing Kilimanjaro together. It's been on my bucket list for as long as I can remember."

I didn't take my hand away and we sat for a long time, saying nothing, staring into the flames, content to just stay there holding hands. I felt at peace—it was a novel experience to be sitting quietly and contentedly with a man I hardly knew. The strange thing was that I felt like I did know him.

I was sorry when we realized that time was marching on and the kitchen would soon close, and as we dragged ourselves away from the fire to go inside the lodge, the spell was broken. We chatted some more, but I think we both realized that the time outside had been special. He asked more about my trip to San Francisco and seemed pleased that I'd loved the place so much. "It's good that you're reminding me about it," he said. "I've been dreading going back, maybe because I don't want to go to New York. My time in Africa has made me realize that I'm not really a city guy."

"Well, I believe San Francisco is a city," I remarked, laughing.

"Yeah, but it's small and there are lots of wide-open spaces around it. You don't have to go far to find wilderness."

"I didn't have the chance to do that," I said. "Next time..."

My heart pounded when he said, "Definitely, and next

time I'll show it all to you, Joanna. When can I see you again?"

I told him we'd be returning to the hide the next day.

"Great. I'll be there too," he said. "I'll see you then, although your friend might not let us talk."

I shrugged and said, "Hopefully she'll have a good night's sleep and be in a better mood. When are you going back to Durban?"

"Next week, on Friday. Can we get together then?"

I tried to sound calm when I replied, "I'd like that. How are you getting back?"

"In one of those taxis I'm sure you've seen. You know the ones, jam-packed with people. Mpilo and I will be squashed in with chickens and a goat or two." He laughed.

I couldn't resist the impulse to issue an invitation—anything to ensure I'd see him again. "Would you like a lift? We'll be going back on Friday as well." I didn't care what Gabby would have to say about the offer; she'd probably grumble, especially as it was her car, but I told myself that it would be an opportunity for her to be civil instead of grumpy.

His face lit up. "Oh, my God, yes please. Taxis and buses are not my favorite forms of transport—and I really want to see you again. But is there room for Mpilo? I can't abandon him."

"Sure. Of course. Not a problem," I replied.

Suddenly, everything seemed right with the world, and although I didn't want the night to end, we both knew there was another early start ahead of us. It was easier to say goodnight, though, knowing it wasn't goodbye. There was a spring in my step as I made my way to bed, hoping that Gabby would be asleep. Thankfully, she was.

She was in a slightly better mood when she woke the next

day; I guess her headache was gone and the issue with her husband was sorted. While the going was good—before she developed another headache or something—I decided to break the news to her that I had offered the two men a ride. She raised her eyebrows and I braced myself for a stormy rebuke, but she merely shrugged and said, "OK."

Even though it was early in the day, it was already hot and steamy. Fortunately, the hide was situated under trees and covered with thatch, so it was relatively cool. Ryan smiled when we arrived, beckoning me to stand next to him. "I kept this spot for you," he whispered, and kept watching me as I walked towards him. I mouthed, "Thanks," and smiled, feeling my heart rate go up.

I was thankful that Mpilo steered Gabby away from us, pointing out some scarlet-chested sunbirds. She was quick to start photographing them and paid little attention to me or Ryan. It wasn't long before I noticed some impala at the water's edge, looking agitated. I'd managed to get a few good shots of them when they suddenly took off into the bush and the reason why became apparent—a pride of lions had arrived for their morning drink. The watering hole immediately became their domain, fifty yards or so away from us. I was so excited that my hands were shaking; I could tell Ryan felt the same way when I heard him murmur, "Holy shit."

They were magnificent cats; three lionesses, eight cubs, and one big male with a dark mane. The cubs kept out of his way and once they'd quenched their thirst, they began to play—wrestling and chasing each other. The adults took their time, crouching down to lap the water, and I managed to get two shots of a lifetime. The first one was when I photographed the male lion drinking—his reflection appeared upside down in the water in front of him.

I was in the right place at the right time and caught the moment on camera; it was magnificent. Then he looked up, and through my telescopic lens, his cold, golden eyes seemed to be staring right at me. I caught that moment as well and that was the second shot of a lifetime.

When they finished drinking, the pride meandered away—leaving the water hole for other animals to take their turn. I stared at the spot where they'd disappeared with my heart pounding, totally under the spell of the bush. Nobody said a word for some time. It was Mpilo who broke the silence. "I'm telling you, man, I've never seen lions here before. We're so lucky we saw them—and close up like that too. Sheez..." He smiled at us and said, "You guys brought us good luck."

That did it for Gabby. She was the one who then made a plan for meeting them the following Friday. They high-fived us as we took our leave and Ryan held my hand just a little longer before letting it go.

Gabby was in a much better frame of mind afterwards. The lion sighting had lifted her spirits and the following days, spent photographing the estuary and the surrounding area, went by without any hitches. I especially loved Lake Nhlange in Kosi Bay, where our evening pictures were exceptional because of the soft light—but nothing compared with my photographs of that lion drinking at Nsumo Pan.

And although I didn't have a photograph of the scene next to the campfire with Ryan, I had an indelible memory of it in my mind. Mkuze had claimed a place in my heart forever.

# CHAPTER 15

Ryan and Mpilo were ready and waiting when we arrived back at Mkuze. Gabby's SUV had lots of space and as they placed their bags next to all the cameras and luggage already there, Ryan remarked, "Wow, there's some serious photographic equipment here."

"We're serious about what we do," I replied, laughing.

"And we're good at it," Gabby added. "Since we left here, we've been up in St. Lucia and taken great photos of the estuary and the wetlands. The lighting's been perfect."

"Do we get to see any of them?" Ryan asked.

"Not yet. We have to edit them first," I replied.

"I'm a patient man. I can wait."

I glanced at him when he said this and he winked at me. I blushed and quickly looked away—but I was smiling as I did so.

When Gabby turned on the radio, conversation became difficult between the front and back seats. Ryan and Mpilo were obviously exhausted; they spread out, put their heads back and closed their eyes. I glanced at them from time to time; they were out for the count. Although I'd hoped to spend the four-hour journey chatting to them, I took the opportunity instead to study Ryan's face by putting my sun visor down and looking at him in the mirror while he slept. He had strong features—a well-defined jaw and high cheek bones. Every now and then he stirred and smiled in his sleep, making me wonder what he was dreaming about. He seemed happy, and I felt happy looking at him.

When we reached Durban, they both woke and sat up. Mpilo rubbed his eyes, while Ryan stretched his arms over his head and looked out the window, frowning. The streets were crowded and the traffic noise was jarring after the stillness of the bush. Already I missed the tranquility of Mkuze and empathized with Ryan's feelings about city life.

Gabby turned the music down and said, "Fellas, where can I drop you off? We're going to our office in Musgrave Centre. Where are you heading?"

Mpilo looked around as if he were trying to figure out where he was. "Um, yeah, Musgrave Centre will be good. Thank you. There's a taxi rank in Greyville not too far away. Ryan, you'll be able to get a taxi back to your place from there."

"Oh, we're close to Greyville now. We can drop you there," I said. "Or you can come to our office, if you like. I can run you home later."

"No, no. Don't drive to the taxi rank. It's too busy. I see where I am now," Mpilo replied. "I don't know what Ryan wants to do, but you can just drop me off here. I'll walk—look, you see over there? That's where the taxi rank is. It's not too far." He pointed to a crowd of people about half a mile away.

Ryan grinned. "Go for it, Mpilo. But I'll take Joanna up on that offer of a ride home."

Gabby was happy not to go any further. She stopped the car, popped the hatch door open for Mpilo to collect his gear, and we waved goodbye. But just as Gabby turned the car around, Ryan remembered something and yelled, "Hang on a minute." Leaping out, he ran towards his friend, shouting something about returning a book. He'd just caught up with Mpilo when we heard the first shots. They sounded like firecrackers.

Suddenly people started running in all directions—many were heading straight towards us. There were screams and more shots, then more shots again. I put my head out the window and screamed, "Quickly, get back in the car." But neither of them heard me—and Gabby wasn't waiting. She started to rev the car, anxious to get away from the trouble as the gunshots carried on and on.

There was no way I could abandon these guys. I shouted at Gabby to stop. She shouted back at me not to be stupid, but when she saw me trying to open the door, she slowed down long enough for me to grab my things and jump out. In retrospect, it was a dangerous thing to do. Maybe it was my photographer's instinct that drove me to do it, but I think it was more likely the urgency to reach Ryan that motivated me.

As I ran in the direction he'd gone, I began taking pictures, hardly knowing what I was recording. I just kept shooting at whatever I saw, knowing I could edit all the shots later. People were rushing past me screaming and wailing, even when the gunshots had stopped. As I fought my way against the crush of people racing in the opposite direction, I saw cars and bakkies shooting past me, and sirens racing towards the taxi rank as the first responders made their way to the scene. I kept on taking photographs—but when I arrived at the place where the shooting had happened, I stopped in horror, staring at the carnage. It looked like a war zone. There were bodies strewn across the street with blood everywhere. Wounded people were moaning in pain, slumped next to the dead. Taxis were on fire, with screaming passengers scrambling to escape the flames that were engulfing them. Children lay among the dead and wounded, some of them lifeless, some whimpering, others screaming.

My heart was pounding as I scanned the scene, searching for Ryan and Mpilo. Suddenly I spotted Ryan; he was the only white face visible in this multitude of people. I made my way to him as best I could, stepping over the dead and injured. When I touched his arm, he spun around in alarm. He was on high alert and his ashen face revealed the shock that he, too, was experiencing. "For God's sake, what are you doing here?" he asked, putting his arm around me and holding me close. That's when I started to shake.

I leaned on him for support and cried, "Holy Mother of God. I came to see if you were OK. Gabby drove away, but I made her stop and let me out. I couldn't leave you stranded. Where's Mpilo? Oh, my God, this is horrific. What the heck has happened?" Shell-shocked, I stood close to him for a few moments until the photographer in me took over and, even though I was shaking, I began to record what I was seeing once more. Ambulances and fire engines continued arriving and paramedics were getting to work with the injured.

"Where the hell does one start to help? Dammit, I wish I could see where Mpilo is," Ryan muttered.

I said nothing as I continued photographing, but it wasn't long before a woman, with blood pouring down her face and a bleeding baby tied on her back, started shouting at me. I realized that her anger was provoked because I was photographing her suffering—and I felt ashamed. I stopped immediately but soon other people joined her, their faces looking murderous. My heart began to pound and I broke into a sweat as the mob grew nearer, when suddenly, like a guardian angel, Mpilo appeared out of nowhere and positioned himself between us and them. Pulling off his own hoodie and grabbing another from his backpack, he threw the garments to us, shouting, "Guys...put these on. Hide your faces. Go. Get away from here quickly. Hamba."

The urgency with which he spoke left no room for argument. Much as we wanted to help, we did as Mpilo ordered and fled the scene, leaving him behind to assist the injured. We didn't stop running until we were safely in Musgrave Centre.

There was no sign of Gabby or anyone else when we collapsed in the office. Adrenalin had kept us going, but suddenly we were drained. It was then that Ryan told me he'd seen two white pick-up vans with armed men in the back, leaving the crime scene. Something registered in my brain. I beckoned him to follow as I headed to my cubicle and began looking at the photos on my camera.

"What are you doing?" he asked.

I didn't respond, but kept going back frantically from one photo to the next. Suddenly I found something. "Look at this." I enlarged the picture as much as possible and handed my camera to Ryan. "See anything interesting?"

He examined it and said, "No, can't say I do. It's a street scene."

"Here, look with a magnifying glass. Two white bakkies are heading away from the taxi rank. Are those the ones you saw—the pick-ups?"

Ryan looked carefully. They were slightly blurred and small, but yes—he seemed to recognize them. His eyes opened wide and he said, "You need to text this to the police."

"Absolutely. They'll have equipment to get greater detail. They might even get the number plate on one of the bakkies. Look, it's there in the photo, but it's too small for us to read here."

"Joanna, you're awesome. Let's get this into the right hands immediately."

The police were able to decipher information that we hadn't been able to see—and a short time later the search was on for the owner of that white bakkie. It was registered to a Petrus Botha. Within a few hours, they'd found him and made an arrest. He had gone on a shooting rampage with another person—the accomplice was still at large, but Petrus was locked up.

Despite being in shock, I felt a rush of pride, recognizing the value of my work. I didn't resist when Ryan put his arms around me and held me tight. "My God, you are something else," he whispered. I closed my eyes, wanting to push the rewind button and go back to Mkuze a few days ago; I wanted to erase today. When he wiped away the tears on my cheeks, it was comforting—and I felt reassured when he said, "It's OK. You're safe now." I was thankful to be with him.

We went back to my apartment to watch the news unfolding on television. Memory of the carnage haunted us; neither of us wanted to be alone and the pride I'd felt in my work evaporated. "I can't bear to look at those photos anymore," I said, as Ryan kept scrutinizing them. "Stop doing that. I know I can sell them and make money, but it doesn't seem right—profiting from someone else's misery."

"I don't agree. People need to see the terrible thing that happened. Pictures speak volumes—they're stronger than words. That's what war photographers do; that's their job. They inform, and they provide records for posterity," Ryan said. "I think you should sell these to whoever will give them the greatest coverage. It'll be an opportunity for the country to see what hatred does."

"This isn't war, though. This is a crime scene..." I began, but I was interrupted by Ryan's phone ringing.

He looked at the caller ID and said, "It's Mpilo." His hands were trembling as he hit the speaker button.

Before he could say anything, we heard Mpilo's voice; it sounded hoarse. "Ryan, are you OK?"

"Yeah, we're good. Where are you? Are you OK?"

"I'm fine. I'm still at the taxi rank. I'm helping injured people here. Sheez, there are so many of them. But please, I need your help my friend; Reverend Dlamini and that little boy were here today in a taxi."

"What? You mean Jabulani? Oh, shit!" Ryan exclaimed. "Were they injured? Are they alive?"

"They're OK. But the boy is screaming. We can't get him to stop. The priest says they were getting out of Joseph's taxi with two other boys from the orphanage when the shooting started. One of the boys was killed. The other one, Andile, is injured."

Ryan looked dumbstruck. He stood quite still with his mouth agape.

"Those other boys were standing right next to Jabulani. The little guy saw everything. He was right there," Mpilo continued.

Finally, Ryan found his voice. "Oh Jesus, I don't believe this. What about Mandy? Was she there? Please tell me she wasn't there too." The color was draining from his face.

"No, just the priest and the boys."

"Thank God." Ryan took a deep breath and said, "Where are they now?"

"Andile has been taken to the hospital, but the priest and Jabulani are still here. Reverend Dlamini is trying to help all these injured people, but we don't know what to do about the little boy."

"I'll call Mandy," Ryan replied. "Maybe he'll calm down if he's with her. Poor kid."

"No, wait. It's not safe for Mandy to come here. People are angry. She can call me and I'll bring Jabulani to her."

I didn't know what was going on, but without any explanation to me, Ryan hit another number. I could see he was shaking. The phone rang and rang before going to voice mail, and I heard him say, "Mandy, it's urgent; call me as soon as you get this message."

He began pacing as he told me how he'd met these two people that Mpilo was talking about, Reverend Dlamini and a little boy called Jabulani. Ryan and Mpilo had been in a taxi with them when it ran out of petrol, leaving them all stranded in the middle of nowhere while Joseph, the driver, went for help. He added that there was also a woman called Mandy who'd been in the taxi. She was now teaching Jabulani to speak English. "He's an orphan and she's got some crazy idea that she wants to adopt him. She wants to take him to America. It's ridiculous. God—where is she? Why won't she answer her phone?"

"Wait a minute. Who exactly is Mandy?" I asked.

"I just told you; she was stranded with us that day in the middle of nowhere. She's also an American, a friend of mine. We were in the Peace Corps together in Namibia—we were traveling to Durban in that taxi, the one that ran out of petrol."

"Is she your girlfriend?" I asked.

He had his back to me when I asked this question, but I saw him stiffen. “No, she’s not,” he replied, turning around to face me. Then he added. “We argue a lot—we’re kind of like oil and water. She’s a friend, that’s all.”

I said nothing, but suddenly I felt wary. When he tried to call Mandy again a few minutes later, I suspected there was more to it than he was telling me. And when he phoned someone else called Ramona and asked her to check whether Mandy was in her room, I was convinced of it. I was feeling so many emotions caused by all that had happened in one afternoon that I didn’t think there could be room for any other emotion. But there was. Jealousy squeezed itself into my heart.

# CHAPTER 16

Mpilo soon called again to say that he had the priest and child with him and he wanted to meet as quickly as possible. Ryan had him on speaker phone and brought Mpilo up to speed about what had happened—that I had taken pictures of some white bakkies driven by the assassins, and that we'd given the images to the police. One of the shooters had already been apprehended, but there was at least another one still at large. I heard Mpilo say, "Can you text me those pictures?"

Ryan hesitated for a moment before asking, "Why? Why do you want them?"

"Why do you think? I'm curious. The bastards were shooting us, I want to see who they were."

"OK, but don't do anything stupid, Mpilo." There was silence and then Ryan said, "Come to Joanna's flat on Musgrave Road; it's near Musgrave Centre, right opposite Standard Bank. Come there and I'll watch for you from her window...I'll come and get you."

I texted the photos and waited with him for Mpilo to arrive—I could hear Ryan grinding his teeth and cracking his knuckles as we did so. As soon as the three figures appeared outside the bank, he rushed down to meet them, quickly ushering them up to my flat. The child was covered in blood. He'd stopped screaming, but he clung to the priest murmuring, "I want Mandy." He whimpered as we took him to the bathroom to clean him and it was a relief when we discovered he was uninjured. The blood was not his; it came from Temba, the boy who'd been killed. The child's eyes were large and watery as he stared at Ryan and whispered again, "I want Mandy."

"I know you want her, Jabulani, I know. We all do. We'll find her," Ryan replied in a soft voice. I couldn't help but notice how gentle he was with the child.

The priest, an older man, looked stunned and exhausted as he cleaned himself with the cloths I gave him. When he thanked me, I saw that, behind his spectacles, his eyes were red and watery. As soon as the blood was washed away from the child, Ryan carried the boy to my car—with Reverend Dlamini following in silence, wiping his glasses for the hundredth time. As I fastened Jabulani's seat belt, I noticed Mpilo take Ryan aside to tell him something that caused Ryan to drop his head in his hands. The priest, who was watching the exchange, obviously knew what was being said because he let out an involuntary sob. I heard Ryan groan, "No, no. Not that old man—and Joseph too. No, no. No. I can't believe they were killed." He looked up at Mpilo and swallowed hard. "Are you sure Mandy wasn't there?"

Mpilo nodded. "I'm sure. I promise you, she wasn't there. But it's bad, very bad there at the taxi rank. I can't stay with you. I must go back and help. And you must be careful. When people are angry, trouble can happen quickly. You don't want to be caught in the wrong place, my friend. Stay away. Get Reverend Dlamini and Jabulani back to the orphanage. They'll be safe there." He was agitated as he pressed Ryan's arm. "Go," he said. "Look after them. You're a good man; you're a good friend. Go well." Then, without a backward glance, he made his way back to the mayhem.

Ryan called after him, "*You* be careful," but Mpilo didn't acknowledge he'd heard. Soon he was lost to sight.

After dropping the priest and child back at the orphanage, I returned Ryan to his lodgings. Neither of us wanted to be alone, so when he suggested I come in with him, I accepted the invitation without hesitation. His room was tiny and sparsely furnished—just a bed and a chair, covered with clothing. Exhausted, I barely remember doing so but I collapsed on his bed and fell asleep. I was still there next morning when I discovered that he'd slept in a sleeping bag on the floor.

Voices woke us; they were coming from next door. Ryan jumped up, ran out at speed, and I heard him shouting, "The least you could've done was return my call." With a sinking feeling, I knew who it was. Despite denying it, I felt certain he had feelings for this woman he'd been trying to reach. Curiosity got the better of me and I walked out to see a man, a woman, and a child. They stood staring at Ryan, saying nothing. The child I recognized; it was little Jabulani. The woman was undoubtedly Mandy and I felt a stab of jealousy once more. How could I compete with this blonde pixie?

As I watched them, the man put an arm around her and said, "I think Mandy's had more important things on her mind than returning your calls."

Ryan stopped abruptly and looked the man up and down. "Who the hell are you?" he asked.

"David Malherbe. And you are?"

I watched Ryan frown and could sense his anger. He muttered something before turning his gaze towards Mandy again and saying, "Would you mind telling me what's going on?"

She spoke for the first time and I heard a soft American accent. "I'm moving out, Ryan. David's offered me and JJ a place to stay while we wait for his passport to arrive. Jabulani is coming back to California with me."

"Dammit, Mandy," Ryan exploded. "We've been through all of that. It's a terrible idea. The kid's a Zulu. He needs to stay here where he belongs."

"He belongs with me," she replied. "He wants to be with me and I don't care what you think."

I stepped forward at this point and said, "Excuse me, but we haven't met either—I'm Joanna Nel. I've heard what you're doing and I think it's awesome, Mandy. Good luck." Turning to Ryan, I said just one word, "Cheers." There was nothing else to say as I walked away.

I could hear him striding after me. "Wait, Joanna. Let me explain," he shouted.

I refused to wait. I continued walking fast and called over my shoulder, "You have explained. I don't believe you, though." He kept coming after me, so I stopped and turned to face him. "Stop fooling yourself. And stop trying to fool me." I wanted to say a lot more, but I turned on my heel and hurried to my car, holding back my tears.

As I drove away at speed, I was trembling with rage. He'd led me on and I'd allowed myself to have silly, unfounded notions. "Just face it," I told myself, "he's a guy on the hunt. A romantic setting doesn't equal romance—all it does is give him an opportunity." I wiped away tears with my sleeve, trying to obliterate the memory of Ryan's face as he looked at that petite blonde—a woman who appeared to have two men fighting over her. Honestly though, by the time I got back to my flat, I was feeling less concerned about Ryan than I was about the carnage I'd seen. The gruesome sight kept coming back to me. I told myself that men couldn't be trusted and I'd be over this American by lunchtime—but the violence was something I'd never erase from my memory.

My photos had revealed such hatred—racism at its worst. I was a Cape Coloured, a woman of mixed race, but I was born after 1994 when apartheid ended. Although I knew race hatred existed, I'd never personally experienced it. I'd witnessed plenty of violence when August went on a rampage—but that had nothing to do with race. I never needed to classify myself or anyone else. I mixed with people of all colors at school and university; we were all just people. Maybe I'd been naïve all this time, wearing blinkers, so I didn't see that hatred was lurking in the shadows, simmering, waiting to erupt. It just needed one small thing, or one person, to ignite it.

# CHAPTER 17

I'd been so distracted getting Jabulani and the priest back to the orphanage that I'd rushed out without taking my phone—and I'd been gone overnight. The moment I walked back in the door in the early afternoon, I saw there were several messages and missed calls from my mom and Tom, but I was exhausted and didn't have the emotional energy to talk to either of them. Feeling totally drained, I just wanted to be alone and sleep some more, so I lay down and closed my eyes, wanting to escape the horror and turmoil I was feeling. I must've slept soundly without hearing my phone ring several more times, and when I awoke, feeling a bit more rested, I texted my parents to say I was fine. Before I could even grab a glass of water, however, I heard pounding on my front door. Thankful that Tom had put a safety chain on it, I called out, "Who is it?"

A voice gasped, "It's Mpilo. Help me, Sisi."

I threw open the door and gasped when I saw him. There was blood pouring down his left leg, and his face was grey. He was groaning as he tried unsuccessfully to steady himself against the door jamb, before collapsing in the corridor in front of me. "Oh, my God," I murmured, dropping down to feel his pulse. Satisfied that he was alive, I ran inside for towels to stop the bleeding and as I made a tourniquet, I saw his eyes flicker. "I need to get you to the hospital, Mpilo," I said to him.

With what little breath he had left, he murmured, "No. No hospital. Take me to Ryan. I've been shot." I don't know how I managed to get him to my car; I guess adrenalin got me going. As I tried to make him comfortable on the back seat, he murmured again, "Take me to Ryan, not the hospital."

"OK, don't worry," I said, which was ridiculous. He was drifting in and out of consciousness and there was everything to worry about. I kept talking, trying to keep him conscious, and drove as fast as I could, thankful to find he was still alive when I got to Ryan's room. It was getting dark when I arrived there and I ran to call Ryan, but there was no response when I banged on the door. Frantic, I was about to phone him when he emerged from the main house and I shouted, "Thank God you're here. Come quickly. I need your help." Without any explanation, I sped to my car and opened the back door where Mpilo lay unconscious, sprawled across the back seat in a pool of blood.

"Oh shit," Ryan said.

As he leaned in to take a look at his friend, another woman suddenly appeared. She pointed to Mpilo and asked Ryan, "Oh hell, is this the guy you were talking about?"

He nodded and made a quick introduction—Ramona Govender was a neighbor living in the main house. I explained how Mpilo had arrived at my flat in a terrible state. "He's been shot. There's a bullet in his leg; we need to get it out. He got really upset when I mentioned the hospital, though; he wanted you, Ryan. My God, he's lost so much blood. He passed out about five minutes ago and stopped responding when I spoke to him. What are we going to do?"

Ramona cleared her throat. “Hell’s teeth. Without medical attention, he’ll be in a really bad way; but if he goes to the hospital, it sounds like he’ll be in trouble. Big trouble.”

I was shaking, desperate to get help for this man who appeared close to dying in my car.

Suddenly Ramona said, “Listen, I know what we can do; let me call a co-worker of mine. His father’s a doctor. I’ll see if we can take Mpilo there.”

We watched her pleading on the phone and I overheard her saying, “OK, I understand, but please try; please. This is desperate. Call me back as soon as you can. It’s really urgent. Please.”

I could see that she was as anxious as we were when she explained what had transpired. “My colleague’s father has retired, so he’s not sure his old man will help. It’s not exactly kosher to extract a bullet from someone without reporting it to the police. The doctor might not agree to do it.”

My heart sank, but her phone rang within a few minutes and when she answered, she said, “Thank you, thank you so much. Text me the address and we’ll meet you there.”

Turning to us, she said, “Right, we’re good. Let’s go. His father has agreed to help.”

Ramona punched an address into her phone and jumped into the front seat next to me, giving directions as I drove. Ryan sat in the back with Mpilo’s head on his lap. The wounded man opened his eyes for a moment, registering Ryan’s presence, and murmured, “I tried to stop them.” Then he lost consciousness again.

I drove at break-neck speed until we came to a narrow road, where I was forced to slow down. When we finally arrived at an iron gate, we were met by Ramona's colleague. He was waiting for us in a car and flicked his lights in acknowledgement, before opening the gate remotely. We followed him up a long drive to a house in total darkness.

"This bloody load shedding. There's no power half the time. Thank God the gate operates on a battery," Ramona muttered. "But I ask you, how the hell is a doctor going to do anything if he can't see what he's doing?"

"Let's hope he's got a generator, or at least an inverter," I replied, feeling similar concerns.

We drove around to the back of the house where there was a small, separate building, also in darkness. As we all climbed out of our cars, I did a double take—because visible in the moonlight was Ramona's colleague. It was the same man I'd seen earlier, David Malherbe. He and Ryan also recognized each other. They both frowned, but said nothing as they lifted Mpilo and carried him to the doctor's office, located in a small building behind the main house. Lit by lanterns, the room looked eerie—and I began to shiver.

David's father was waiting for us, a stern, unsmiling figure. When they placed Mpilo on the examination table, we watched in silence as Dr. Malherbe took a quick look at the injury. Finally, he grunted, "I don't want to know how this happened, do you hear me? But we can't let the poor bugger bleed to death." He examined him further, before adding, "Right. I'll fix him up—and then I don't want to hear anything more about it, and I don't want to see him again. Is that understood? I don't want to know who he is, or anything about him." He looked at each of us in turn and waited for us to acknowledge what he'd said, before setting to work. His wife, who appeared to be his assistant, shooed us out of the examination room into the adjacent waiting area. As I looked around in the dim light coming from a candle, I figured that this place had probably once been servants' quarters, now converted into Dr. Malherbe's consulting rooms.

Ryan immediately began pacing up and down, and when David walked outside into the garden, Ryan followed him. I watched through the window and saw the two men in the moonlight, talking to one another. It was not a friendly exchange and when David drove off, Ryan strode back inside. His face was grim and he was breathing heavily as he sat down next to me. After a few moments of awkward silence, he muttered, "I wonder how long we're going to be here? We can't leave yet."

"Of course not," I replied, although I wished I could leave. I didn't want to be mixed up in this situation now that I had grave doubts about Ryan. Mpilo was his friend and his responsibility. I pointed this out, saying, "What are you going to do with Mpilo? Where will you take him?"

Ryan put his face in his hands and groaned. "Oh crap, I hadn't thought about that."

"He's going to need someone to look after him," I said.

It took only a moment before he looked up, his expression brighter, and said just one word, "Mandy." That name again. I felt a chill run down my spine.

Ramona overheard us. "What? Are you crazy? You can't expect Mandy to take care of him!" she exclaimed. "She's looking after that child already."

"No, you don't understand. She's moved out of her room. Mpilo can stay there and *I'll* look after him. He can't go back to the township; it would be too risky. There'll be police searches—and informers too, probably. Anyway, he needs someone looking after him. I will."

"That's a fantastic idea; I didn't know Mandy had moved out. And didn't Mpilo say something to the effect that he was trying to stop the crowd?" Ramona asked. "It's a good defense. If he needs it, I'll defend him. But it would be better if he escapes prosecution in the first place—then he won't need any defense. Best keep him out of sight."

I hadn't realized that Ramona was an attorney. As it turned out, although Mpilo was a victim in a shooting incident, he was also in luck—he had found a doctor, an attorney, and a good mate. Maybe Ryan wasn't so bad after all, but I still didn't trust his intentions towards me. I reached across and touched his arm, saying, "You're a loyal friend; Mpilo is very lucky." I couldn't stop myself from adding, "And so is Mandy."

Ryan raised his eyebrows, then stood and beckoned me to follow. Hesitant at first, curiosity got the better of me and I followed him outside. Once the door shut, he put his hands on my shoulders and said, "Joanna, there's nothing between me and Mandy, I promise you. We've traveled together and worked together. Things looked like they might get serious at one point, but they didn't. It doesn't work that way with us. She can actually be a pain in the ass. Trust me, she's a friend—that's all; nothing else." He slipped his arms around me and pulled me close. "Now I think we are good for each other, though."

I wanted to believe him, but I froze and said nothing. What I thought was: *Don't lie. I saw how you looked at her.*

I think he read my mind because he frowned and said, "So much has happened with you and me, in such a short time. You had me hooked already at Mkuze, sitting next to the fire. We didn't need to talk much—it was just good being there together. It was magic. And as if that wasn't enough, you came and rescued me—and, what's more, your photographs helped catch the perpetrators of all this. What would I have done without you? What would the police have done without you? I've never met anyone like you. You're awesome."

It was flattering to hear this, but I was still wary. Was it a glib tongue or was he sincere? I had to say what was on my mind. "I saw the way you looked at her."

"I don't know what you saw, but you're imagining things."

"I'll tell you what I saw—a blond bombshell. You couldn't keep your eyes off her. That's what I saw, Ryan."

He shook his head and sighed. "Joanna, stop it. She and I are like oil and water, like I said. Yes, Mandy is good-looking, but I'll tell you again—she's a pain in the ass. My only desire, as far as she's concerned, is that she would shut up and be sensible about that child. Now my feelings for you are quite different—and quite truthfully, I prefer brunettes with long legs and big brown eyes."

My armor began to crack a little as we stood together in the moonlight. I didn't resist when he pulled me close, burying his face in my hair and whispering, "This feels so right, so good."

Ryan and Ramona helped me scrub the inside of my car while we waited for the doctor to finish his work. The blood stains on the leather would need something more than soap and water to clean them, but fortunately the seats were dark so the marks weren't too obvious.

It was almost three hours before Dr. Malherbe considered it safe for Mpilo to leave. When they eventually emerged from the operating room, Dr. Malherbe entrusted the patient to Ryan, with stern words. "This guy had a lucky escape. The bullet lodged in his leg close to the femoral artery; it missed by little more than a few centimeters. I wouldn't have been able to save him if it had been any closer—he would have bled to death in minutes. It was tricky getting the damn thing out, but fortunately I was able to remove it without too much damage. I've cleaned the wound, stitched him up, and given him antibiotics—but he's weak. He lost a lot of blood and his body is in shock. He could do with a blood transfusion, but he'd need to be in a hospital for that so it seems he'll have to manage without one. It's imperative he rests and drinks a lot of fluids. Now, who's going to look after him? You?"

"Yes, sir. I am," Ryan replied, adding, "I'm very grateful for your help. I don't know what happened to him. He's a good friend of mine. He was probably caught in crossfire somewhere. He was an innocent bystander, I'm sure of it."

The doctor grunted again. "They all say that—*it wasn't me, it wasn't my fault.* If I had a rand for every time I've heard that, I'd be on a bloody first-class trip around the world, not sitting around patching up stupid buggers who get themselves into trouble with the police." Despite his gruffness, my heart warmed to him when I noticed that he refused payment as he sent us on our way.

With Mpilo lying in a wheelbarrow, we moved him to the car. He was weak, but as we fastened his seat belt, he murmured, "You guys saved my life. Thank you. People were going crazy. I thought I was going to die."

"You'll be OK now," Ryan reassured him. "I'm taking you back to my place until you're stronger. Don't try and talk. There'll be time enough when you're better."

Mpilo nodded, but he was eager to make something

clear. "I tried to stop people from rioting. Everybody was going mad. Some guy saw the picture Joanna sent of the bakkies, and he went wild. That's all it took to get everybody going crazy. They attacked every white car they saw. Somebody in one of them started shooting and that's how this happened," he said, pointing to his leg. "Too many people have died. I'm lucky I wasn't one of them, my brother."

# CHAPTER 18

After leaving the three of them at Ryan's place, I headed back to my flat, ready to clean the mess on my doorstep—but somebody had already done so. The trail of blood left by Mpilo was all gone, and I found a note stuck on my door that read: *OMG! Are you OK? I'm so sorry I left you. Call me. Please tell me you're not hurt.*

Gabby must have come looking for me. I checked my phone and saw numerous messages from her, as well as from my mom and dad. I texted Gabby back to say it was Mpilo's blood, not mine, and thanked her for cleaning up, adding that it had been my choice to get out the car, so she shouldn't worry about it. After that, I collapsed on the couch and fell asleep before I could reach out to anyone else. Sometime later, startled by a loud noise, I shot up, disoriented, trying to figure out where I was and what was happening. It took me a few moments to realize it was my phone, and another minute to locate it. I was still groggy with sleep when I heard my mom saying, "Joanna, is that you?"

"Yes, of course."

"It doesn't sound like you. Are you OK?"

Hearing her voice, the anguish of the last days was suddenly unleashed. I began to sob as I described what had happened at the Greyville taxi rank and explained that I'd been there, taking pictures. She seemed much calmer than I was. When I finished telling her about my part in it, she said, "I'm proud of you, Joanna. I always knew I had a strong daughter."

"I don't feel strong right now. I'm crying like a baby," I replied.

"Strength isn't the absence of fear, liefling. It's the ability to cope with it. That's courage—and you have it in spades."

Her quiet words had a calming effect and my sobs began to subside as she continued speaking to me. "I don't have to tell you to stay safe; I know you're sensible and will do that, but I'm so relieved you're back in your flat. Your father heard from Walter Gibson that you'd left Mkuze and that you were back in Durban—one of your co-workers said she'd left you near the scene of the attack. We've been sick with worry, trying to reach you."

"It was a slaughterhouse, Mom, except it was people being killed, not cattle. How can anyone commit such atrocities? It was senseless, random killing of innocent people. Who could do such a thing?"

"My liefling, listen to me. There are wicked people everywhere, but plenty of good people too. Don't let something like this make you think that the whole world is bad. The world is what you make it and it's how you react to evil that defines your life. In the battle between good and evil, I believe good will always triumph. If we don't believe that, there's nothing left to hope for in this world. We have to have hope."

I took comfort in my mother's calm words, longing to see her and feel her embrace. It was amazing that she could think like that after the treatment she'd received from August Nel for so many years. I didn't know whether I could believe her, but I wanted to do so. Tom called shortly after Mom. "Do you want to come back to Cape

Town?" he asked. "Durban is a tinder box. There's plenty of work here for you; this is home. It's safe here. You don't have to worry about August any longer—he's a toothless old dog. There are lots of people here who miss you and would like you to come back."

I found myself smiling. That sense of belonging was a tempting draw card, but I was enjoying my job here in Durban. And there was Ryan. Meeting him had changed everything. Maybe he was leading me on and I felt my chest constrict when I thought about him and Mandy, but I wanted to believe in this American guy. Somehow, I was going to have to find a way to put my doubts aside and trust him.

"Don't worry about me here. Things will calm down soon and in the meantime, I'm quite safe. I won't do anything heroic," I replied.

"You've already been heroic," he said. "I've heard all about it from your mother. She called to let me know you were safe. Joanna, please, I beg you, if you won't come home, at least promise to keep away from trouble spots—and taxis. I've only had you in my life for a year or so; I want you in it for many more. Promise me."

"I promise."

# CHAPTER 19

The commitment Ryan showed towards his friend impressed me. He never wavered in his role as caregiver, never expressing anything other than encouragement and concern for Mpilo, and always maintaining a cheerful attitude. I had deadlines to meet for the tourism board which distracted me from the horror I'd seen, but it also meant that Ryan and I didn't have much time to meet. We spoke every day though, and every time I saw his face pop up on my phone screen, I felt happy. I began to believe in him a bit more, especially when I inquired after Jabulani; I was pleased when Ryan admitted that he didn't know much because he'd had little contact with Mandy. However, he reported that Reverend Dlamini said the child was doing better in her care, and that the injured boy, Andile, was out of the hospital and back at the orphanage. This was all good news.

The streets seemed to settle down, although there was a strong police presence that was both unnerving and reassuring at the same time. More perpetrators were apprehended, from both the initial attack at the taxi rank and the subsequent revenge shootings. It was a tense time, but I kept my promise to Tom—I stayed close to home and the office.

Fortunately, I didn't need to go out in the field; I was busy putting a proposal together for an opportunity that had arisen with a travel magazine called *Outlook*. When

Gabby handed their proposal to me, she said, "This came for the two of us, but I can't take it unless I want a divorce. Anyway, I owe you this, Joanna. I still feel bad leaving you at Greyville, even though you turned out to be such a superhero. Maybe if you get this plum assignment, you'll forgive me."

"I've told you before; it was my choice and you have nothing to apologize for." She stood watching as I read the project description, and smiled when I exclaimed, "Wow!"

"Yup, I thought you'd like it," she said.

*Outlook* was the South African edition of an English magazine with large readership, both domestic and overseas. They'd been running articles on art and architecture from around the world; now they were looking for a photo journalist to create a pictorial essay on that subject in the Western Cape. Our work for the KZN Tourism Board had caught their eye, so they included our advertising agency in their search—specifically mentioning me and Gabby.

"Are you sure you don't want to take a stab at this, yourself?" I asked her.

"Quite sure. I've been away from home a lot already and I'd have to be away again. It would be too much. I can't even think about it. My husband would be wild. But I think you should give it a go."

"Thanks, Gabby, this is huge." I hesitated a moment, and then blurted out something that had been bothering me. "Can I say something to you please? You've become a friend as well as a workmate, and I value your friendship. I know it's none of my business, but I'm going to say this anyway, because I care about you. You see, my mother was married to a man who was a control freak. In fact, he was a bully. He knocked the shit out of her to a point where she forgot how to stand up for herself. Please don't let that happen to you."

She stared at me, wide-eyed. At first, she said nothing, but then she nodded and murmured, "Good luck with the application," before walking away.

A few days later, I found a potted plant on my desk with a note that read: *It took a lot for you to say what you did. Thank you, I appreciate it. Gabby.*

I discussed the job with Ryan and appreciated his enthusiasm. Tom was also supportive. He listened to my ideas, fine-tuning some of them and adding suggestions. I desperately wanted the job; perhaps it was an effort to wash away the memories of Greyville from my mind that I wanted to show positive images. Ironically, it was probably my photos from Greyville that stood out when I submitted my CV to *Outlook*.

I anxiously awaited an answer from them and tried to manage my expectations, but the first thing I did each day was check my inbox. Every day, Gabby would raise her eyebrows when she saw me, questioning and wondering, and I'd shake my head. When the answer finally came, it was sent to Walter. He summoned me to his office and his face gave nothing away as he signaled me to sit down while he ended a phone call.

"Yes, I'm sure we can make this work," I heard him say. "Thanks for getting back to me. I'll let her know."

He ended the call and drummed his fingers on his desk as he looked at me. I held my breath and stared at his face, trying to read his thoughts. He would be an excellent poker player; he gave nothing away. Finally, he started to laugh. "You were born under a lucky star, Joanna.

They love your proposal. You've got the assignment if you want it." Stunned, I was at a loss for words and simply stared at him. "It's a one-off thing," he explained. "They want you on loan from me to do this project, but I've said that you need to finish whatever you're working on here first. That needs to be done quickly; they want you to start next week, if possible. Will that work?"

I nodded as Walter went on to describe how *Outlook* would be paying my salary for the duration of the project. In addition, they would give me a travel allowance to go wherever I saw fit, but I needed to check in with him regularly, as well as give a weekly update on my progress to the editorial staff at *Outlook* for their approval.

I was over the moon. Much as I'd fallen in love with San Francisco and looked forward to visiting there again someday, I relished the thought of returning to my roots and traveling around the Western Cape on an assignment.

I immediately began to plan in detail how to proceed with the work. The logical starting point seemed to be Cape Town, the Mother City, located on the southern tip of the continent. The Castle, the oldest existing building in South Africa was there, dating from the 1600s. After that, I could focus on the Cape Dutch architecture that developed later. I'd have no difficulty finding material—the difficulty would be trying to decide what should be included or omitted. And I needed to research contemporary material, as well. There were so many artists and so much art for me to uncover—I wondered whether Tom might give me permission to include his photograph of my mother.

It had been a month since Mpilo was shot, during which time Ryan and I saw nothing of each other. When I called to tell him that I'd got the job, he also had good news; Mpilo was well enough to start classes at university and would be remaining in Mandy's room. Reverend Dlamini had checked with the landlords who were happy to help by not charging him rent while Mpilo was at university. (So, my mother was right—there are good people in the world.) But the best part of the news for me was that Ryan was freed up and we would have time to be together at last. I was excited about that, and I was impressed by the degree of care he had shown towards Mpilo. Ryan Thompson was also a good person; I was beginning to believe I could trust him.

# CHAPTER 20

The senior editor at *Outlook* magazine went out of her way to accommodate me—even providing me with an allowance for an assistant, since Gabby had chosen not to be part of the assignment. I was quick to ask Ryan to help me. As an American, he would provide a different perspective that would appeal to a wider audience overseas. Keen to explore the Western Cape, he accepted immediately and we made plans to get going the following week.

My little Fiat was cramped with the two of us, as well as all our luggage and equipment crammed into it—but I didn't care. I was happy, and every kilometer we traveled made me feel even happier; we were getting further away from Mandy and I was letting go of my jealousy. I surreptitiously took note when he made phone calls; they were usually to Mpilo, never to her.

It was a two-day journey and we shared the driving through territory that was new for both of us. The Karoo was different from anything either of us had ever seen and we marveled at the endless, open spaces that seemed to be populated by more sheep than people, battered by dust storms, and dotted with windmills. But even though it was a long journey, we never felt tired or bored; when we weren't chatting, we listened to music or audiobooks, and I kind of wished we could keep driving forever.

We stopped overnight in some little dorp whose name I don't even remember, unwinding as we climbed out the car and stretched our legs. There appeared to be only one hotel in the small town and we made our way there, praying they would have accommodation for us. They did, but it was an awkward moment when the receptionist announced there was just one room available. It felt even more awkward when we entered the room and saw only one bed. Ryan looked at me and smiled. "Do we flip a coin?" he asked.

I said nothing. Ryan appeared to sense my embarrassment and I was thankful when he suggested we head out and find something to eat. We were both starving.

It was an old-fashioned hotel with a large, musty dining room. Several other diners were already seated, dressed to the nines, which made us feel extremely underdressed—we hadn't even showered yet. But hunger drove us to ignore stares as we were shown to a table by a waiter who appeared to be the maître d' hotel. Dressed in a white suit with a red sash draped over his shoulder and across his chest, his smile was as wide as the sash. Large mirrors in ornate frames, almost holding onto reflections of years gone by, covered the walls—and in one corner stood a glistening, grand piano. A man in a tuxedo sat playing the instrument, smiling and singing songs from a different era. He was playing "Strangers in the Night" as we inspected the menu, and continued to play several variations of it until someone sent a request for "Moon River." After that, he broke into "Tea for Two" and "Yes Sir, That's My Baby." When he started playing "My Bonnie Lies Over the Ocean," Ryan groaned. "I think it's time we changed things up here, don't you? I'm going to make a request, but I'm not telling you what it is. You'll find out in a minute."

The pianist acknowledged us with a smile and when

he began to play "Help," I started giggling. Any intended irony escaped the man as he continued with a repertoire of Beatles music, ending with another request from Ryan, "If I Fell in Love with You." This time I didn't giggle when Ryan took my hand and began to mouth the words.

The pianist finally took a break and wandered over to our table. We were enjoying local venison with a bottle of pinotage, and he joined us for a drink. The man was so amiable that we ended up buying his CD—even though we didn't own a CD player. *Does anyone still own such a thing*? I wondered.

When we left the dining room, we both started laughing. It had been such a bizarre evening that I'd forgotten about the problem of only one bed. But as we returned to the room and I took my turn in the bathroom, showering and brushing my teeth, I thought about it again. And I thought of my friend Shazza, remembering how she'd made a conscious decision at university to lose her virginity. She'd discussed the matter with a few of her close friends, including me, and told us that she had in mind a guy she'd been out with once or twice. He was a good candidate, she claimed, because he was super attractive and, more importantly, he'd had experience. There were two friends who supported her, and another who was shocked by the notion. I felt differently. "Losing your virginity shouldn't be so cerebral," I'd said.

"Why not?" Shazza had replied. "The first time I ate oysters, I was with someone who showed me how to do it. I love oysters now, but I bet if I hadn't been shown how to eat them, I'd still be chewing away on them and wondering what was wrong with me—or them!"

I couldn't help laughing at her analogy, although I didn't agree with her. I was laughing again now, thinking about it. Shazza was a character; I missed her. When I came out of the bathroom, Ryan asked what was so funny; I just smiled and shrugged. I didn't tell him, of course, but climbed into bed while he took his turn, showering. When he emerged from the bathroom, I discovered he was a guy who didn't normally wear pajamas, but for discretion's sake, he'd put his boxers back on. He informed me that he usually preferred sleeping butt naked—like the day he was born.

Looking at him standing there, I could feel myself blushing—and my pulse rate was rising fast. He was good to look at when he wore clothes, but even better without them. I'd not seen this much of his body before; he was muscular and tanned—and I felt a strange stirring. We said nothing for a few moments and a question mark was almost visible in the air between us—until I lifted the covers and beckoned him.

Well, Shazza was wrong; I didn't care whether he was experienced or not. In fact, I didn't want to think of him being with someone else. I didn't want to know. And I didn't want to think about Mandy. All I knew was that being there with him felt wonderful. And when he removed my pajamas and we lay together, his flesh on mine, my body came alive in unexpected places. Nothing had ever felt so exciting in my life before—and no experience was necessary.

We stayed with my mom when we got to Cape Town. She had us sleep in different rooms—I knew she would; I shared with her, and Ryan used my old bedroom. He accepted this without any comment, and I was actually quite pleased to have some distance from him. Although our overnight stop had been amazing, it had complicated things. I was happy to apply the brakes.

He and my mom got on well immediately, just as I thought they would. But while Ryan was eager to meet my family and see where I'd grown up, I hated being back in the house with all its memories. Mom hadn't even begun clearing out August's room yet. "I don't want to jinx anything," she told me. "The moment I go in there, that will be the moment he fully recovers and wants to come back."

"That's not going to happen, Mom," I objected. I wanted her to throw out all his stuff and start a new life, in a new place, as soon as possible—and I found it hard to hide my feelings. "He's not coming back and you should move on. Sell the house and find somewhere else to live. Get rid of everything that was his."

She shook her head and explained that Esther wanted to move into this house but didn't have quite enough money to buy it yet. "I'm prepared to let her have all the time she needs," Mom said. "I'd love to just give her the house, but that wouldn't be fair to you and Emma. Anyway, I need money to buy somewhere else to live."

I couldn't argue with that, but when she allowed me to help her clear the front room, I said, "Getting rid of all this stuff of his makes me think—maybe I should get rid of my surname too. I might change it to Montgomery. Joanna Montgomery. How does that sound?"

I looked to see her reaction and was surprised when I saw a pained expression on her face. She shrugged and murmured, "But I'm Petra Nel." I didn't understand why, but I realized that I'd upset her and it probably wasn't worth the effort of trying to make the change.

Ryan met my sisters briefly and they greeted him cordially, which was a relief. I was a bit nervous there might be some residual resentment, but there wasn't. They were welcoming and happy to meet him. After a brief visit, we left them to visit Tom—I was eager to see my dad again and keen to check out his new place. I wanted Ryan to meet him as well. My mom was with us; she hadn't known about the plan of going to Tom's and she was not pleased with this development. I explained to her that time was short—a weekend was all I had—and I needed to pack in as much as I could before I started working on the assignment.

She grew very quiet as we got closer to Camp's Bay, and when we walked into Tom's new flat, her eyes showed her astonishment. She had never been inside any home belonging to him before. From his balcony, he had a beautiful view of the beach—which in itself was quite a feature, but the interior could've won an award from Architectural Digest. Tom clearly didn't need Cynthia's help to decorate; he had his own style. He'd kept the furniture from his home office, but that was all I recognized from his old home. Everything was simple and contemporary, and on one wall of the living room was his pride and joy—the photograph that had won that competition all those years ago. It was in a striking silver frame with double matting to set it off—the outer matting was grey, and the thin, inner strip was black. It looked stunning.

I turned immediately to see how my mom would react, half expecting her to be embarrassed. She didn't appear to be. She stared at it, but said nothing. My dad was also silent as he watched her. Ryan was outside on the balcony, too busy looking at the view to observe either the photo or the interaction between my parents. I was pleased; it was a private moment that I didn't want him to witness.

The silence in the room was broken when my mom made a simple statement. "You were a brilliant photographer. You should have continued." She didn't look at my dad when she spoke; she merely stared at the photo.

He glowered, and for a moment I thought angry words were about to be uttered, but Tom was prevented from saying anything when Ryan re-entered the room. He was eager to explore the beachfront and Tom offered to go with him—I think my father wanted to escape my mother's presence.

As Mom and I watched them from the balcony, I took the opportunity to ask how she felt about Tom. She sighed. "He's a good man."

"Well why..."

She immediately put her hand up and stopped me. "Don't. Don't go there. I'm still married—and so is he. It isn't simple. Tom is angry with me. Love has turned to hate for him. I don't think he'll ever forgive me for not telling him he had a child. And he's right; it was cruel of me. It wasn't fair to him or you. I'm sorry, Joanna, really sorry. In hindsight, I know what a bad decision I made, but I can't undo it."

"Mom, I forgave you long ago. I was angry with you for a while, really angry. But I realized what a predicament you were in and that helped me understand why you did what you did. I had to let go of my anger. Do I wish things had been different? Definitely. But as you say, we can't change the past; we have to move forward. My point is, if I can forgive you, I'm sure Tom can as well."

As she reached out and took my hand, I could see tears in her eyes. "Our worlds are so different, Joanna. I knew that at the time, but the way we were meeting, it didn't seem to matter. Nothing mattered. We were divorced from reality. We met in a studio and that became our world. It would never have worked outside that environment. I never said so to him, but it was madness to even think we could be together openly. And nothing's changed in that regard."

"I don't understand what you're saying," I said.

She sighed. "I would never have been able to fit into his privileged world. I grew up dirt poor, a Cape Coloured from the wrong side of the tracks. There was no way I would've been accepted in his circles, and he wouldn't have been comfortable in my world either. We were crazy about each other, but we were lovers; that's all we could be."

I stared at her, shocked, and shook my head. "I can't believe what I'm hearing. Apartheid had ended. It was history. There was nothing to stop you being together publicly."

"Don't be naïve, my liefling. Just because the laws had changed didn't mean people's attitudes had changed. He was still a white man, living in a wealthy environment; I was still a Cape Coloured woman from Salt River. Yes, I'd moved up in the world, but not enough to live in his fancy world. I was still a second-class person."

I thought I would explode. "Apartheid will never end if you keep it alive in your head," I said. "You're every bit as worthwhile as Tom. In fact, when you think how much you've had to overcome in your life, I'd say there's even more worth to you. He had everything handed to him on a plate. Get over it, Mom. Nobody cares about the color of your skin anymore. Stop being a victim."

She turned and looked away and I wondered if I had said too much; I was surprised by her words when eventually she spoke. "I'm afraid it's not that easy to erase the past. No matter how much life changes, the past is always there. It shapes us, for better or worse. It makes us who we are."

"Oh, rubbish. The past doesn't define who you are unless you allow it to do so. Don't limit yourself by becoming a prisoner to the past. Please...let go of all that history." The ensuing silence was charged with emotion as we stood side by side, staring at the ocean. I was trying to understand where she was coming from, but I couldn't do so—and I'm sure my impatience showed.

Eventually she said, "What about you and Ryan. Do you love him?"

It took me a long time to answer. Finally, I replied. "I don't know. Perhaps. I like him a lot, I really do, but I don't know if what I'm feeling is love. I don't know what love feels like."

"Come," she said, and took my hand. She led me back into the living room where she pointed to the photograph on the wall. "It's simple. That's what it feels like."

"Liberating?" I asked.

"That, and so much more... It makes you feel complete. When you find it, you'll know what love is. And then you must treasure it. Don't let it slip away."

After a weekend of family time, it was time to get to work. I spent an afternoon with Ryan, photographing Cape Town Castle, which had been built at the beginning of European settlement at the Cape. There was loads of history surrounding it—but the more I thought about events that took place in the seventeenth century, I realized I was making a huge mistake. I was ignoring what had existed here long before Europeans landed in Table Bay. How could I even think the castle should be the starting point?

I should be looking at the art of the San people who were here long before Europeans arrived—that should be the beginning of my photographic essay. It was a huge 'aha' moment. There was no architecture remaining from those days, but there was plenty of art left behind—it was painted on rocks. I needed to find it.

With that realization, the time had come to leave Cape Town. I made some inquiries and soon we were heading to the Cederberg, an area I'd never been to before, but I was told it was a good place to scope out rock art. The drive was only a couple of hours and I felt both excited and anxious about what we might discover—what if reports were false and there wasn't much to see? Where would we go then?

I didn't need to worry. There was plenty to see when we arrived—so much so that I would've been unable to find words to adequately describe what I saw. Thank goodness I didn't need to try, my camera was able to do that for me. It was spellbinding, looking at people and animals drawn on the rock face, thousands of years ago, right in the same spot where I was standing at that moment. This was where the San people had used charcoal, fat and droppings to make depictions of their lives, and as I stood gazing at their artwork, I began to shiver—not from cold, but from wonder.

Yes, this was the perfect starting point of my photographic essay.

# PART 2

# PETRA

*When truth is replaced by silence,*
*the silence is a lie.*

—YEVGENY YEVTUSHENKO

# CHAPTER 21

It was late in the day when the cops arrived at my door—will I ever be able to forget their words? "Petra Nel, you're under arrest for the murder of your husband, August Nel."

As I sat locked in a jail cell waiting to appear before a magistrate, those words echoed in my mind with disbelief. *Murder—you're under arrest for murder.* How could that be? I sat shivering in semi-darkness while the stench of vomit and urine from the adjacent cell made my stomach heave. (All the drunks were locked up next door and—despite the horror of my situation—I was thankful to be alone in this cell, rather than with them.) My mind was racing. How could I be responsible for my husband's death? He had died in hospital ages after I hit him, and besides that, he'd also had a stroke. Why was I being charged with his murder now? It didn't make sense. I'd hit him in self-defense because he was attacking me with a knife. What was I supposed to do—stand there and get killed?

There was no lightbulb in the cell, but twilight revealed the grimness of my surroundings—a bunk, a blanket, and a bucket. I tried to stay calm, not knowing how long I'd be detained in this place. *Don't panic,* I told myself. *It's important to keep a clear head. There's been some mistake and you'll be out of here soon. Stay calm.* I tried to think about other things to distract myself, but my thoughts constantly turned to August, the man I was now accused of murdering. Would I ever be free of the stranglehold he'd had over me all these years? Even in death, he was tormenting me.

My thoughts drifted to how young I was when I married him. It had been financially imperative to do so; my mother was a single parent on death's doorstep, and we were dirt poor. There was no other way out of poverty. When August Nel wanted a wife to give him an heir, he bought a house for my mother and gave her money for medical treatment, in return for my hand in marriage. She was financially secure for the first time in her life and so was I—but my shoulders sagged thinking about what the marriage had brought with it.

I moved to the furthest corner of the cell, trying to get away from the stench emanating from next door. It reminded me of how I used to hide when we lived in the Bo-Kaap with August's dad, at the beginning of our marriage. I was afraid of my father-in-law. He had a quick temper, just like his son I soon learned. It was difficult enough to keep out of his way when our first child was born, but impossible when a second baby arrived soon after. The only way I could escape was by going out with the children.

Curled up in a corner of the cell, I remembered the relief I'd felt when August bought a house in Woodstock and for the first time in my life, I lived in a place I could call my own. It made me almost smile, despite my current surroundings, remembering how grateful I felt. It was a fixer-upper with a tiny garden, surrounded by bigger homes, and August kept his promise—he bought a place for my mother, not too far away. Seeing her happiness and renewed health made my sacrifice worthwhile, I suppose.

The neighbors weren't as welcoming in Woodstock as they'd been in the Bo-Kaap, but I didn't mind. I loved taking the children for walks in the neighborhood, often drawn to a huge Milkwood tree on Treaty Road that was over five hundred years old. People said convicts used to be hanged there, and slaves were sold under the tree until 1834. That made me go cold. I would find myself staring at it, trying to imagine what those souls felt. Some of them might have been my ancestors, dragged to this place from Malaysia or Central Africa. Were they as afraid as I was now, sitting in this cell?

My thoughts were interrupted by cursing coming from next door. "I said shut your fokken mouth. Get out of my way. And piss in the bucket, not on the floor, you filthy animal."

I cringed. The anger reminded me of August's friend Hendrik. He visited our house often; the two of them would eat the dinner I'd cooked, before retreating to the front room. Hendrik never thanked me; instead he went out of his way to be insulting while trying to amuse my husband. "It's a pity your wife never met your mother," he said once. "She might have learned how to cook a decent meal." They talked as if I wasn't there, never lifting a finger to help while I cleared the dishes and washed up. If I complained to August, he grew angry and that wouldn't end well. In fact, Hendrik's visits often resulted in August getting violent, so I kept quiet and tried to ignore the insults. I was always pleased when they finally retreated to the front room. That was August's domain. They both chain smoked; I didn't like going in there and they didn't like me joining them. I was content to withdraw to my bedroom—thank goodness, we had separate bedrooms. That sent my thoughts back along another path.

Before we were wed, August had insisted I go for a medical exam. It was an unpleasant experience and I shuddered remembering it, but I was pronounced healthy—and a virgin, which maybe was the purpose of the visit as far as August was concerned. My thoughts turned to our wedding night. A young and inexperienced bride, I dreaded what was to come, but August drank too much so all that happened was that I listened to him snoring. (He later used this affliction as a reason for us to have those separate bedrooms when we moved into our house in Woodstock; I was more than happy to agree.) When he awoke the morning after, he took a moment to focus as he grabbed his glasses and searched for me; I'd stuffed tissues in my ears and moved to a chair in the corner, distancing myself from the snoring. When he spotted me, he said, "Come here, Petra. Show me what's hidden under that pink thing you're wearing."

My mother had bought me a negligee with a matching gown for a trousseau. Although she'd made my wedding dress, which was very plain and simple, she'd insisted on buying this bedroom apparel for the honeymoon. That was a joke; the honeymoon was all of one night at a small hotel and it held no happy memories for me.

When I didn't move, he said sharply, "Do you want me to come and take it off?" I remember mumbling something in confusion and the next thing I knew, he walked over, picked me up and dropped me on the bed, tearing at my negligee as he did so. I gave an involuntary cry when I heard it rip and tried to stop him from damaging the garment further. "Oh, come on, Joanna. Are you trying to play hard-to-get? It's a bit late for that, woman."

I shook my head and sat up, pulling the negligee over my head to stop him damaging it further. As he stared at my body, his face showed no emotion. Embarrassed, I tried to cover my breasts—I'd never been naked in front of a man before. I heard him clear his throat and saw him take off his glasses, before removing his underpants and dropping them on the floor. I began to tremble, watching as he reached down to fondle himself. When he was aroused, he pushed me back, forced my legs apart, and lowered himself onto me. I braced myself when he said, "Let's do this thing. It's why we got married."

I don't believe he wanted to do it any more than I did. It didn't last long. Intercourse was perfunctory and painful—and that was the end of the honeymoon. Nine months later, I produced a daughter.

My thoughts were interrupted by a sudden uproar next door, bringing me back to my current location. I covered my ears as I heard a loud crash and a cop began shouting at the inmates. I held my breath, anticipating something terrible might happen, but the noise stopped, allowing my thoughts to return to my firstborn child.

I was delighted the moment I saw Esther, but August didn't disguise his disappointment. He wanted a son so badly that I barely had time to recuperate from childbirth before he returned to my bed and set to work again. A second daughter, Emma, arrived one year later. Once again, he was displeased and showed no interest in the baby. After a few years without me getting pregnant again, he insisted that I take my temperature daily to judge when I was ovulating. At the appropriate time, I had to inform him and he would proceed to my bed. He studied recommendations for different positions that supposedly increased the chances of having a boy. He tried them all.

Nothing worked.

I dreaded the monthly assault and although he grew angrier as time went on, I was content with my two little girls, Esther and Emma. They were happy children and gave me a reason to get up each day, but August had very little to do with them. He was not unkind, he just displayed no interest and they kept out of his way. Without them, I would've been lost. When they started school, I decided to go back to work. Tempted by the idea of extra income, August agreed to let me take a job at a clothing company—reassured that the bookkeeping department was exclusively women. I found it strange that he never looked at me with interest or desire, but he didn't want anybody else doing so either. I was a jealously guarded possession, but I was not loved.

My thoughts turned to that job and for a while I was transported from this dank cell. It was an exciting world; there were always dressmakers and designers milling around. I was quick to get my work done and find an excuse to go walkabout, just to see this other world. It was on one of these sorties that I noticed a particularly good-looking man staring at me. I felt myself blushing and looked away, making my way back to my desk as quickly as I could. The man was Tom Montgomery.

I'd no sooner sat down than there was a tap on my shoulder. I looked up and there he was, smiling at me. He said that the firm was looking for photographic models to show off the new summer line, and he wondered whether I would be interested in trying out. For a nanosecond, I thought I should get permission from August—but as this man smiled at me, the moment passed. I agreed to give it a go.

It was a strange sensation. Shy as I was in front of Tom

and all the others in the room, I wasn't shy in front of the camera. I adored the clothing and how they made me feel; soon I was making suggestions about what would work well. I posed in ways to show every garment to its best advantage. I noticed that Tom Montgomery was present whenever I was modeling and soon we began to chat; I no longer felt shy around him. I presumed he was a photographer, but actually it turned out he was in management.

The year was 1994, a momentous year when we won our freedom from apartheid and I, a Cape Coloured, was no longer labeled a second-class citizen. This was my country at last, and I had my rightful place in it. I got to vote for the first time in my life and I remember what a festive day it was as lines queued for miles to reach ballot boxes. I was glad to get time off from work to cast my vote, joining a long line with co-workers. I was relieved I didn't do it with August breathing down my neck, telling me who to vote for.

At Tom Montgomery's request, I was soon spending more time modeling than working as a bookkeeper. August didn't need to know that. Everything in the summer collection suited me well; the clothes were crisp and beautiful—there were lots of bright colors and miniskirts. I felt a moment of embarrassment posing in a bikini, something I'd never worn before, but I felt more assured when Tom smiled at me and nodded. The evening collection was dramatic; designers were using a lot of silk. I loved one black dress in particular. It was a sleeveless wraparound, with a miniskirt and a deep V-neckline. When Tom handed it to me and said, "We want you to wear this next," I was thrilled. Never in my life would I have an occasion to wear something like that, but it didn't stop me wanting to try the dress on. When I did so, I stared at the mirror in amazement. It was a perfect fit and showed some cleavage that modesty would normally have prevented me from revealing. When I emerged from the changing room, I could tell that Tom liked what he saw. He smiled and said, "That dress was made for you. It just needs some jewelry to finish it off." With that, he produced a string of faux pearls from a box of accessories and put them around my neck. I could feel his breath on my neck as he fastened the clasp, and his hands lingered a moment once he had it tightened. It sent a shiver down my spine and as I posed in front of the camera, I knew I was posing for Tom. Remembering that moment made tears spring to my eyes. I wiped them away and tried to obliterate my surroundings; I needed to focus on something other than my present situation.

After we'd finished the shoot that day, I got a message to go to his office. I was unsure what to expect, but he put me at ease immediately. "Petra, you've done a fantastic job modeling for us. Thank you. We're giving you a bonus and hope that you'll agree to help us again with next season's collection. In fact, we'd like you to be our in-house model." With that he passed me a very generous check.

I gasped when I saw the amount. He smiled and said, "Modeling is very lucrative and you've got what it takes."

I tried murmuring my thanks, but he stopped me and said, "Actually, there's something else I wanted to ask you." He took a deep breath and began to speak quickly. "I'm an amateur photographer, a wannabe really, so I've been coming to all the shoots, trying to pick the brains of the professionals. Here's the thing, there's a competition offered by the Arts' Council to celebrate our new South Africa. The theme for it is liberation. Entries can be in any medium and I want to enter a photograph." He stopped for a second and took another deep breath. "I would love you to model for me. You're such a natural. Would you be prepared to do that? I would pay you of course."

I felt myself blushing as I stammered a response. "I, I...yes, I would love to, but I won't accept any payment."

He opened his mouth to speak and I stopped him immediately. "You said yourself that you're an amateur photographer—well, I'm an amateur model!"

I loved hearing his laughter. His face lit up and his eyes twinkled. "That's fantastic. Thank you," he replied.

There were some practical matters that needed to be sorted out. Tom rented a studio in an old warehouse and our plan was to meet there on Saturdays. I decided to explain my absence to August by saying I had to work overtime, which was somewhat true, and Tom—I presumed—said the same thing to his wife. I had noticed his wedding ring; I didn't really care. We weren't doing anything wrong. I took my daughters to my mother's every Saturday, and August spent the day smoking, drinking and playing cards with Hendrik. He barely noticed I was gone. Often, by the time I returned, the two of them were as drunk as the creatures in the cell next door to me and I'd retreat to my mother's house with the girls. I didn't want them to witness their father like that.

The first Saturday that Tom and I met, we brainstormed ideas on how to express liberation. We tried going to the beach to play around with poses. First, he had me jumping into the air wearing a bikini; another effort had me leap off a rock and he photographed me in mid-air. He also tried having me emerge from the water, dripping wet, like the birth of Venus, but when we returned to the studio, we both began to laugh at our efforts. "They're pretty corny really; all we can say is that we've made a start," Tom said. "So, are you OK to meet again next Saturday?"

"Of course. And I'll be thinking of ideas between now and then," I replied. In fact, come to think of it, it was all I did think about and I was counting the days until we could meet again. I suppose I was really more interested in being with Tom than in the competition, but I knew how much it meant to him and I wanted to come up with a good idea. In the end, I did—and it was a very good idea.

"I think this has to be more than one photograph," I told him.

"No, it can't be," he replied.

"It can. Hear me out." I surprised myself with my boldness, but Tom was eager to hear what I had to say and didn't seem in the least taken aback. "You can superimpose one photo over another and present it as one photograph. In one, I'll be cowering—and in another I'll be bold and strong."

His face broke into a smile immediately. "That's brilliant, Petra. I think you've hit the nail on the head. That's why last week's efforts didn't do it for us. It needs the contrast to show the liberation." He showed me the prints we'd taken before; they were good pictures, but nothing special. "They don't express anything except your joie de vivre," he said. He looked at me and said, "Are you always this full of life?" I smiled and looked away, without answering.

And that was the birth of our brainchild. Wearing the black dress borrowed from the collection, I posed, crouching low to the ground—but it seemed awkward. I made a suggestion that I turn around and have my back to the camera. He liked that idea and I heard his camera clicking away.

For the next pose I faced the camera, standing tall and looking up, with my arms stretched upwards and my legs astride. He took many photos of these poses and we both felt exhilarated by the progress we'd made.

I couldn't wait to see the photos and the moment I did, I knew we were on the right track. I also knew immediately what else was needed. Tom read my expression and frowned. "What's on your mind? You look disappointed."

I shook my head. "No, I'm not. Not at all. But I think there's something we can do to make them even better."

"Oh?" he said.

I took the two photographs that I considered the best; one where I was scrunched up in a tight ball with my back to the camera, and another where I was doing the forward-facing pose. "What if you made this one small?" I said, pointing to the crouching one. "Small and a little out of focus."

"OK..."

"And then make this other one crisp, much larger, and more imposing."

"Yes, I like it. And they should be in black and white. It's much more dramatic."

"Definitely." I took a deep breath before adding, "There's another thing that would make the composition even more dramatic."

"What's that?"

I remember how I stared at him, nervous to say what was on my mind. I knew my idea was a good one but I wasn't sure how to say it.

"Well?" he urged. "Your ideas have been fantastic, so don't be afraid to express them. This is a team effort, Joanna."

I swallowed hard and said, "What if we did them

again, but this time I'm naked?"

His eyebrows shot up. "Oh!" he exclaimed, and said nothing more.

I couldn't make out what he was thinking. I remember feeling anxious that he might think badly of me. After a moment, however, he exhaled loudly and said, "It's actually what I've been thinking, but I didn't feel I could ask." I can still picture how intently he looked at me and said, "Are you sure you'd be comfortable doing that, Petra?"

I said nothing, but walked over to the single chair in the studio and began removing my clothes. When I turned to face him, neither of us spoke as I moved into position. Crouched down, with my head tucked below my knees, I heard the camera clicking as he moved around the room, taking shots from different angles. Finally, he said, "Right. I've got that. Let's have you turn around now."

I stood up and faced him. Nothing more was said as we stared at one another, but my heart was pounding and my body tingled. His gaze slowly drifted up and down my body, before our eyes locked. After what seemed an eternity staring at one another, he half-smiled and gave a silent nod—and we got to work once more. I stood astride and arched my back, lifting my arms upward with my hands stretching for something beyond my reach. My head was tilted back so that my face was not visible—only the end of my chin could be seen—and I could feel my hair cascading behind me. Completely free of inhibition, I bared myself to him. It was exhilarating.

Once again, I could hear the camera clicking multiple times. Still nothing was said, until finally I heard him exclaim, "My God, Petra, you are a thing of beauty and grace. I don't know how you can hold that pose so steadily. You're a marvel." A moment later, I felt his hand under my back.

"Come, you can straighten up now," he said—and as he pulled me up, I found myself cradled in his arms. It was like nothing I'd ever felt before as his hands brushed over my breasts, and I knew that whatever the consequences were, neither of us could stop ourselves from what was about to happen.

I closed my eyes now, remembering that moment when he'd touched me, remembering how my body had quivered.

# CHAPTER 22

It was bittersweet remembering my time with Tom, but when I heard shouts coming from the crowded cell next door once again, my thoughts quickly returned to August and the reason why I was locked up here. The angry shouts were a reminder of how August grew more and more aggressive. Even though I rushed back from work each day to fetch the girls from school and prepare dinner before he got home, he was never satisfied. On a good day, he would eat his meal, then get up and leave the table without saying a word. On other days, however, he would tell Esther and Emma to go to their bedroom before dragging me to the front room. There he would find something amiss. One day he pointed to an ashtray filled with stompies, and shouted, "What sort of woman are you, leaving your house so filthy?" Before I could reply, he threw the heavy ashtray at me. His aim was good and it hit me in the face, showering me with cigarette butts. Another time, he pointed to the windows and said, "Just look how filthy those are. What's more important to you, your home or this stupid job you've got? You should be grateful that I bought you this house."

He didn't expect me to answer, but I did. "I love my job, August. I need..."

I wasn't able to finish before he slapped me. "Don't answer back," he bellowed. My hands shot up to protect myself as I saw him getting ready to strike again; I quickly turned away to avoid the blow but he grabbed my hair and yanked it. "If those windows aren't clean tomorrow, you can forget about that bloody job. This is your work right here, in this house. Do you understand?" he shouted.

Fighting back tears, I stumbled to my room with my head throbbing, thankful that he'd insisted we have separate bedrooms. I remember thinking at that moment, *I have to leave him. This isn't safe.* If only I'd had the courage to follow my instincts.

I threw some clothes into a suitcase and was about to do the same for my daughters when there was a loud crash as he kicked open my door. Oh God, I remember how he took one look at my packed bag and said, "I wouldn't do that if I were you. If you go, I'm telling you, you'll never see Esther and Emma again."

"You can't do that," I replied with my heart racing. "The court favors the mother in custody matters."

"I told you not to answer back. Are you deaf, woman? Or just dumb?" He sneered and added, "No court will give a woman custody if she's homeless—especially if her mother's homeless too. Do you think your mother owns that nice place I bought? It's in my name. She'll be out on her ear immediately if you leave, and the two of you can sleep on the streets with that pathetic brother of yours. Is your wonderful job going to pay enough to support the three of you? It would be a pleasure to see you all starve and I'll tell you once more, you'll never see your children again if you leave."

Speechless, I stared at him and felt my world crumbling. I watched as he turned, locked the door and slowly removed his belt. Bracing myself for a beating, I shut my eyes and crumpled to the floor. The room seemed ominously silent, with just the sound of a clock ticking. When nothing happened, I looked up and saw him looming over me, wearing only an undershirt. He was menacing as he looked down at me, his face filled with anger. He pulled me up, threw me onto the bed, and ripped off my clothes.

I cried for mercy. "Please, no, August. Stop it. Please don't hurt me."

He ignored my cries and pinned my arms down with force, bellowing, "Shut up."

His weight as he lay on top of me was suffocating, and the pain was excruciating as he thrust himself into me over and over again, grunting and sweating. "Dammit. Give me a son," he screamed in my ear. "What's the matter with you, woman?"

When he finally climbed off me, I wanted to throw up. I felt defiled. Rolling over, I buried my head in my pillow, sobbing—but this was a mistake. My bare bum was a tempting target for him and before he left, he whacked me twice with his belt for good measure. "Just remember who's boss around here," he shouted. As I heard him pulling up his trousers and storming out the door, I lay very still, choking on my tears, thankful it had been only a couple of lashes.

I was relieved that Esther and Emma were safely in their bedroom–but a few minutes later, they appeared in my room with tears streaming down their cheeks. Their terror was apparent as they clung to me without speaking; they knew to keep very quiet. Trying my best to comfort them while attempting to hide my injuries, I knew that I was trapped. I couldn't get away. He was a monster who would stop at nothing to get his way. I had to protect my mother and children, even at the price of my own happiness. As long as I stayed here and kept the peace, they would all be safe.

As I sat shivering in the cell, remembering the years of abuse, I realized how glad I was that August was dead. Even though I was locked up in jail on a charge of murder, I was free of him—and that freedom was worth everything to me.

I called in sick the next two days, giving myself time to ice the swelling around my eye, and of course I cleaned the windows. By the time I returned to work, concealer did a fairly good job of hiding the damage to my face, although it didn't go unnoticed by Tom. He followed me into the coffee room and I saw him clenching his jaw as he stared at me. His eyes were flashing as he reached out to me, but I flinched when he touched my bruised arm.

"My God, Petra," he gasped. He was prevented from saying anything more when two people came through the door, unaware of the tension between us. Instead he said to me, "Can you see me in my office please?"

I didn't want to see him. I didn't want to discuss what had happened. I wanted to forget it, so I didn't go.

Our photographic composition won first place in the Arts' Council competition. I could tell immediately what had happened because of the expression on his face as he walked through the bookkeeping department. He had a broad smile and gave a surreptitious wink as he walked past me. Later I saw a newspaper announcement posted on the notice board in the coffee room. It read: *Thomas Montgomery, an amateur photographer, walked away with the recent Arts' Council Prize. Tom and his unknown model captured the exhilaration of freedom in their portrait, LIBERATION.*

There was a lot of conjecture at Sudar and Green

about who the model was, but we kept quiet. I was determined to remain anonymous, happy to bare myself to Tom but not expose myself to everybody else. While he took all the accolades, I was more than satisfied to stay in the background, simply knowing that we had won. I glowed with the praise I received from him in private. "This is more thanks to you than me, Petra," he said. "It was your brainwave to show the contrasting poses, and it was definitely your beauty that expressed what we were trying to say."

"It was your skill that captured it, though," I replied.

He hugged me then and said, "I couldn't have done it without you. You are my muse. You're my everything." I would never forget those words, even when his love turned to hate.

Locked in a bleak cell, I sobbed as I thought back to those days. Yet, despite the pain caused by them, it was those same memories—which I had not dared reflect on for such a long time—that kept me going through a long night of incarceration. And so, I continued to cast my mind back…anything rather than think about what might happen the next day.

We continued to meet every Saturday at the studio. Tom often brought flowers for me—especially proteas when he could get them. "Their beauty is as unique as yours," he would say. "There's nothing quite like them anywhere in the world. You're my South African flower, Petra—not just beautiful, but strong and resilient. You're not some delicate rosebud."

It became our secret code at work when he would sometimes have a small bouquet of proteas delivered anonymously to my desk. Everyone presumed they'd come from my husband—that he was trying to make amends for giving me another beating. (It was impossible to hide all my cuts and bruises, no matter how hard I tried.) I let them believe the flowers were from August, but I knew who had sent them and I glowed with happiness.

I thought back to that Saturday, as we lay together on a blanket. Tom frowned while he examined the bruises and welts caused by August's belt; the swelling was completely gone, but he could see the bruises that had turned yellow and purple. I remember how he implored me to leave August. "If I could lay my hands on him, I'd kill him," he muttered, appalled by what he saw. "You have to go to the police, Petra. You have to report this domestic violence. He can't do this to you." Holding me close, very gently so as not to put pressure on my injuries, he said, "I'm going to get a divorce. I want you to leave this brute and marry me."

How I wish I'd said yes. There was nothing I wanted more, but it could never work. I didn't say that he was living in cloud cuckoo land. In reality, there was no way we could be together other than in our little nest. The outside world wasn't ready to accept us as husband and wife, even though it was legal now that apartheid's draconian laws were a thing of the past. And besides, August was capable of enormous cruelty; his threats were not idle. I knew that he would prevent me from seeing my daughters and evict my mother—and they were my responsibilities. Tom assured me that he would take care of them like his own, but he didn't understand what August was capable of. He would come after Tom and me; he'd hunt us down and our lives would be threatened. No matter how much Tom begged me, I would not agree to marry him. Besides, as long as I kept a clean house and had his meals on the table at the right time, August kept out of my bedroom. That was where the worst damage was done.

Tom and I continued operating this way for about eighteen months, meeting every Saturday. For the most part, things settled down more smoothly at home, except for occasional bouts of rage when something upset August. This happened once when someone showed him a magazine advertisement with me in it, modeling bikinis and miniskirts. He erupted with rage, hitting me and throwing me against a wall, screaming that I was nothing but a whore. I thought he'd discovered I was having an affair, so it was a relief when he showed me the magazine and I realized that my real transgression remained undetected. It was all I could do not to laugh.

With a black eye to show for my troubles, I received a scornful sneer from Hendrik when he next came to the house. August had wasted no time showing him the advertisement—even though he said it was humiliating. When my husband found fault with me, it usually coincided with one of Hendrik's visits—for some inexplicable reason, that man disliked me.

I concocted a story at work about falling on some stairs. Not many people bought it, and Tom definitely knew it wasn't true. Once again, he begged me to leave August, and once again I told him I couldn't. My fear of my husband was so great that it outweighed the faith I should've had in the man I loved. How I wish I'd had the courage to leave; none of this would've happened if I'd done so. I wouldn't be sitting in jail, waiting to appear before a magistrate on a charge of murder.

# CHAPTER 23

The pain was intense as I thought back on those times. It was torment to remember how happy I'd been then and what my life had come to now. They'd been the happiest eighteen months I'd ever known. Life had been worthwhile, despite the abuse at home. It seemed as if nothing could destroy my joy—until I awoke one morning, knowing something had gone horribly wrong. Despite our precautions, the unthinkable had happened.

I began to shake, remembering that fateful morning when I barely made it to the bathroom before throwing up, and the smell of food made my stomach churn as I tried to cook August's bacon and eggs. I bought a home pregnancy kit that afternoon, but I needn't have bothered. It was a foregone conclusion what the result would be.

When I rode the bus to work next morning, my daughters' faces kept coming to mind. I was their security. I had to protect them from August's violence; I had to stay close to them. And my mother and Willy; their lives also depended on me and my marriage. It was imperative that I figured something out quickly because a baby was growing inside me, so I didn't have the luxury of time to make plans. I stared out the window at passing traffic, but I saw nothing. Instead, my mind went around and around trying to decide what to do, realizing that my options were limited. There were only three...

- *I could have an abortion.* Laws had recently changed which meant I could now do this legally.
- *I could leave August* for Tom and hope that I could get my daughters away with me. That would be unlikely though—and besides, he was still a married man.
- *I could stay with August* and pretend it was his child. I shuddered at the thought of that.

I quickly ruled out having an abortion. I couldn't end the life of this small being that was mine and Tom's; I just couldn't. I loved the man and I wanted to have his baby; it was a piece of him. Leaving August was what I really wanted to do. Tom said he would divorce his wife if I would leave August, but could I be sure of that? What if I left August and Tom didn't get a divorce for some reason? What if his wife wouldn't agree to give him one?

I squeezed my eyes shut and imagined how happy he would be if I went straight to his office and told him he was going to be a father. I tried to picture his face; I was sure he wouldn't care about any consequences at Sudar and Green. We could make a plan to get my girls and move somewhere safe until we could both get divorced. I grew excited thinking along those lines, but in my heart, I didn't believe it could work. Our worlds were too different. It was a fairytale to think we could overcome the obstacles that would be in our way. Deep down, I believed that his career would come to a grinding halt if I were his wife, even though apartheid was a thing of the past. I was a Cape Coloured. I wouldn't fit into his world, and he wouldn't want to live in mine—besides, we'd never be safe from August's wrath.

Just thinking about August made me shiver. He would

want revenge if I left him; I would never be safe, no matter where I went. His violence would rise to a whole new level, of that I was certain—and Tom wouldn't be safe either. August was capable of anything. I wouldn't put it past him to engineer an accident that conveniently got rid of us, and then what would happen to Esther and Emma? They would be left to his mercy, a quality he didn't have. And my mother? What about her? Willie would have to support her and he could barely make ends meet for himself because his education was such that it didn't offer him too many opportunities. It was an impossible situation.

My stomach was in a knot when I climbed off the bus and walked into Sudar and Green, but my mind was made up; there was only one option. Before I lost resolve, I went to the HR department and handed in my resignation, giving no explanation. I knew that I couldn't spend one more day near Tom because I would weaken—and that would spell disaster. Time was not on my side.

"What on earth has happened? You look terrible. Please reconsider," the head of human resources pleaded.

I apologized but said I didn't have a choice.

"Can you at least give us two weeks' notice so that we can find a replacement for you?"

I swallowed hard and shook my head. "I can't. It's not possible. I'm sorry."

There was only one more thing left to do, but before I made my way to Tom's office, I made a detour to the toilet to throw up again. My legs could hardly carry me as I headed up the stairs to knock on his door. He looked surprised when I entered and his concern soon became evident when he saw my stricken face.

"Petra, what is it?" he asked.

I closed the door behind me and stood looking at him,

longing to tell him that I was pregnant with his child. When he got out of his chair and walked towards me, I couldn't help but take a step towards him—but then I stopped myself. With my eyes squeezed tightly shut, I thought: *Petra, don't go one step further. You have to do this. There's no other way.*

It was easier not to look at him as I delivered the story I'd worked out. Staring out the window, I said, "He's found out, Tom. I don't know how, but August knows about us."

"Oh God," he said. "How on earth did that happen? We've been so careful. Don't tell me he's laid a hand on you, Petra." With that, he rushed towards me, but I was quick to put my hands up, stopping him.

"Please don't, Tom. Don't touch me."

"Oh God, he *has* beaten you again," he said. "My God, I've seen it happen too many times and this is the last time he's going to do it. If you won't do so, I'm going to report him to the police—that's if I don't kill the bastard first." His eyes were flashing as he looked at me.

All I wanted to do was fall into his arms and tell him the truth. How I wish I'd done that. It was the hardest thing I'd ever done when I stood my ground and stopped him. "No, it's not safe anymore. It's over, Tom. I'm sorry, there's no other way; there's too much at stake. We can't see one another anymore. It's all over between us. Please, if you love me, let me go. Don't try to contact me again." Choking back tears, I looked at him one last time and whispered, "I'm sorry." My heart was breaking as I rushed out the door before he could stop me. I didn't speak to him again for nearly twenty-two years.

There was still an even harder thing to endure, however. That night, after dinner, when I'd put the girls to bed, I steeled myself and made my way to the front room. Hendrik was there as usual. He looked up and said, "Petra, this is a surprise."

"Yes, it is, I'm sure. But if you don't mind, I'd like a bit of time with my husband. You're monopolizing him."

His eyes almost popped out of his head and August looked equally astonished.

"Well, it seems that suddenly three's a crowd," Hendrik said. "I'd better be going, then. See you tomorrow, my friend." With that, he glared at me, got up and left.

"What's all this about?" August demanded. "I don't appreciate you chasing Hendrik out of my house."

It took all my courage to smile at him and say, "I've been taking my temperature again, August. I know how much you want a son, and I really want to give you one. The thing is, I'm getting older and soon it will be too late to try for another baby. I'm ovulating right now. If we seize the moment, maybe we can... you know... make your dream come true." He stared at me and for once in his life he was speechless.

It was as much as I could do not to throw up yet again as we moved to my bedroom and August tried to impregnate me with his Y chromosome sperm. When he left my room, he offered me his thanks instead of his belt, and I lay in bed crying as if my tears would never stop.

The only other person who suspected the truth was my mother, but even she didn't know the whole story. I couldn't burden her with the knowledge that she was one of the reasons I had to stay in this unhealthy marriage. I went to her the next day—and every day—for a couple of weeks, until my morning sickness subsided. She cooked meals for me to take home during that time, sparing me a duty that was too difficult to perform without throwing up.

A month later I stopped the charade and announced to August that I was pregnant. Overjoyed, he didn't do any calculations and for the ensuing months, he treated me with remarkable consideration. He even bought a car to make my life easier. It was a sturdy Volvo that I'm still driving, twenty-two years later. He was convinced that the baby was going to be a boy—that God was finally giving him what he wanted.

I'll never forget the day Joanna was born. The onset of labor was quick. I made it to the hospital in the nick of time, thanks to my mother's help. Remembering the searing pain of the last two births, childbirth was not difficult this time around because I accepted the offer of an epidural. It seemed only moments before I heard the doctor say, "It's a girl." He held her up for me to see briefly, before a nurse took her away to be weighed and washed. She didn't cry at first, and in desperation they had to give her oxygen to get her to breathe. My new baby looked very different from the way her sisters had looked at birth. She was pale, with very little hair, and what hair there was, was fair. She had baby blue eyes that stared right at me when she was placed on my chest, as if she was recognizing the bond between us. She'd arrived three weeks early and there was concern about the maturity of her lungs, but my little girl was strong. Even then she was a fighter; a healthy baby who grew into a strong woman.

Needless to say, August was beside himself with rage that I had given him yet another girl. He left the hospital without even looking at her. I was thankful that he was not in the delivery room when she was born because I was able to enjoy the first moments of Joanna's life with unadulterated love and joy. He didn't return to the hospital to visit and when I arrived home with her, he glanced at the new baby wrapped in a shawl, only to let me know in no uncertain terms what a failure I was—and what a disappointment she was to him. He didn't care what name I gave her, which left me free to call her Joanna, after Tom's mother—at least there would be some connection to her father, even if she wouldn't know it. August never held her, nor did he look at her until she was a toddler—when he couldn't avoid seeing her running around. Like the rest of us, she was forbidden to go into his bedroom, and was only allowed into the front room when he summoned her there to issue an order, or to reprimand her. But Esther and Emma loved her immediately and treated her like a living doll. They helped me bathe her and sang lullabies to her; they read her stories and delighted in her smiles. She, in turn, grew to love them and her eyes lit up when they returned from school each day. They marveled at her blue eyes, which turned brown after several weeks. In addition to that change, her blonde curls turned into dark brown waves, and her pale skin became olive in the sunshine. Soon she looked more like us.

I clutched my breasts in the dark cell, remembering how I would watch her little mouth sucking as I fed her, longing for her real father to see her. My heart ached for him—many a time I was tempted to call and tell him about his child, our child. One time when I had her in the car, on an impulse, I drove to Sudar and Green. She fell asleep on the way there, looking angelic. I was in the parking lot, about to take her out of her car seat, when I saw him come out of the building with two other men. They walked by, about twenty yards away. If he'd looked my way, he would have seen me, but he was facing in the other direction. My pulse was racing; if he'd been on his own, I would've called out to him. Instead, I buckled Joanna back into her seat and closed the door quietly, thankful she was still asleep. I returned to the driver's seat and stared at him, aching for the man I loved.

The sight of him, even at a distance, reopened the painful wound I'd inflicted on myself a year previously. The way he walked, the backward tilt of his head when he laughed, the way he expressed himself with his hands—all of it was so familiar that it took me right back to our studio days, our happy days.

"What have I done?" I thought. "Is it too late to make amends? Is it possible to repair the damage I've done? Can I call out to him and say I'm sorry? Can I introduce him to his daughter? Will he forgive me, or will he hate me?" So many thoughts raced through my mind as I watched him, willing him to turn around and look at me.

He didn't turn, though. He just kept going. Bereft, I watched him walk further and further away—and my heart broke all over again.

As I sat in the stinking cell, I told myself to stop remembering Tom; I'd kept him out of my thoughts for so many years and now I was tormenting myself by dwelling on the heartache. It was better to think about Joanna instead. She had always brought me such joy. Through the years, I recognized many things about her father in our daughter. Her eyes sparkled like his; she also had his strong jaw and engaging smile. They were constant reminders of him. A clever child, she was awarded a bursary to attend a private girls' school where she received an outstanding education. (Poor Esther and Emma had not been as fortunate; like me and Willie, they grew up in the days when schools were segregated, so their education was very inferior to the one their sister received.) Joanna's school reports revealed that she had exceptional talent in art and that she was a diligent student. *She is a good all-rounder*, was a frequent comment at the bottom of her yearly report. At the end of her matriculation year, she received the Principal's Prize for excellence.

I was sure all this was inherited from her father. My academic career had not been illustrious at all. It had been a struggle to finish school for Willie and me because of our dire financial situation at home; I was often absent to help in the shop. I imagined how proud Tom would've been of his daughter and wished he could know about Joanna. It wasn't possible, however. It had to remain a closely guarded secret. So, it was just me, her grandmother, and her sisters applauding her success when she finished high school. August was busy elsewhere. I was thankful I'd had the foresight to save enough money to send her to university, with a small additional student loan. August wouldn't agree to pay her tuition but I wouldn't let that stop her. She was accepted at UCT and we were both over the moon with excitement. This was what she'd always wanted and she needed to follow her dreams. I was proud that she forged ahead, despite the obstacles he put in her way.

I couldn't believe that August had the audacity to brag about her achievements. It made my blood boil. I'd hear him telling Hendrik how well Joanna was doing, that she was the first Nel to go to university. You would've thought he'd encouraged her all along if you'd heard him speak. It was all I could do not to shout out, "But she's not yours. She's not even a Nel. She's mine; mine and Tom's." What I didn't realize was that it was a sales promotion on August's part; he was putting my daughter onto the marriage market. He had his eye on Hendrik's son and wealth.

# CHAPTER 24

A loud crash brought me back to my present circumstances and I saw police officers running to investigate what was happening. There'd been shouting all night as drunks made a ruckus in the adjacent cell, cursing and retching. Fortunately, they were handcuffed so there were no punch-ups, and the cops—satisfied that no harm had been done—moved away. One of them looked in on me while passing and said, "You'll be up before a magistrate later today; your attorney is on his way."

He seemed kinder than the other cops who'd brought me in. Those guys had simply banged on my front door, announcing that I was under arrest for the murder of August Nel. Just like that.

I was stupefied. "What?" I'd gasped. "What are you talking about? He died ages ago in the hospital. Nobody murdered him."

Dogs were barking next door and neighbors were staring out their windows, watching to see what was happening. One of them called out, "Should I phone Esther for you?" All I could do was nod as I was pushed into the back of a police van.

The commanding officer at the station was more accommodating. He handed me a phone and said, "I'm not at liberty to discuss the case with you. The investigating officer will do that, but you can call an attorney."

I didn't have an attorney so I asked, "Can I call my

daughter instead?"

He shrugged. "Please yourself, lady. You can make one phone call, that's it."

Joanna was beside herself when I reached her and explained what had happened. "That's bullshit, Mom," she said. "How can they do this?" I heard Ryan's voice in the background and a second later she said, "I'm on my way back to you and we'll get an attorney. You'll be out of there soon. You've done nothing wrong. Trust me; you're not guilty of any crime."

I felt a little better after talking to her. Joanna is one of those people you feel safe with. Like her father used to be for me, her confidence was reassuring. Suddenly I felt like the child in our relationship. It seemed wrong to be taking her away from work, but I didn't know what else to do; I couldn't manage without her and the one night I'd spent in a cell was enough to convince me I wanted all the help I could get.

The same cop arrived a little later to cuff me. He escorted me to an interview room, where an attorney sat waiting for me. My handcuffs were removed and I heaved a sigh of relief as I was offered a seat. A middle-aged man introduced himself as Ben Pistorius, explaining that he'd been called by a contact of Joanna's in Durban to represent me. Bewildered, I stammered that I couldn't afford to engage an attorney. He smiled and reassured me, "Mrs. Nel, it's all been taken care of. Don't worry about that—just tell me what happened on the day that your husband had this accident."

Ben Pistorius had a kindly face and I felt slightly better as he pressed me to tell my version of what had happened. He took notes as he listened and asked questions. I answered, describing how August had come at me with a knife and I'd picked up the nearest thing to defend myself. It happened to be a cast iron pan with hot oil in it.

"May I call you Petra?" he asked. I nodded and he continued, "Let's just back up a bit here. Why did he come at you with a knife? What provoked that?"

"He was always attacking me, Mr. Pistorius. I have scars all over my body to prove it."

"Had he ever attacked you with a knife before?"

I shook my head. "No. That was a first. That's why I fought back. I knew if I didn't, he would kill me."

"The prosecution will argue that you killed him, though. The coroner's report states that the cause of death was a blow to the back of the head. This could be a charge of culpable homicide—or murder, I'm afraid. It could go either way."

My heart was pounding. "But I didn't kill him," I cried out. "I injured him—I don't deny that, but I was injured too. I was fighting back. He stabbed me with a sharp kitchen knife—you can see the slash down my arm here where he cut me. When I hit him, he fell backwards and knocked his head on the kitchen counter. I saw blood coming from the wound."

"That could be the cause of death, then. What was the counter made of?"

"Concrete."

"Ah, that makes it very possible. Where did you hit him?"

"I think it was on his forehead. I mean, it all happened so quickly I can't be sure exactly."

Ben Pistorius nodded slowly. "Tell me what you did when you saw him on the ground."

"I ran to my brother's house as fast as I could, to get away. I was bleeding from the knife wound and there was hot oil burning my arm. I was in pain. I needed help. I was terrified."

"So, you left your husband lying on the kitchen floor, bleeding?"

"Yes. I had to get away before he attacked me again. I didn't know he was unconscious—I didn't stop to check. He had a stroke too, I don't know exactly when. But, like I told you, I got away as fast as I could and my brother rushed me to the hospital. I think he also called my daughters to tell them what had happened; maybe he didn't call them all, but I know he called Joanna. The police came to the hospital later and questioned me; they had to, because of the knife wound which the doctors had reported to them. I told them that I'd left August on the kitchen floor, so I suppose they sent someone to check up and that's when they found him. When they saw my injuries, and the other scars on my body, they concluded that I'd acted in self-defense. I heard nothing more from them."

"Is that right!" my attorney exclaimed. "If that's the case, I wonder why they're charging you now. It doesn't make any sense. The man was in hospital for ages and he's been dead for some time." He stared at me as he drummed his fingers and I felt as perplexed as he did. "You're sure there's nothing else you've forgotten to tell me?" he asked. "What made him attack you?"

I didn't want to explain all the details about the photograph, and Joanna, and the second phone; that was all too personal and private. So, I shrugged and said, "Who knows? Sometimes he just felt like attacking me. He was a bully."

He continued staring at me and after a while he said, "You're telling me everything are you, Petra?"

I nodded.

"Right...well I'm meeting with the prosecutor in ten minutes. Maybe we'll speak again after that. They must have some new evidence to reopen the case. If you're sure that's all you can tell me, I'll go and hear what he has to say."

I was taken back to the holding cell but it wasn't long before the same cop returned and said, "Come on. He wants to see you again." Once again, I was handcuffed and led to the interview room. Ben Pistorius looked less kindly now. As soon as I was seated, he said, "You didn't tell me you were having an affair, Petra. That's what provoked August to attack you with a knife, and not only that, there was motive there for you to kill him. The prosecution will argue that you wanted out of the marriage." He shook his head and said sternly. "I've asked you to tell me the whole truth, not just part of it. Now, can you explain again what happened that day?"

I realized that I couldn't hide anything if I wanted to get out of this mess. Nothing could be private anymore; Ben Pistorius needed to know it all. My heart was thumping in my chest and I shut my eyes tightly, squeezing back tears as I explained what had happened more than two decades ago when I discovered I was pregnant—how I'd walked away from the affair and pretended the baby was August's. Then I fast forwarded and told him how August had wanted to force Joanna into an arranged marriage, but that I couldn't let it happen. I described how I got her away to her biological father and explained about the two phones I'd bought. I told how I'd hidden a phone in the kitchen so that my daughter and I could communicate safely, and how—when August had discovered it—he realized that it had been me who'd helped Joanna to escape.

He also read text messages and realized that Joanna was not his daughter.

Ben Pistorius listened carefully without interrupting, and when I'd finished the saga, he said, "So are you saying that this affair ended before Joanna was born and that you never saw the man again?"

I nodded. "I didn't see him again until I needed help getting Joanna away. He didn't know about his daughter until then. He never knew I was pregnant."

He frowned and said, "Let me get this straight. Who was Joanna's biological father?"

I swallowed hard and said, "The man I was having an affair with, Tom Montgomery."

Drumming his fingers again, he asked, "I see. Did August know that?"

"No, I told you, he only discovered that information when he saw a message on my phone. And like I said, Tom didn't know either." I choked on my words as I said, "The first time that Tom knew about her was when I called him for help."

He frowned. "Petra, explain to me then why August attacked you. What exactly did he see on your phone that enraged him? What was in the text?"

I sighed and my head dropped to my chest as I tried to choose my words.

"Petra, I need to know. I don't want any surprises in court. I need to know the full story."

I had no option but to explain about the photograph. As he listened, he seemed to grasp what had transpired. When I'd finished telling him about the competition, and how Joanna had sent me a photo of the original, which August then discovered on my phone along with her message, Ben nodded. "Right. Now I get it," he said. "And by a strange coincidence, I actually remember that photograph. I saw it on display in the Barnard Gallery. It caused quite a stir. Had your husband not seen it before?"

I shook my head. "Art wasn't the sort of thing that interested him."

"Well, well, well. So that was you, was it? Mm, I can see why a man would react the way August did when he came to that realization. That definitely provides him with motivation for what he did—and it further explains why you had to defend yourself." He smiled at me and said, "Petra, this is a dream case. I never like to be too confident about these things, but I feel pretty good about this. Are you certain that your affair ended more than twenty-one years ago and that you're not withholding any information?"

"I'm certain."

I was ushered into the magistrate's court for a remand hearing and as I was led to the dock, my heart skipped a beat. Joanna was sitting on a bench at the back of the room, and although everything was a blur, I could see Ryan seated beside her and Tom Montgomery on the other side. It was humiliating. I wished nobody was there to see me like this. But when my daughter smiled to give me encouragement, despite my embarrassment, I almost cried with relief that she was there, my Joanna.

It was amazing how swift the process was. The magistrate seated himself at the bench in front of the court. He looked formidable and my heart missed a few beats when I saw his stern expression; no smile had ever graced that face, I felt sure. The lawyers seated themselves at the bar in front of him; Ben Pistorius was nearest to me, and a rather grim looking man was seated a distance away from him. This man, the prosecutor, was quick to address the magistrate. "Your Worship," he said, "we have sufficient evidence to hold Petra Nel on a charge of murder." My head began to spin as I heard this man explaining why he had a good case against me. What he said was so different from what happened that it made no sense.

Ben Pistorius showed no reaction as he listened, nor when he stood up to respond. He cleared his throat and in a calm voice said, "Your Worship, I have evidence that proves my client acted in self-defense against an attack on her person by August Nel. The man was wielding a kitchen knife and he stabbed her." He turned and gestured towards me. "As you can see, Petra Nel is a small woman. August Nel was a large man; she would be unlikely to attack him unless she feared for her life. I will prove beyond reasonable doubt that my client was the victim of an attempt on her life." He let that thought linger a moment before saying that I was not a flight risk. "Therefore, I am requesting bail," he added.

The answer seemed a long time coming, but eventually the magistrate spoke. "This appears to be a prima facie case. The court will set a trial date and bail is set at R50,000. Mrs. Nel, you must surrender your passport."

I gasped and murmured, "I, I... don't have one, Your Worship." I started to shiver, knowing also that I didn't have money to pay for the bail.

He coughed. "Right, well, once your bail is paid, you'll be free to go until your trial. You must remain in Cape Town and report twice a week, every Monday and Friday, to the Woodstock police station in Victoria Road."

I had no idea what was going to happen, but the bail must have been paid quickly by someone and I was free to go later that day. (I suspect it was Tom, because nobody else I knew could afford that sort of money.) The trial date was set for three months' time—three months in which to prepare and agonize about the future.

Despite my attorney's optimism, I felt I was living on a knife's edge. Ben Pistorius advised Tom to stay away from me; he and Joanna could communicate because they were father and daughter, but a big piece of the argument in my defense was that the affair between me and Tom had ended over two decades ago. There was no need to make that request to Tom; it was obvious that he only tolerated being in my presence for Joanna's sake. For my part, I felt embarrassed and uncomfortable in his company. We were worse than any estranged divorcees.

It turned out that the prosecution's new evidence had come from Hendrik, who had barely left my husband's bedside in hospital. He claimed that on August's deathbed, my husband said I'd attacked him with a knife, and that it was as he'd wrestled the knife from me that I'd been wounded. August was defending himself, according to his friend. Hendrik made a further outrageous claim that August fell because I pushed him over, then hit him repeatedly as he lay on the ground. His account portrayed August as the victim and me as a violent aggressor.

When Ben explained to me what the prosecution's case was, I was filled with disbelief and bitterness. August could barely grunt a response, let alone say all that. I remembered all the times those two men had cloistered themselves together behind closed doors in my house; I was expected to keep out of the way, but still wait on them like a servant. And when I thought how the two men had planned to marry my daughter to Hendrik's son, suddenly I knew what this was all about. I was quick to share my suspicions with Ben Pistorius; Hendrik couldn't forgive Joanna for running away—and when he discovered that I was complicit in her escape, he was set on revenge.

His eye brows shot up. "That's very interesting. So, your husband and this man were often cloistered behind closed doors, you say. What exactly was the relationship between August and Hendrik?" he asked.

"They were old friends. They'd known one another since childhood," I replied.

He looked at me long and hard before asking, "Was it platonic, or was it more than that? Were they lovers?"

Taken aback, my immediate response was, "Oh no!" But I felt a wave of horror sweep over me. Closing my eyes, I tried to block out an image of these two men in a sexual relationship—my husband, who had sired two children with me, and this other man who had accepted my hospitality for years, but who now made outrageous allegations against me. The picture wouldn't go away and unwelcome thoughts kept springing to mind—the fact that August had married late in life but had never courted me, he'd simply bought me. And sex was never anything more than a means to reproduce for him; he wanted a son to continue his business. I felt he despised me at times. And as for Hendrik—well, he was always there, always insulting me. They were as thick as thieves. Had I been naïve not to suspect something was going on between them? It had never dawned on me to question their relationship.

I almost gagged when eventually I looked up and said, "I haven't ever thought about it before."

"Well?" He waited for a response.

"It's possible, I suppose," I said after a while.

Ben nodded and said, "That could be useful."

I panicked. "But Mr. Pistorius, it's just conjecture. I

have two other daughters. August was their father. It would be humiliating for them to have that relationship questioned in court. I can't agree to that. I mean, it might have been the case, but we don't know. It's only conjecture—and it's slanderous. We don't know for sure." I didn't want to believe it.

"Petra," he responded. "We're fighting for your reputation here, not August's. And let me point out that your daughters won't be happy having you go to prison either, so stop trying to protect them. They're in for rocky times, whatever happens. Their father was a violent man who attacked you on many occasions with a belt, sometimes with his hands. This time he went further and used a knife. That is indisputable; you have scars to show it was the case. We are trying to save you and anything we can use to do so, we must. If he might have had a homosexual relationship with Hendrik, I want to throw light on that possibility. It's not considered a crime any longer, but it would bring into question this man's accusation."

With a heavy heart, I realized the logic of what he was saying and I nodded when he asked, "Were his daughters aware of how he beat you up?"

"Well, there you are. This might not come as a surprise to them. I presume they also saw that this man, Hendrik, was a big part of their father's life. It isn't a big leap to question the relationship. They'll be able to testify to that. Of course, we can't state that they were definitely lovers, but we can allude to it without saying so in as many words. Your daughters' evidence would be helpful for that."

"No," I shouted louder than I'd intended. "Please don't put them through that ordeal. It would be cruel."

He sighed and said, "Petra, please focus here on your defense against this allegation. Either Hendrik is lying, or

August was lying—if that is in actual fact what he said on his deathbed; I am not aware that there were any witnesses to confirm he said it. If that's the case, well—it's hearsay and inadmissible; I'll have it thrown out. Furthermore, it begs the question, why didn't Hendrik go to the police immediately? Why did he wait so long after August supposedly made this accusation on his deathbed, to report the matter?

"We have to show probable reason why Hendrik is lying. We have a good one—actually two good ones; revenge because his friend/lover died, and revenge because his son was rejected by your daughter. He knows that you helped her get away and he's embittered. Rest assured, Petra, the case against you is weak." He was smiling as he spoke.

His reassurances should have been comforting, but they weren't. I had the sword of Damocles hanging over me while I awaited trial, and my thoughts were in turmoil as I tried to digest this idea about August's relationship with Hendrik.

# CHAPTER 25

## ESTHER AND EMMA

Esther and Emma were stunned when Joanna called them from her car as she headed back to Cape Town. They stared at one another in disbelief when she said that their mother had been taken away by the police, charged with murder. Esther recalled that somebody had left a garbled message on her phone saying something about the police, but it had made no sense. Now it did. The sisters began peppering Joanna with questions, to which she replied, "I've told you all I know. A friend in Durban has referred us to an attorney who'll defend her. Mom hasn't done anything wrong, so, don't panic."

"Don't panic! Our mother's been charged with murdering our father and you say don't panic!" Esther cried.

"And geez, Joanna, I know she has to have an attorney, but how are we going to pay for one?" Emma asked. "I'm working more hours than there are in a day already..."

She was cut short by Joanna. "It's all taken care of."

Esther frowned. "How? Attorneys cost big bucks. Where're you getting that sort of money?"

"It's all taken care of," Joanna replied. "Someone is paying all the legal costs."

"OK, spit it out," Emma said. "It's your father who's paying, isn't it?"

Joanna took a deep breath before she replied. "Yes, it

is. I called him immediately I heard from Mom."

Esther and Emma said nothing as that information sunk in, until Esther murmured, "Thank God for that. Are they together again?"

Joanna sighed. "No. Far from it. Listen, I'm sorry, it must be weird for you right now. Your father died so recently, and now this has happened. It's a double whammy for you."

There was a moment of silence before Esther replied, "It is, Joanna. It's all weird, but you know, everything about Pa was weird. He wasn't mean to us like he was to you, but..."

Emma finished the thought for her. "I hated him sometimes when he hurt Ma. He was cruel. Even so, I can't believe she killed him deliberately. No way."

"She didn't," Joanna responded. "I'm sure of it. Mom has a hard time killing a mosquito. I'm on my way and as soon as I know more, I'll call you."

When the call ended, the two older sisters sat in silence, wishing they could contact their mother in jail, but it was not possible to do so. She was allowed no visitors. "I'm frightened," Esther spoke so softly that her sister hardly heard her. "I can't believe this is happening."

Emma nodded as she searched for a tissue in her pocket. "This is a nightmare; our mother accused of murder! I can't believe it either, but why do you think Ma called Joanna first?" She blew her nose and added, "Do you suppose it's because we were always so close to one another that Ma and Joanna developed a special bond? Is it because we excluded them?"

"Maybe. Things changed after Joanna was born. I understand why that happened now, but I didn't then. I resented it. I was the oldest, but Ma was always closer to Joanna," Esther replied.

"She was protecting her from Pa, I suppose. We didn't need the same protection. We were a dysfunctional bunch, weren't we? God, I just hope this all ends quickly and Ma is acquitted. It really is a nightmare. I wish I could wake up and find that it was just that."

Esther nodded. "I know. I feel so helpless. To be honest, I didn't feel all that sad when Pa died, but this...I can't bear it. Not our Ma. Even though she had plenty of reasons to kill him, she wouldn't have done so. She just wouldn't—even though he was so mean. I never understood why he was like that. It was lucky we had one another, Em. Poor Joanna, it was different for her. You know, when Pa introduced me to Sol and talked of marriage, I was horrified at first. But then he got mad about something and had one of his rages—and suddenly I couldn't stand it any longer. I couldn't wait to get out of the house. It was the easiest way of doing so because I didn't have money or a decent job. I didn't want to leave you there, but things worked out fine for both of us. Sol's a good guy and it was easy to love him. He's kind to me and the kids."

Emma nodded. "I felt the same as you—I couldn't wait to get away, especially after you left. It was lucky I met Sol's cousin at your place and we really liked one another. Pa didn't know that; he thought he'd engineered everything. Isaac and I were planning on getting married anyway."

Despite the tension, Esther smiled. "Our father was a control freak; I'm glad you outsmarted him. He thought he could do whatever he wanted."

"Except get a son," Emma replied.

"I know, poor Joanna. Jislaaik, he was so mad that she was a girl. Remember when he came back from the hospital after she was born. We were dying to know what had happened, and all he said was, 'I don't want to talk about it.' I was afraid Ma had died. Do you think he knew she wasn't his child?"

Emma shrugged. "Maybe he had his suspicions and that's why he beat Ma so much."

Esther nodded. "Could be... he definitely got worse after Joanna was born. He wanted a son so badly; sons-in-law didn't do it. He wanted Marius for Joanna because Hendrik was such a close friend, but Marius is such a slob. Ugh. And can you imagine Pa's rage when Joanna ran away? I'm glad I wasn't there to see it. I bet he took it out on Ma."

"Oh God, poor Ma. I can't believe this. Our mother isn't capable of killing anyone. It's rubbish. I don't understand what's happening," Emma replied.

Immediately they heard she'd been released on bail, Esther and Emma rushed to be with their mother at her house. Joanna was there already. She informed them about Hendrik's accusation and explained the attorney's defense strategy, adding they would likely be called to testify about their father and Hendrik. "He wants to suggest that perhaps they had a homosexual relationship," she explained.

"What on earth are you saying? No. That's not true," Esther said. Her hands shot up to cover her mouth.

"What sort of nonsense are you talking, Joanna?" Emma added. "Jussus, that's a shocking thing to say. That's a load of rubbish."

"Not at all. I don't think it's rubbish," Joanna replied. "We can't say for sure, but it might've been true. They had such a weird relationship. Anyway, this is a fight to save our mother, whatever it takes. I'm sorry that it's embarrassing for you, but think what's at stake. We have to defend her. You know she had no intention of killing your father—and she didn't do so. He died from knocking his head as he fell, so it wasn't murder. And he had a stroke; he could've died from that; I wonder what his death certificate states. Anyway, he died in hospital many weeks later. You have to do this for Mom."

Petra listened to her daughters and finally said to them, "I am so sorry it's come to this. You must do whatever you think best. I don't know what went on between August and Hendrik, but I'll tell you something—Hendrik made up this whole story. He's a vindictive man."

Long after their mother and sister had gone to bed, Esther and Emma sat talking, finishing a bottle of Pinotage. "The more I think about it, it does seem possible that Hendrik and Pa were...you know..." Emma began.

Esther took another sip of wine and said, "I would never have come out and said so, but I agree. Their relationship was odd. Pa was much closer to Hendrik than anyone else; they were always together and it was the only time Pa ever smiled. He wasn't happy around us. And think about when Pa was in hospital. Whenever we went to see him, Hendrik was there, watching over him like a mother hen."

"And remember how he fell apart when Pa died, sobbing and screaming like a banshee. He was beside himself."

"Mm, and when I think back, it was often when Hendrik left the house that Pa would hit Ma and scream at Joanna—even us sometimes, if we got in the way."

Emma nodded. "Exactly, and we were never allowed

into his room. Why did he and Ma have separate bedrooms, anyway?"

Emma topped up their glasses and said, "I never thought about that before; that's not normal. Us three girls were all squashed into one small bedroom, while he had the biggest room, and Ma had that other little one."

"Joanna stayed in Ma's room for a time when she was little, until she got moved in with us. Pa insisted on that, probably so that he could go and beat the crap out of Ma without being seen," Esther replied.

"Ja, but we could hear it happening. He couldn't hide the sound effects."

They opened another bottle of wine and as Esther held her glass up to the light, she said, "It'll be very embarrassing to testify about this in court, Em." She paused a moment, then added, "If it's true, I feel kind of sorry for them though, Pa and Hendrik. To tell you the truth, I wouldn't have cared about them being together, if Pa had just left Ma alone. He was vicious."

"I know," her sister replied. "It's tragic that he and Hendrik felt they had to hide their feelings for one another, if that's what was happening. I bet Ma would've been happy for Pa to go, as long as she was looked after financially. He didn't like to part with his money though, so that might've been a problem."

"Jussus, you aren't kidding about that," Esther agreed. "He was as tight as a tick on a dog's bum."

"But maybe it would've been worth it for him to get what he wanted, and Ma would've jumped at the opportunity, for sure. It would've been so much better for everyone if they'd just been honest, but Ma and Pa both had so many secrets," Emma said, filling her glass once more.

"Ja, they sure did. I know it was against the law to be

a homosexual when Pa was young, so they would have needed to keep it a secret, but it's accepted now. It's legal," Esther added. "It might've seemed strange at first, but we would all have been OK with it. It would've been so much better for them to be honest. He and Hendrik could've lived together; it would've been better than Pa beating the crap out of Ma in frustration. It wasn't her fault."

"I suppose they were old school though, and not ready to come out. They were trying to pretend they were straight. It's crazy. Nobody gives a shit anymore. Half the people I work with are gay—and proud of it."

"It's the same in the fashion world. Nobody cares about anybody else's sexual preference these days."

"Ja, but we don't know for sure that the two of them were gay," Emma reminded her sister.

Esther screwed up her face and said, "I bet they were. We were dumb not to realize it before. Everything points to that, let's face it."

"Mm, I agree with you. We just didn't see it, though, did we? Man, there has to be something we can do to help Ma. What if we go to Marius and talk to him?"

Esther frowned. "Oh hell, I haven't seen him in ages. He was an odd sort of guy. A bit of a dork."

"I know. He was a pain in the arse, but think about it...he wouldn't want this brought up in court. Maybe he'll have some ideas about what to do."

"Hey, Emma, that's not a bad idea. Yes, maybe we should try and talk to him." Esther took another swig of wine and added, "It might be awkward, given the whole situation with him and Joanna, but who cares? We've got nothing to lose."

"That's right. Nothing to lose and lots to gain. Not a word to Ma, though."

# CHAPTER 26

## MARIUS

Marius Abrahams was surprised to receive a phone call from Esther Nel, now Esther Coetzee, and it was with mixed feelings that he agreed to meet her. Although they'd known one another as children, he hadn't seen her in years—besides, it had been humiliating when her youngest sister made a fool of him. Furthermore, her mother was being charged with murder... When he thought about that, he decided he'd actually had a lucky escape; it would be embarrassing being a member of that family now. He'd always suspected that August and Petra Nel were not happily married, but he would never have imagined it could result in murder.

He thought about his father's fury when he discovered that August had died. It was worse than when he discovered his friend was in a coma after being attacked by Petra. "If only I'd been there, this would never have happened," Hendrik Abrahams had told his son. "I'll never forgive her, the bitch. She's going to pay for this. You just wait and see."

His father would be even angrier now if he knew that Marius was speaking to Esther, but she had impressed upon him how urgent it was—and something in her voice made him agree to this meeting. The problem was that since his wife had died, Marius had become slack about tidying up; there didn't seem much point. He kept meaning to increase the hours his domestic help came—maybe to work for him full-time, but he'd never got around to doing it. He raced around now, tidying his big house before Esther's arrival.

When his father had suggested this marriage to Joanna Nel, Marius had not been interested, but after seeing a recent photograph of the young woman, he changed his mind. She was extremely beautiful, like her mother, and come to think of it—his life felt empty these days. It would be good to have companionship again, and a partner in bed would also be welcome. The nights were lonely, although nobody would ever replace his Avril. She'd been dead eight years now, but he still thought about her every day. And he wanted children; he and Avril had not been blessed with any. He was even more impressed when he discovered that Joanna would have a bachelor's degree from UCT. He felt that would be a good thing for a mother to have, although she wouldn't have to work ever; her job would be bringing up their children.

He'd been nervous, but excited, going to meet Joanna Nel after so many years. The last time he'd seen her she was still in junior school, a gangly little girl whose teeth seemed too big for her mouth. Not anymore—her smile couldn't be more perfect. She was a beauty.

He'd spruced himself up as best he could—made a trip to the barber and even bought some new clothes. His heart was racing when he and his father arrived at the Nel's small house, as he tried to picture what his future bride would look like in the flesh. It came as a shock when the door opened and he saw August Nel's face. The man was hyperventilating as he beckoned them inside, slamming the door behind them. It was Mrs. Nel who said,

"Joanna's not here, I'm afraid..."

She didn't finish before August Nel exploded. "She's run away."

This came as a surprise to Marius. He hadn't ever considered Joanna's feelings about the matter at all. He'd presumed she was in agreement with the proposal—there were such obvious financial advantages for her. It was totally unexpected to be met by a storm of cussing and fist-pounding from August, with Petra cowering in the background. It was a horrible scene to witness.

Marius had flinched when August announced, "We'll find Joanna, don't you worry. I'll get her back and this marriage will go ahead. She's a spirited filly, that's all. But it will be all the more fun for you to tame her; you'll have to break her in. You'll enjoy that."

Marius had surprised himself when he took a step back and said, "No. Definitely not. I can't marry somebody who doesn't want to marry me. It'll never work. I won't do it."

He remembered his father and August impressing on him that the marriage was in everyone's best interests, that he shouldn't be so sensitive about it, but he'd remained adamant. "No. It's in everybody's interests except Joanna's. It's not going to happen." He'd walked out the door and returned to his empty home. His father didn't speak to him for weeks after that. It was only after August Nel was rushed to the hospital that he heard from his father again.

The doorbell ringing made him shove a last bunch of papers into a drawer and slam it shut. With a quick glance in the mirror, he ran his fingers through his hair, wiped his brow, straightened his back, and opened the door. There stood Esther, with her younger sister in tow. They both looked tense. "I hope you don't mind, but Emma wanted to come as well, and I feel more comfortable having her with me for support," she said. "Thank you for seeing us on such short notice."

Marius hesitated a moment, looking from one woman to the other with a sense of dread. He took a deep breath before saying, "Come in. Please sit down. Tell me why this is so important."

Esther spoke first as she sunk down into an armchair. "We're hoping that you'll have some ideas about what we can do... Oh goodness, this is really awkward." She crossed her knees and then uncrossed them, shifting in her seat while searching for words.

Still standing, Emma showed no reluctance to speak her mind. "I'll come straight to the point, Marius. We've found out that our mother's defense attorney is going to suggest our fathers, yours and mine, were in a homosexual relationship."

"What?" he gasped. "That's nonsense. You're bullshitting me. That can't be true." Again, he looked from one to the other and saw the seriousness in their faces. They were not kidding.

"A lot of dirty linen is going to be aired in court and both our families are going to be dragged into this. At first, our reaction was just like yours, disbelief," Emma continued. "But when we thought about it a bit more, it all began to add up. We think it was very likely true."

Marius was speechless as he stared at them.

Esther added, "Your father was always at our house and the two of them—your dad and ours—would be together, on their own, never with my mother—except at meals. They were sometimes in the front room, talking, drinking and playing poker; but very often they were in

Pa's bedroom, 'working.' The door was closed, maybe even locked. We were never allowed in there. That was taboo."

"That doesn't mean what you're saying," Marius objected. "They were both married men with children; I've never heard such a load of bullshit. This is ridiculous. I won't listen to this rubbish."

"We don't like it any more than you do, but it's not ridiculous. Maybe we were naïve about what was going on, but if you'd seen them together in our house, you would realize that it's very possible they were—um, you know—lovers," Esther said. "We can't say for sure, I grant you that, but there's a lot of evidence that points to it. And I'm telling you, Pa was always especially cruel to our mother after a visit from your dad. You probably don't know this, but he beat her. She never reported it to the police, but it happened. And think about this; your father only had one child—you—and then your mother left him. Why did she do that?"

Marius opened his mouth to argue, but Esther stopped him.

"No, listen to me. *Our* parents had us and no more children for ten years, and then only because our father wanted a son. There was never affection between our parents. I'm sorry, I know it's a shock, but that's why we wanted to speak to you. It's going to be extremely embarrassing for all of us when this comes out in court—and it will. I know it will."

"I don't believe any of this. What you're suggesting can't be proven."

"Maybe not in a court of law—but in the court of public opinion, suspicion will be enough to find them guilty," Emma replied.

"We will be asked to testify, and you might be too," Esther continued. "So that's why we came to you, to try and brainstorm. What can we do to stop it, Marius? I mean, I know homosexuality isn't illegal any longer, so you don't have to worry about your father being charged with a crime, but this would be such an embarrassment for both our families, wouldn't it? Just think of the scandal."

"That's why we came to you for help. Have you got any ideas?" Emma asked as she seated herself on the arm of Esther's chair. When he didn't reply, she added pointedly, "The whole of the prosecution's case seems to rest on your dad's statement, which is after all hearsay we are told—unless you know of any witnesses." She paused and added, "Do you?"

Marius collapsed onto a couch and shook his head. "I...I don't know. How would I know? I wasn't there. Maybe there was a nurse present at the time. Who knows?"

Emma continued, "Well, your dad will be grilled with questions in court about his relationship with our father, and it will all be under oath. He can't perjure himself and tell lies because he'll go to prison if he does. But without his statement, I suspect the case would be nothing. It might even be thrown out."

When Marius looked up at Emma, she was staring at him as if her eyes would drill right through him. He recoiled when she said, "And don't forget that it's a lot more than our families' reputations at stake. It's my mother's life."

He felt weak as he rose to show them out. "Thank you for warning me about this. I realize why you wanted to meet so urgently. Let me give it some thought. I'll see what I can do," he murmured.

# CHAPTER 27

I found it hard to get up each morning while I awaited trial. It was a relief to be asleep—until nightmares took away even that comfort and my nights became as much a torment as my days. I couldn't face the indignity and shame of going to prison if I were found guilty of this outrageous charge.

After a week, during which time I hadn't spoken a word, Joanna said to me, "Mom, you have to do better than this. I ask you what you want to eat and you don't answer; I put food in front of you and you don't touch it; I try and speak to you and you don't even register that I'm doing so. You can't go on like this."

I turned my head away.

"Mom," she raised her voice. "For God's sake! I know this is a terrible situation, but we're all fighting it. Esther, Emma, Tom, Mr. Pistorius—we're your team; we're working for you. You need some fighting spirit as well."

I still said nothing. They weren't the ones in the dock. How could they possibly know the humiliation and fear that I felt?

"Listen Mom, here's what I'm going to do. I'm going to stock your freezer with food, and then I'm going to leave. I don't feel that my being here is helping you—maybe it's even an irritant, and I've got work to do. Ben Pistorius has promised to keep us all in the loop. If there are any developments, you'll be the first to know, so please keep your phone with you at all times." A frown formed on my daughter's brow as she stared at me, before adding, "What happened to the amazing woman in that photograph twenty something years ago?"

Her words cut through the fog I was living in and I felt my throat constrict. My voice sounded strangulated when I turned to her and said, "Don't go. Don't leave me."

My youngest daughter didn't hesitate. She put her arms around me and held me tight. She was now the one who said nothing when I murmured, "I wish that woman could come back. Those twenty something years have been hell."

I heard nothing more from Ben Pistorius once he'd notified me of the trial date. It was hard to know what to make of his silence; I wished he would call and yet I dreaded speaking to him as well. Joanna agreed to stay longer, making only short day trips to keep working on her assignment, and I made an effort to be more communicative. It wasn't easy, but once I began responding, I felt less isolated. Esther and Emma visited every day and I could see that they were relieved by the change in me. My three daughters frequently had their heads together, deep in discussion; they didn't include me and I was satisfied to simply watch them while I could. If I were to be imprisoned, it could be a long time before I had that pleasure again.

I was outside in the garden when Joanna handed me her phone, saying that my attorney needed me urgently. As usual, I'd left my phone somewhere and, in desperation, he'd called Joanna. I couldn't read anything from her expression and mouthed, "What does he want?"

She shrugged. "I don't know. You're his client, not me. You really need to keep your phone with you, Mom.

Especially now. I'm putting it on speaker so that I can hear too."

My hand trembled as I took my phone from Joanna and cleared my throat. His secretary asked me to hold for Mr. Pistorius and although it was only a few seconds, it seemed like an eternity until I heard his voice saying, "Are you ready for this?"

I grunted something unintelligible. Joanna had been watching me; she put an arm around me and I leaned against her, afraid to breathe. Esther and Emma rushed to listen as well. We could hear papers rustling and the seconds felt like hours as we waited for him to speak. Expecting the worst, I could feel my chest constrict, but what we heard in the end, was a loud guffaw. "Petra, your problems are over. Hendrik Abrahams has withdrawn his statement."

I just about dropped the phone. "What?"

"Yup, you're a free woman. The case against you has been dropped. There'll be no trial. It's over."

"What? I can hardly believe it," I stammered. A smile spread across my face as an unbearable weight started to lift. Joanna leapt into the air, whooping and hollering, while Esther and Emma high-fived one another, laughing like crazy women—and my tears began to flow. They were tears of joy, as well as relief. Over the noise my daughters were making, I heard Ben say, "Your legal problems are over, Petra, but Hendrik Abrahams's are just beginning. He'll be facing charges of perjury. If I were his attorney, I'd get him to admit guilt and make a plea bargain. Fortunately, I'm not his attorney. What a git that man is."

My energy level exploded with an adrenalin charge. We were all laughing hysterically as I joined in my daughters' triumphal dance—until I collapsed onto a bench, gasping for air. When I finally caught my breath, I managed to say, "I wonder what on earth made Hendrik do a thing like that, make a false statement and then withdraw it?"

Emma was still bouncing around but she looked at her sisters and winked. "Maybe there's such a thing as divine justice."

"Well, maybe that awful man has a conscience after all," I said. "I mean, when I think of all the meals I've cooked for him in this house, and all the hours he's spent under this roof, I couldn't believe he'd make up such a story."

"Oh Ma, just face it, Hendrik is a fokken doos," Esther replied, sending her sisters into peals of laughter.

I had an urge to reprimand all of them—especially Esther for such bad language, but I bit my tongue; now wasn't a time to be considering good manners. In that instant, though, I noticed a strange look pass between Esther and Emma. I'd seen a similar look pass between them when they were younger and up to something. I was too exhausted to question them about it and a second later they were laughing again.

Looking at my three daughters standing together, united in their love for me, I didn't think I could ever be happier than I was right then. It didn't matter to them that I'd been unfaithful to August, or that they had different fathers. They made no judgment calls; I was simply their mother.

# CHAPTER 28

I felt sad that Joanna would soon be leaving, although I understood the importance of her job; my youngest daughter is an ambitious woman who has always set high goals for herself. I was grateful she'd taken time off from a big assignment to support me through these difficult weeks, and then she stayed close to home once she started working again.

Ryan had kept away and it was a pleasure to see him when he reappeared one day, dressed all in white and very flushed. I could tell he'd been running. "How lovely to see you again. Where've you been all this time?"

He smiled and replied, "Joanna's father offered me a roof over my head. We've just been playing tennis at Kelvin Grove; geez, he's a hell of a good player. He lent me all this gear to play at his club, but I'm not sure why—there were lots of people who weren't wearing white."

"Well, I suppose he's a traditional sort of man—old school," I said, thinking how different Tom's world was from mine. I've never been to Kelvin Grove and I've never played tennis.

"I guess my clothes are a bit tatty after two years living in the bush. That's probably why… he was just too polite to say I looked like a tramp."

I smiled. "I'm glad he's looked after you."

"Oh, he sure has. He even took me to a cricket match at Newlands. I didn't see the point of the game I must admit, and it took such a long time that I could've read all of *War and Peace* while it was going on. It was fun, though."

I laughed, but before I could answer, his phone buzzed. He grabbed it and said, "Oh, it's Joanna texting me; she wants me to meet her at the shops. I won't be long. We'll be right back."

I had a warm feeling as I watched him walk away; he was a kind, considerate young man. I wasn't surprised that Tom had helped him; he would do anything to help his daughter—and getting to know her boyfriend would be important to him. With a sinking feeling I thought that I, on the other hand, didn't deserve the generosity he'd shown by hiring an attorney to defend me.

Immediately, painful thoughts came flooding back. I remembered that awful day when August proposed that Joanna should marry Marius. I'd known immediately what I needed to do. I remember how I'd waited until my husband went out before calling Sudar and Green, and how my hand was shaking as I asked for Tom Montgomery. When his administrative assistant had questioned the purpose of my call, I remember saying, "I'm an old friend trying to reach him. Tell him it's Petra."

When she'd asked me to hold the line, I remember how I began to sweat. It seemed an eternity before she came back and said, "Mr. Montgomery will take your call now. I'm putting you through."

His voice sounded exactly the same and my heart skipped a beat when I heard him say, "Petra? Petra Nel?"

I had to stop myself from crying; there were important matters to be dealt with and I couldn't let my emotions get the better of me. Steeling myself, I said, "Yes, it's me. I'm sorry to spring this on you, Tom, but I need your help.

Can we meet?"

"Why? What's going on?"

"I'd rather not tell you over the phone, but it's urgent." When he didn't respond immediately, I said, "Please Tom, can you meet me?"

"When?"

"As soon as possible. Now?"

"Where are you?"

"At the Waterfront."

"The Waterfront is a big place. Where exactly?"

"At the Mugg and Bean. Please can you come?"

I heard him clear his throat before replying, "I'll see you there in half an hour."

I was waiting when Tom arrived and I watched as he made his way to the table. We recognized each other immediately but he didn't smile; he looked concerned. I had a sinking feeling that the concern would quickly switch to anger when he heard what I had to say. We stared at one another in awkward silence and although I longed to fling my arms around him, too much water had traveled under the bridge to do that. He looked as handsome as when I first saw him—perhaps even more so, with grey hair now that made him look distinguished.

"What's happened, Petra? What's so important that after twenty-two years of silence, you want to see me suddenly?" he asked. "Wait, before you tell me, let me get some coffee. Maybe I need a shot of something in it... You've got yourself coffee already, I see. Can I get you anything else?"

Fighting back tears, I shook my head and tried to compose myself while I waited for him to return. My eyes never left him as I stared at his back, noting the way he moved and the way he held himself. It was all so familiar and I felt a yearning that I'd long suppressed. My heart was pounding; I wasn't sure whether that was caused by the thrill of seeing him again or by fear of what I was about to confess. The moment I was dreading arrived all too soon when he sat down, placed his coffee on the table, and said, "So, what is it, Petra? What help do you need?"

I stared into his eyes, wishing he could read my mind—that I still loved him after all this time. I think he might still have had some feelings for me, otherwise he wouldn't have agreed to meet me. Neither of us spoke for a few moments until he said again, "Well, Petra, what is it? What help do you need?"

I took a deep breath and squeezed my eyes shut. And then I had to say it; I stated the simple fact. "It's not actually me that needs your help—it's our daughter."

I'll never forget the look on his face at that moment. His eyebrows shot up almost to his hairline and he opened his mouth to speak, but no words came out.

"We have a daughter, Tom. She's the one who needs your help urgently, not me."

His expression changed. Now he was frowning. "What are you saying?"

I closed my eyes again and prayed for help in choosing my words. Feeling my hands trembling in my lap, I didn't look at him until he said, "In God's name, what are you saying, Petra?"

My voice was as shaky as my hands when I answered him. "I left you twenty-two years ago because...because... because I was pregnant with our baby."

"What?"

Suddenly my words came out in a torrent. "I didn't know what to do, Tom. August would've killed us if he'd discovered the truth. I had to protect us. I had to protect my family. I didn't know what to do, so I did the only thing I could think of—I pretended the baby was his."

"You did what?" The color drained from his face—and then just as quickly, the blood came rushing back and he turned red.

"Our daughter is twenty-one. Her name is Joanna."

He exploded. "I don't believe this. You're telling me that when you walked out of my life with some BS story—you were actually pregnant with my baby? And you let that monster be the father to my child?"

I gulped and nodded.

"My God. How could you do that, Petra? Were you insane?"

"Yes. I think I was."

"You had no right to do that. How dare you? I don't believe what I'm hearing."

I tried to explain the position I'd been in—how afraid I was that August would evict my mother and take my daughters from me. Tom shook his head in disgust and said, "You know I would've done anything to support you. I told you that. But you walked away and gave my child to another man? I assume you slept with him to make it seem plausible."

I nodded again. "I had to."

"That's despicable. You disgust me."

"No, you don't understand, it was disgusting for me. But I didn't know what else to do. I was afraid he would do something terrible to us. You know how violent he is."

Tom clenched his jaw. His eyes were cold and his expression dismissive when he said, "Does she know about me?"

I shook my head. "No, she has no clue. She's about

to graduate from UCT but August has plans for her. He's trying to marry her off to some wealthy widower, twice her age. She won't do it, but her life won't be worth living if she stays under August's roof. She's got no money and I've got nothing left to give her after paying her university tuition. She has to get away as soon as she finishes her exams in three weeks' time; it's imperative. That's why I've come to you for help."

I'd brought a photograph of Joanna with me. I handed it to him, trying to steady my hand as he reached for it. I remember how he stared at it for a long time and I watched his face going through many emotions before he murmured, "She's beautiful." He looked up at me for a moment and shook his head. "To think I would never have known about her if this hadn't happened. I can't believe you could do such a thing, Petra." Turning his attention back to the photo, his eyes were watery when he said, "Bring her to me as soon as you can. I'll do whatever I can to help her." He was frowning again when he added, "You've got a lot of explaining to do to her, as well. I hope she can forgive you for all your lies. I can't. I won't. How could you profess to love me and then do something like that? You deprived me of the one thing I wanted more than anything in the world. You knew how much I wanted a child."

"I'm sorry, Tom. I've never stopped loving you. It broke my heart to do what I did, but I couldn't see another way out. You don't fully understand how violent August is—what he would have done if he knew the truth. You only saw the tip of the iceberg. I had to protect us all; you, me, my children, and my mother as well. He threatened to evict her if I left him, and he said I would never see my children again. He's a cruel man."

"And that's the man you gave my child to? My daughter, my flesh and blood, was brought up by that brute? For God's sake, what were you thinking? Petra, let me tell you this, I'll help Joanna in any way I can; I can't wait to meet her. But you—my God, I can't believe what you did. You lied. You cheated me out of my child's life. You cheated her too, with your lies. You deserve to rot in hell for this."

Those words burned into my soul, replacing the words I'd held dear all these years, that I was his muse. I could tell that he didn't even want to look at me as he wrote his address and cell phone number on a piece of paper, which he thrust my way. "Here, give these to Joanna once you've explained to her who I am. Let me know what plan you make to get her away. I'll be waiting."

He got up and left without glancing at me—and I wondered just how many times my heart could break.

Joanna remained outside talking on the phone when she and Ryan returned—and I stood watching them through the window, fighting back tears as I recalled those painful moments with Tom. *Why do you do this to yourself, Petra? Stop thinking about these things. It's over now,* I told myself.

When Ryan came inside, he could see that I was upset. I was touched when he immediately took my hands and said, "Mrs. Nel, you've lived through a nightmare. I hope you'll be able to put it all behind you."

His gentleness caught me off-guard and suddenly I couldn't stop my tears. This upset him and he immediately tried to apologize. "I'm sorry, I didn't mean to make you cry." He seemed to be searching for words to comfort me and said, "I'm in awe of you and your daughters. You're such brave, strong women." As I grabbed a tissue and blew my nose, he added, "I have to tell you something though—Joanna won't be happy until you're happy. She worries about you."

I blew my nose again and said, "But Joanna is very happy with you..."

He took a deep breath and looked away. Now he seemed to be the one struggling with his emotions when he turned back and said, "I'm in love with your daughter, Mrs. Nel, and I think she cares about me, too. But I feel that she puts up a wall between us. It's like one step forward and two steps back."

My heart went out to him. "There's a reason for it," I said. "It goes back to her childhood, I'm afraid. You see, my husband was a cruel man. I did my best to protect her, but she lived in constant fear of him. She was always on her guard."

He frowned and said, "I've never seen anyone more fearless than Joanna. You should've seen her at that shooting we witnessed in Durban. She rushed back to find me, despite the carnage everywhere."

I gulped. "So, you were there too. I knew Joanna was there, but I didn't know she ran back because of you. I thought she just happened to be in the wrong place at the wrong time. Do you mean she actually made a choice to go there and find you, despite all that was happening?"

He nodded.

"Well, I would say that gives you a clue that she cares about you, Ryan, and she hadn't even known you very long. Yes, Joanna is brave, very brave. It takes courage to overcome fear. She's learnt to do that through the years; I'm afraid it's made her wary, though."

He glanced out the window to make sure Joanna was

still outside and out of earshot, before he asked in an undertone, "Did August beat her?"

I shook my head. "No. He gave her the odd whack, but he saved the beatings for me." When I saw Ryan recoil at those words, I tried to explain. "There were other ways he hurt her. He was a bully. He never praised or encouraged her; he shouted and demeaned her. Fortunately, her sisters watched out for her and she knew only love from them and me. We tried to make up for his cruelty."

"It must've been very difficult for her—and you," Ryan said.

"I'll tell you something, if I had my life over, things would be very different. But hindsight is a wonderful thing, isn't it? I made a huge error of judgment when I left Tom Montgomery—one I'll regret to my dying day." My voice was shaky when I added, "I hope that as she gets to know her real father, Joanna will learn to trust more readily."

Ryan nodded. "She trusts *him* already; it's me she's not so sure about. Tom was the first person she turned to for help when you were arrested."

"Trust has to move from her head to her heart. When that happens, I think you might find that the wall comes down and she'll let you in. You'll just have to be patient."

# CHAPTER 29

After Joanna and Ryan left, I decided to tackle August's room; it was high time I sorted through his stuff. Oh my goodness, the moment I opened the door, I was overwhelmed by the smell of tobacco permeating the place, triggering bad memories, and I felt prickles down my spine—as if he were still standing behind me. I could almost hear him saying, "Hurry up cleaning here, then get out. I'm busy." In fact, I was so alarmed that I turned around to make sure I was alone. Reassured, I took a deep breath and did what I'd wanted to do for years—I went straight to his desk and looked for a key to open those mysterious drawers.

He'd always locked them, and I'd always wanted to know what was in them. I justified my curiosity by thinking there might be legal papers that needed to be read, before the thought struck me: *I don't need an excuse for anything anymore. I can do whatever I like, whenever I feel like it.* The realization that I was free at last felt good. I was giggling like a child as I began searching for the key, which I soon discovered in a box of pencils.

My heart started racing as I opened the top drawer, unsure what to expect. To my surprise, it was neatly organized. August was a slob about everything else because he expected me to clean up after him, but his finances were kept in an orderly fashion. The drawer contained a cheque book, some bank statements, and his share portfolio. Although I'd been a bookkeeper, it took me some time to decipher these documents, and when I did, I thought I must be mistaken. The amount of money he had salted away was considerable, and I checked again to make sure. My God, I thought, how could he let his daughters struggle so much financially when he could easily have helped them? They'd had to wait until he died to get anything from him. It was typical of him. He was selfish, as well as cruel. I pushed the drawer shut and banged my fists on the desk, feeling both relief that there was plenty of money for all of us, and anger that he had made us suffer needlessly all these years.

Before I opened the other drawer, I took a deep breath. What surprises would I find here, I wondered? And when I saw that it contained a photo album, I suddenly felt cold. Why was the album locked up?

The pictures were all of August and Hendrik. In them, the two were smiling broadly while engaged in different activities. Here they were in a sports car, and there they were climbing Table Mountain; here they were playing cricket, and there they were fishing off rocks somewhere along the coast. As I browsed through them, I felt saddened that the happy young man in the pictures, so full of life and laughter, had turned into such a beast through the years. I wasn't surprised that there were no photos of me or the children, but I did find a picture taken on our wedding day. It made me gulp. In profile, he and Hendrik were facing each other with glasses raised in a toast. The photo had obviously been handled a lot and had come loose from the page; I turned it over. Written on the back were the words: *Forever your best man. Nothing can come between us. Love you always, H.*

I swallowed hard and pushed it aside, trying not to

read too much into the words, but there was more to come.

Concealed in an envelope was a recent selfie of the two men—I could see August's arm outstretched, holding the camera. A sheet discreetly covered their lower bodies, but otherwise they were naked in this bed right here behind me. No words were necessary for this photo; August's happy smile said it all as Hendrik kissed him on the cheek.

My hands started to shake. I hadn't wanted to believe it, but it was true; they had been lovers. I threw the thing back in the drawer, slamming it shut. My stomach heaved and I began to retch. Suspicion had been bad enough; reality was worse.

August had married me because he wanted someone to give him a son; I had married him because he was my meal ticket out of poverty. It was a marriage of convenience for both of us, a working arrangement. We'd used one another and we both knew it. I hadn't wanted to believe Ben Pistorius when he tried to concoct a theory that August and Hendrik might have had a sexual relationship, even to use in my defense, but this photo changed everything. All the time he'd been married to me—even before he'd married me—August had loved Hendrik.

I was stunned. He'd been deceiving me, leading a duplicitous life, betraying me since the day we were married. I began to shake with rage. Banging my fists on the desk over and over, I screamed, shoving everything in front of me onto the floor. Then, opening the drawer and snatching the photo again, I was about to rip it into shreds—when I suddenly stopped and caught my breath. A terrifying prospect dawned on me. What if Hendrik tried to attack me again? It was quite possible. He hated me and blamed me for August's death; he was capable of anything. I stared at the wall for a few moments, gritting my teeth—and then I exhaled loudly, realizing I had nothing to fear. This photograph would protect me. August and Hendrik had gone to great lengths to hide the true nature of their relationship; if Hendrik knew that I had this evidence revealing that they were gay—and I intended to let him know that I did—he wouldn't dare try anything. The photo would guarantee my safety—and I would store it securely in a safety deposit box at the bank where he couldn't get his hands on it.

When I looked at the bed behind me, I shuddered. Was this where August had found happiness? He'd hidden his love away, like the photo locked in a drawer. It became clear to me in that moment, that trying to keep his secret hidden had eaten away at August, eventually turning him into a violent monster. Shame on him. But what about me? I'd found love elsewhere—and then lost it. A good man's love for me had turned to hate, because of my lies. *My* deception was just as bad. Not only that, I'd fooled August into believing another man's baby was his. So, double shame on me. Both our lives had been full of secrets and silent deceit.

Pacing up and down the house, my shock and anger gave way to grief—and it was at that point that I collapsed on my bed, sobbing uncontrollably. Had August only had enough courage to be honest, everything might've been different. He and Hendrik could've lived together openly and I would've walked away without a grudge. It would have been a relief for us all—him and the girls. It had been an unhappy home, despite my best efforts to protect the children. You can't disguise misery and abuse.

My mood spiraled downwards after that; I didn't get

out of my pajamas and I didn't even brush my hair or teeth. I lay in bed for days, staring at the ceiling, getting up only for necessities. All I wanted to do was sleep. I didn't want to speak to anyone, so when my daughters called, I told them I was busy. It didn't take long for me to start thinking bad thoughts about myself. I couldn't stop dwelling on the pain I'd caused Tom, and the unhappiness Joanna had endured because of my decisions all those years ago. Tom's words rang in my ears: You disgust me. My life seemed pointless. What had always been most important to me was my children—but they no longer needed me. They'd made their own lives as I'd hoped they would, and I didn't want to be a burden to them. The second most important thing in my life had been Tom, but he despised me. That bridge had been burned. My life was now without purpose.

It had been a week since I'd conversed with anyone, and I hadn't eaten or drunk anything more than water and crackers during that time. Hungry, I made my way to the kitchen and as I looked around the room, my thoughts returned to the terrible day when August had attacked me with a knife. It was right here that it had all happened. The scene replayed in my mind and I felt myself shaking, confirming what I needed to do, what I'd known all along. As soon as possible, I had to move out of this house with all its unhappy memories. Esther could have it. With the inheritance from her father, she could afford to buy the place now and I could offer it to her at a price that was reasonable, just enough for me to find a small flat for myself.

Things moved quickly after that and within a month, I closed the door on the house and moved into a rented apartment in Vredehoek. Here I could take my time finding a new home to buy—one that would have no memories jumping up to haunt me. It was a relief to be in a new neighborhood where I could be anonymous, without people asking after my well-being while talking behind my back. Esther was welcome to all the neighbors at the old house. Eventually they would grow tired of the scandal, but seeing me carted away in a police van and knowing that I'd been charged with murder would linger on their lips and in their minds for a while still. It would be better when they no longer saw me. For the first time in months I felt calm, able to sleep at night without waking in a sweat because of nightmares—and as I regained my equilibrium, I recognized I had much to be thankful for. I could've been sitting in prison if it hadn't been for the support I'd received. I'd already thanked my children and Ben Pistorius, but I knew there was someone I had not thanked yet—and so I sat down and wrote a long overdue letter.

*Dear Tom,*

*Thank you for taking care of my recent legal costs. It was magnanimous to do so after the way I treated you. I cannot find adequate words to express my regret for what I did all those years ago. I made the wrong decision leaving you, but I was afraid and unable to think straight. As a consequence, I hurt a lot of people and I would like to explain, if you would be willing to listen.*

*I hope that you will find it in your heart to forgive me. I also pray that your relationship with our daughter will continue to flourish.*

*Joanna cares a great deal about you.*
*I have the utmost regard for you, Tom.*
*You deserved much better treatment from me.*
*I am so sorry.*
*Sincerely,*
*Petra*

I suppose it wasn't unreasonable to hope that he would at least hear me out, but days went by and I heard nothing from him. I was determined not to fall into that dark hole again where my life seemed pointless, so I tried not to dwell on it—although I was constantly looking in the post box for a reply, or checking my phone for messages or emails. In an attempt to put the matter out of my mind, I offered to help Esther sew beadwork on a wedding dress; it was an intricate design and required all my concentration. We chatted intermittently as we worked and I was happy hearing how she was settling into her new home. Clearly, bad memories didn't bother her and I was thankful that at least I had protected her from those.

It wasn't long before the subject of Tom arose; I felt uncomfortable as she questioned me. "Did you love him, Ma? More to the point, do you love him still?" she asked. When I didn't answer, she added, "It's OK. You can be honest with me. After all that's happened, you don't have to pretend. I always knew your marriage was miserable. I don't really understand why you stuck it out."

I dropped some of the beads I was working with and cursed, bending down to pick them up as they scattered over the floor. It gave me time to compose myself before answering her. "I was trying to protect you and Emma," I said.

"Well, I suppose you did what you thought was best,

but you didn't really spare us. We could see what was happening. Anyway, enough about that—what about you and Tom?"

"There's nothing to tell and I don't wish to discuss it anymore," I replied.

"He seems to care about you still, Ma. Why else would he pay your legal fees and be in court for your appearance?"

"It was for Joanna's sake, not mine. I don't think he cares at all about me, but his daughter asked for help and he gave it. He would do anything for her. Whatever was between him and me ended a long time ago."

I didn't tell her about the letter I'd written to him. It still remained unanswered.

# CHAPTER 30

## TOM

Tom Montgomery was on a conference call when the day's post was delivered to his inbox. There wasn't much of it these days as most communication came electronically, but a pale blue envelope marked personal caught his eye. He put it to one side and concentrated on the phone call he was making about the workers in Zinkwazi who were threatening to strike. Production was running late for GREEN and the situation was serious; he needed to get to the factory in person to deal with the situation.

After a further call to his assistant to get him onto a plane to KZN as soon as possible, he turned his attention to the pale blue envelope. The writing seemed vaguely familiar and his eyes scanned to the end to see who it was from. When he saw Petra's name, he stiffened. Whatever she wanted now, he thought, was of no concern to him and as he read her words, there was ice in his heart. He didn't care what excuses she offered, they couldn't alter the fact that she'd cheated him out of twenty-one years of his daughter's life. For that, he would never forgive her. Her behavior was as dishonest as Cynthia's had been in their divorce proceedings.

There was one more paper in the mail for him to sign, from Cynthia's lawyer. She was driving a hard bargain but he no longer cared about that either; he just wanted the marriage to be over. Cynthia had found herself a tough legal team and they seemed out to get him for everything he had. God almighty, after months of wrangling he was giving her the house and—even though she earned as much as he did—he was giving her a huge cash settlement. She wanted more, though. He was convinced she didn't want any money going to Joanna. She was jealous of his daughter.

With a flourish, he signed the final document and heaved a sigh of relief. At last he would be a free man.

# CHAPTER 31

"Maybe you should go back to work, Ma," Emma said. She was visiting me and I could see the concern on her face as she spoke. It was obvious why she felt this way; my flat was untidy, my bed was unmade, and I was still in pajamas at 3:30 in the afternoon. "It's time to put all that's happened behind you and move on."

I looked away and swallowed hard. It's easy for people to say things like that; they don't know the guilt I feel, and the dark thoughts that swirl around in my head.

Emma continued urging me to make some changes. "Word has it that Yellow Wood Barn is short-staffed and desperate for help," she continued. "When you worked there for a while, you enjoyed it. You were good at your job—I'm not sure why you left. You're an amazing baker, Ma; your pastries are superb. I learned everything I know from you. They'll take you back in a heartbeat, and once you're busy working again, you'll feel happier. You've got too much time to sit and think. It's not like you to live like this. You've always been house proud, but look at this place; it's a small flat, yet it's wall-to-wall mess."

"It's load-shedding," I said, defending myself. "You know what it's like."

"Oh rubbish. You can't blame it on load-shedding. You don't need electricity to tidy up. Sorry to be blunt, but it's time you pulled yourself together and got on with your life."

I had no energy to explain anything to her, and frankly, I didn't care. I'd sunk back into that dark hole and nothing interested me. I wished I could close my eyes and not wake up.

"I'm really worried about you, you know," Emma continued. "Esther and I are going to call Joanna and..."

"No," I shouted. "Stop it. I'm sick of being told what to do and I do not want Joanna brought into this. She's got her own life to live, and you and Esther have too. I appreciate your concern, but keep your parenting skills for your children—not me. The best thing you can do for me is leave me alone. I need to lick my wounds."

"What are your wounds?"

I looked at her in amazement. "I can't believe you're asking that. I'm a widow..."

"Well, that's not a bad thing, given what your marriage was like."

I glared at her. "I was married to him for 36 years. Suddenly it's over and I get accused of murdering him. And I discover that he was in a relationship with that awful man all these years. How do you think that makes me feel?"

"I'm sure it's horrible for you to think about him and Hendrik, so don't. And the case was thrown out, Ma. You got a *get out of jail free card*."

Although I turned away from her so that she couldn't see my tears, I couldn't disguise the tremor in my voice when I replied. "The only man I've ever loved despises me—for good reason. Life is all about choices, Emma, and I made some bad ones. Now I'm paying the price."

She put her arms around me and said softly, "You did what you thought was best at the time. I understand that. You've paid the price already by living in purgatory all these years. That's over now."

"It's over for me, but not for Joanna and Tom."

"Why? They're delighted to be in one another's lives, and Joanna is flying high with this job of hers. She couldn't be happier. She's a hot shot photographer and her work is in demand."

"I know that and I'm proud of her. Yes, I suppose she's fine, but Tom will never forgive me. He lost twenty-one years of his daughter's life."

Emma hugged me in silence and allowed me to cry on her shoulder. When I stopped sobbing, she finally spoke. "You can't change what happened, and you can't make Tom understand if he's not willing to try. I get it, and so does Joanna; she's not bitter. What's eating you up is what Tom feels about you. And you know what, Ma? Screw Tom. If he wants to be hard-arsed, that's his choice. Let him stew in his anger, but please don't let your choice be to stew in guilt. You did what you thought was best at the time. C'mon, Ma, please let it go and make a new life for yourself. Maybe you're suffering from PTSD; maybe you need to see a therapist, or join that support group for abused women that you mentioned. But in the meantime, I think you could help yourself by moving forward and letting go of the past."

Without saying another word, she began picking up the mess all around us. Shamed into action, I began to help her. It took twenty minutes to tidy the flat, at which point she said, "That looks much better. Now, I'll wait here while you jump in the shower and get changed, and then we're all going to have dinner together—you, Esther and her family, me and my family. Please don't argue unless you have something better on your calendar."

Fortified after an evening with my children and grandchildren, I decided to do as Emma had suggested. She was right; I did have too much time to dwell on things—in fact, I was wallowing in remorse. No good could come of that. I'd reached out to Tom to try and make amends and there was nothing more I could do. My guilt had become a tumor; it was up to me to cut it out and get rid of it.

Before I could lose resolve, I checked online and saw that the Yellow Wood Barn was indeed hiring. Emma was right, I had been happy when I worked there and so, without calling first, I determined to seize the moment. I dressed smartly, put on some makeup, and checked my appearance in the mirror. I'd lost a lot of weight and my face was a bit drawn, but otherwise I wasn't too bad for a middle-aged woman. I made my way to the Yellow Wood Barn—taking some pleasure in having a purpose once more. Everything was going to get better. My spirits lifted even more at the familiarity when I walked in the door and saw some of my former workmates. A chorus of voices shouted various greetings: "Petra! Nice to see you. Welcome back. How are you?"

I felt myself blushing. The warm reception was just what I needed. Looking around, I said, "It's good to see you all, too." After a moment, while they looked at me expectantly, I added, "Is Mr. Poulton here?"

"He's in his office, but you'll have to wait. He's being interviewed by some foodie magazine. They've been at it for an hour, so I don't think it can go on much longer," my friend Lela said. "Why don't you have some coffee and something to eat while you wait? You need some fattening up! We've started making apple and brie pies; it's a new recipe and I think you should sample one. Here, come and talk to me in the kitchen while I work. I'm making a fresh batch because this morning's first lot sold out, and the next batch of bread is ready to come out the oven. Maybe you can lend a hand—nobody else comes close to your baking skills, Petra. Honestly. You need to come back."

I smiled and said quietly, "That's why I'm here. I want to come back to work."

Lela did a little jump and clapped her hands. She grabbed my arm and dragged me into the kitchen, whispering, "Ag, I heard about your husband. Good riddance, I say." When I looked away, she was quick to apologize. "Sorry, it's not my place to say that. Come, have your coffee and pie, and then you can get to work. My God, we need you."

For the first time in days, I laughed. "I'd better talk to Mr. Poulton first, don't you think?"

"Why?"

"Well the last time I checked, he was still the owner of the Yellow Wood Barn. Have you taken over from him?" I was smiling as I spoke and bit into the pie I'd been offered. My reaction was just what she'd hoped for. "Man, this is good. I love the mixture of flavors—and the pastry is so light."

Lela beamed. "That's high praise coming from you, Petra. It was my idea, but I had a hell of a job trying to get Mr. Poulton to give it a try. He can be such a stickler about stuff. I finally persuaded him that customers are always keen to taste new things, as long as we don't take away the old favorites. It meant a whole lot of extra work for me, but he agreed. I'm so happy you're coming back."

Just then, the kitchen door opened and Mrs. Poulton appeared. "Hello, Petra, I heard you were here. We're free now; won't you come through to the office? My husband is waiting for you; we can talk there."

Lela was beaming as she winked and gave me a pat of encouragement when I walked past her. "Thank God you're back. You're an answer to a prayer," she said, loudly enough for Mrs. Poulton to hear.

I followed her into the office and felt a shiver when I looked at my former boss. An austere man, he had started this bakery and café thirty-five years ago. It had been an immediate success and remained a place of note in the area. He got up and shook my hand, saying, "Please, take a seat, Petra. I gather you want to see me. What can I do for you?"

The courage I'd felt earlier started to drain away. I'd left my job here in awkward circumstances and I felt embarrassed, remembering them. Nursing a black eye, I'd had to call in sick for three days after one of August's batterings. When I'd limped back to work, Mr. and Mrs. Poulton took in my appearance and told me to go home immediately, until I felt better. "You're so pale," Mrs. Poulton had said. She was a motherly individual and I appreciated her consideration.

Mr. Poulton had agreed with her, but added, "I can't have you working here looking like that. If a food inspector came and saw you, he'd be asking questions about this establishment—and about you. You might find it awkward answering those questions. What goes on in your home is none of my concern, Petra, but what goes on here is definitely my business." As I'd turned to leave, he'd added, "And give your husband a message from me. Tell him that men like him should be locked up."

I cried all the way home and when I walked in the door, I heard August and Hendrik talking together in the bedroom. I was surprised they weren't at work.

"What are you doing here?" August asked. He looked annoyed by my unexpected appearance as he stormed into the hallway.

"I… I got sent home," I replied.

"Why? What did you do?"

I turned away and said, "Nothing. I don't want to talk about it."

August grabbed me. "Answer me. What did you do?"

"I'm telling you. I didn't do anything, but they won't have me at work with a black eye. That's why. Mr. Poulton sent me home."

He shook my shoulders and shouted, "Did he ask how you got a black eye?"

I looked away and replied in a whisper, "He said it wasn't his concern what goes on in my home." I chose not to relay the entire message.

August looked like he was about to explode. "Jussus, what exactly does he mean by that? You go right back there and tell him to stick the job up his arse. No, actually, I'll go there right now and tell him myself. How dare he say a thing like that? What is he implying?"

And so, that ended my job at the Yellow Wood Barn. Apparently, August made such a scene that Mr. Poulton called the police to have him removed from the premises.

There was an awkward silence now as Mr. Poulton cleared his throat and said, "I was sorry to hear about your recent troubles, Petra. I know things have been difficult for you."

I looked down at my hands that lay folded in my lap, and rubbed my ring finger. I no longer wore a wedding band, but there was an indentation where it had sat on my finger for over three decades. When I lifted my head, both he and Mrs. Poulton were staring at me. "I'm so sorry about what happened that day my husband came here. He was a difficult man. I didn't want to leave my job here, but he wouldn't let me come back."

"I gathered that. He made that very clear," Mr. Poulton replied. "The staff were all sorry to see you go."

"And we were extremely worried about you. I wanted to come to your house and check up on you, but I didn't dare. Your husband had warned us to keep away. He was in such a rage when he came here that I thought it might make matters worse if I attempted to reach out to you," Mrs. Poulton added.

"Yes, well, that's all in the past. What can we do for you today?" her husband asked, glancing at his watch. "I'm sorry I have another meeting in fifteen minutes."

His voice sounded cold. I needed to state my business quickly. "I see that you're hiring and I'd like to come back to work here," I said, and then held my breath.

I saw husband and wife look at one another. She raised her eyebrows and inclined her head, but he frowned at her. It was apparent that they had already discussed this and were not in agreement. He turned to look at me and sniffed loudly before he spoke. "We thought this might be why you were here, Petra, and I'll be quite honest with you; there's been too much scandal to have you come back. You were charged with murder; that's pretty serious. Word would get out, and even if you remained unseen in the kitchen, or in the office doing the bookkeeping, it would be bad for business. This is a respected establishment, a bakery and café where families come to enjoy good food."

I went cold as I stared at him. "But I'm innocent," I said. "The charges against me were false. It was all lies. The case was dismissed."

"I know that, Petra. But while you were an excellent baker, your employment record was not exemplary. You had more sick days than anybody I've ever known. I would have fired you for that, but the union wouldn't allow it. It was something of a relief when you chose to leave, and I'm not prepared to risk taking you on again."

"I stayed away because my husband beat me. That's why I had sick days. You know that, I know you do. You saw firsthand how violent he could be. But he's dead now; he won't be beating me up any more. I'll be here every day, come rain or shine. Please, Mr. Poulton, don't punish me for my late husband's faults. I'm trying to start my life over again," I pleaded. "Please. Please help me."

Mrs. Poulton looked like she wanted to speak, but her husband put his hand up to stop her and shook his head. "No, I'm sorry. It was distressing when your husband threatened me. Not only did I fear for my safety, it was embarrassing with customers and staff watching the whole debacle. It hasn't been easy to forget something like that, but I've closed the book on it now. I'll be happy to give you a good reference if that will help you, but I won't have you back at the Yellow Wood Barn. There are plenty of other jobs in the catering industry. Look for one of those. Now please, see yourself out. I have work to do."

Unable to take in what had happened, I don't know how I made it home. My spirits that had lifted earlier when I'd made my way there, now collapsed like the World Trade Center on 9/11. Stunned, I couldn't even shed a tear as I fell onto my bed and stared at the ceiling once more. Even in death, August was making my life unbearable.

Emma called and I told her in the briefest terms what had transpired. I could tell she was shocked as well, but she tried to console me. "Ma, you don't want to work for somebody like that. You had a lucky escape. Who needs people like that in their life? Screw him. What an arsehole. Better knowing it now than later. There are lots of other jobs out there, don't worry. We'll find something for you, and it'll be much better."

The last thing I felt like doing was listening to well-meant platitudes. My silence conveyed that message to her and she ended the call quickly saying, "I love you, Ma."

Eventually I dragged myself off my bed and that's when I saw the postman through the window. He looked up and waved, giving me a thumbs-up to signify I had mail. If only he'd known what he was delivering, he might not have been so cheerful.

My hands were shaking as I opened the envelope. The handwriting was familiar—it was Tom's. My heart was pounding as I held the note to my chest for a moment, almost too afraid to read it, but then I took a deep breath and reached for my glasses. It was a very short message.

> *Your situation was a heavy burden on Joanna. It was for her sake that I paid your legal expenses. Our paths might cross from time to time because of our daughter. If they do, I will endeavor to be civil. Other than that, I wish to have no further contact with you and I have no interest in hearing any explanation for your disgusting actions and lies. I can never forgive you.*
>
> *Tom.*

# CHAPTER 32

At first I was numb, but after I read his note again, my heart began to pound. Anger boiled inside me like a pressure cooker about to explode. Yes, I was fully aware that it had been a difficult time for Joanna; it had been a difficult time for all my children. But it had been even more difficult for me, dammit. Mine was the heaviest burden, carrying the weight of a false accusation for such a serious crime. I was the one faced with prison time. I was the one whose name was sullied and and I was the one who couldn't get a job now because of the scandal surrounding me. I was the one whose neighbors spoke behind my back with their own conjectures about what had happened—some thinking I had a lucky escape from justice, others thinking I had a lucky escape from an abusive husband. They all had their theories. I wasn't able to escape the scandal by moving. Cape Town seemed to have shrunk to a village where everyone knew my business.

I collapsed onto my bed again, staring at the ceiling once more, but I was no longer thinking badly about myself—my bad thoughts were about Tom. I hated him. I despised him. I crumpled his note and threw it to the floor, then I spat at it in disgust. And I wanted him to know how I felt, so, disregarding his instructions, I took a photo of the spittle running down the paper and texted it to him. Then I wrote a follow-up email:

*I was fool enough to marry August Nel without love because it was a way out of poverty. The abuse I suffered was a heavy price to pay. I was fool enough to fall in love with you and now I'm suffering abuse from you, too. You're as cruel as August ever was. You have a cold heart and I don't believe you ever really loved me. If you did, you would try to understand.*

*Don't worry, you'll never hear from me again.*

*Goodbye.*

I was exhausted, but my mind was racing. Although I wanted to shut my thoughts off and go to sleep, they kept jumping around in my head. In desperation, I went to the bathroom to search the medicine cupboard and soon found what I was looking for. With one sleeping pill in my hand, I stared at the bottle as a new thought began to form. Relief from misery was within my reach. I squeezed my eyes shut and imagined how easy it would be to end it all. When I opened them again, I looked at myself in the mirror and thought, "It would be peaceful. I'd be done with all of this."

But suddenly I thought of my daughters. Horrified that I was entertaining such an idea, I swallowed one pill and put the bottle away. "Pull yourself together," I said out loud. "You've dealt with much greater difficulties than this before. A good night's sleep will make everything feel better in the morning."

I lay down on my bed and waited for the pill to take effect while mentally replaying the events of the day, but nothing happened. I continued to lie there, staring into space, but sleep wouldn't come. In frustration, I returned to the bathroom and picked the bottle up again—perhaps another pill would do the trick. That's when I saw that the pills were past their expiration date.

I wanted to scream. Nothing was going right for me and I sat on the toilet seat with my head in my hands, sobbing. I had to sleep; I was desperate. Perhaps if I took a few more, I thought, there would still be some efficacy in them, enough to put me out for the night. I was apprehensive, but the longer I stared at the bottle, the more the temptation grew—until eventually I emptied the contents into my hand and gulped down a clutch of pills. I didn't count how many there were, I just kept drinking water and swallowing.

Returning to bed, I lay back and closed my eyes, wondering how long it would take. It was a relief when I finally started to feel drowsy—and as I drifted asleep, my misery seemed to float away.

# PART 3

# COMING TO TERMS

*I am coming to terms with the fact that loving someone requires a leap of faith, and that a soft landing is never guaranteed.*

—SARAH DESSEN

# CHAPTER 33

Joanna was checking her emails when she suddenly shrieked, "Oh geez, I need to finish this project quickly. Holy smoke, I can't believe this!"

Ryan looked up from his phone and smiled. Life was never dull with her. "What now?" he asked.

"*Outlook* magazine wants me to finish this project I'm working on quickly, then go and photograph Kilimanjaro. Can you believe it? Me, climbing Kilimanjaro? And get this, they're offering me a full-time, permanent job! Listen to what the senior editor says: *We admire your talent and would like to have you onboard as a full-time photo journalist.* Can you believe it? They want an answer ASAP because this assignment on Kilimanjaro needs to get started pronto. My God, do you realize what this means? They have international readership, Ryan. Who knows what might be in the cards after that—travel to foreign places? Woo-hoo. My career is taking off. I'm a photo journalist."

"That's awesome, Joanna." He watched her excitement, while feeling his heart sink. Where did that leave him? "So, what about your job with the advertising agency in Durban?"

"I guess I'll have to resign." She thought for a moment and added, "I hope Tom won't feel I'm letting him down, but man oh man—this is the job of a lifetime. I'd be crazy not to take it."

"I'm sure your father will be proud of you. He'll understand."

"I hope so. I mean, I love the people I've been working with, especially Gabby, and I'm thankful Tom helped me get the job, but I don't love advertising. This new job is a dream come true; I'll be exploring the continent—the world maybe—camera in hand, without having to come up with cutesy ideas for some bloody thing that nobody needs or wants."

Ryan's smile hid a sense of dread.

"By the way," she added, "the editor says I should take a couple of helpers with me to climb Kilimanjaro—an assistant photographer, and a porter. You interested?"

The smile on Ryan's face stretched so wide that it almost didn't fit his face.

"We should phone Mpilo and tell him the good news, see if he wants to come." She laughed and added, "Do you want to be the porter or the other guy?"

"I'm not fussy, as long as I get to go."

"We need to start the climb on November 30th apparently. When is Mandy's wedding?"

"Sometime in the middle of November," Ryan replied vaguely. (Mandy had felt elated when he'd first told her that the American woman and David were getting married, and especially happy that Ryan showed no signs of disappointment about it. In fact, he seemed genuinely pleased for her—making the last vestiges of Joanna's jealousy disappear. She'd breathed a quiet sigh of relief.)

"Well, we'll have to leave for Arusha right after the wedding. It'll be a bit of a rush—is that OK with you?"

The smile didn't leave his face as he hugged her. "Oh my gosh, no. Joanna, you are the most amazing woman. You make everything exciting, like drinking champagne," he said, holding her face in his hands. "I never want there to be a day in my life that doesn't have you in it. OK?"

"Yikes. That's a big ask," she replied, laughing.

"Not really," he said, running his fingers over her cheeks and hair. "I love you so much." He'd never uttered those words to her before and the moment he said them, he felt her stiffen. Things had been going so well between them that he felt he had gained her trust. Desperate to hold onto her, he whispered again, "I love you, Joanna."

"I heard you," she said, pulling away.

He held his breath, unsure what to say next. He could sense the wall going up around her again.

"How do you know it's love?" She spoke so softly he almost couldn't hear her, but he could see her frown.

He swallowed hard. "Because when I'm with you, I'm happy. When I'm not, I miss you. I haven't analyzed it, but I reckon that's what love is. I know we can't be together every minute of every day, but I don't only want to climb Kilimanjaro with you—I want to be with you always."

"You make it sound so simple."

"It is simple. It's not something I have to think about—I just know how I feel about you."

She sighed. "I envy the way you know your own mind. I wish I could be like that—but I'm not. I don't know... maybe I love you too, I'm just not sure."

His eyebrows rose. "*Maybe* you love me? *Maybe?* C'mon, you've just asked me to climb Kilimanjaro with you. Surely you must love me to do that."

"Well, I'm asking Mpilo to come with me as well. What does that mean? Do I love Mpilo too?"

"It means that you love us both, but hell—please say it's not in the same way."

She started to giggle, and then to laugh. "Definitely not in the same way!"

"You see, that's what I mean. We make each other happy," Ryan said. "And maybe I know your mind, too, as well as my own. I say you *do* love me."

Joanna was still laughing as she nodded and said, "I think you're right. Yes, I do."

*The wall has come down*, he thought with relief. On impulse, he dropped to one knee and said, "Joanna Nel, will you marry me?"

Her laughter stopped and the smile disappeared immediately. She stared at him in silence and neither of them moved. Swallowing hard, she said, "Love is one thing, but I'm not so sure about marriage."

Ryan inwardly cursed himself. Why had he thought for one moment that she didn't still have that emotional barrier? All the signs had been there; it had been wishful thinking on his part. He stood up slowly and watched as she turned away from him.

"I haven't seen marriage work too well. It seems to be an institution destined to make people unhappy," she said, standing as rigid as a soldier on parade.

Ryan cleared his throat, searching for words. "I understand why you're wary of marriage. I get it. Neither of your parents had marriages that worked, and you grew up with that bastard beating the crap out of your mom. Marriage doesn't have to be like that, though." He decided he had nothing to lose by adding, "Come to San Francisco with me and meet my parents. They're growing old together and they're still best friends. They're still crazy about one another. We can have that, Joanna, I know we can. And my parents will love you. I've told them all about you."

She shook her head—the frown was still there. "The trouble is that I keep hearing August Nel saying romantic love is nothing but lust and hormones—and that scares the heck out of me. What if he's right?"

"Oh yes, he was such an expert on love and marriage, wasn't he! Forget about him. He's gone, dead and buried. If you let him cloud your thinking, the past is going to keep messing up the future for you. Put him out of your mind."

Neither of them spoke as she stared at a spot on the ground, lost in thought. She was thinking about her mother and grandmother and their ill-fated love. She remembered how her mother had wished Joanna would not suffer the same fate. And when Joanna had expressed uncertainty about her feelings, she recalled her mother saying: when you find love, don't let it slip away.

Ryan stood watching her, not knowing what was going on in her head. Eventually, when he could stand the silence no longer, he repeated himself. "Joanna, it's a yes or no question. Will you marry me?"

He held his breath as he waited for an answer. Her brow was creased as she seemed to be struggling with her emotions. It was impossible to know what she was thinking—until finally her frown disappeared and she looked up at him with a hint of a smile.

"Can we get married at Mkuze?"

Relief flooded through him as he put his arms around her and closed his eyes. Holding her tight, he whispered, "Definitely. With an orchestra of crickets—and a lion solo for back up. I can think of nothing better."

It was an evening to remember. They dined out, drank champagne, laughed, made love, and fell into a deep, satisfied sleep—only to be jolted awake when Joanna's phone rang, long after midnight.

It was Tom calling her. Glancing at the clock, she could tell from the time and the urgency in his voice that something was wrong. "Joanna, where are you?" he asked.

"In Stellenbosch. Why? What's the matter?"

"Something's not right with your mother."

"What do you mean?" She sat up in bed and her heart began to race.

"I just had a strange email from her. I think you should call her."

Joanna frowned. "Why? What did it say?"

"Never mind. Just call her right away, please."

He ended the call without any explanation and Joanna apologized to Ryan. "Sorry, I just need to check up on my mom." Without waiting for his response, she hit the speed dial button, her heart pounding as she did so. It took a minute for the call to connect, but the phone rang a few times and then cut off. She called again. This time the call was answered, but an unintelligible sound was all she could hear.

"Mom, are you OK?"

There was a muffled groan in response, and then silence.

"Sweet Jesus," she shrieked. Her heart was racing as she called 112 and gave her mother's address. Then she called Esther, who had a key to their mother's flat; her sister said she would be there as fast as she could. Joanna told Esther that she was an hour away but would depart immediately—leaving Ryan to pack their bags and settle their bills in the morning.

"Just go," he said. "I'll make my way back to Cape Town by taxi."

"God, I hate taxis, Ryan, after all we've been through with them."

"That was then; this is now. It's not going to happen again. I'll be quite safe. Just go—drive carefully. And please keep your doors locked."

Esther called Joanna on the road to tell her that their mom was in the emergency room at Groote Schuur Hospital; she had no idea why. Joanna went directly there and sat for an hour and a half waiting with her sisters, not knowing what was happening. They were finally allowed to see their mother when Petra was moved into intensive care, where a young intern explained that their mom's blood pressure was extremely low. This was a concern for the doctors. "I have to tell you," the intern said, "your mother got here in the nick of time. She took an overdose of sleeping pills. We resuscitated her and gave her a stomach pump, but she's not out of the woods yet."

"Oh, my God," Joanna gasped.

"We're monitoring her carefully; she's in good hands." He paused a moment and asked, "Any idea why she might've done this?"

The sisters looked at one another in horror. After a minute, Joanna said, "Her husband died a few months ago..."

"Oh, I see," the doctor said, "but there will have to be a police report, I'm afraid. And, in these circumstances, we strongly recommend counseling. I trust your mother will have the full support of her family as well."

Joanna nodded, while Esther and Emma answered in unison. "Yes, of course. We'll take care of her."

"God, if Tom hadn't called me, and I hadn't called Mom, she might've been dead by now," Joanna gasped.

They were able to see Petra briefly, but she didn't register they were there. It was traumatic seeing her lying with machines, tubes and drips attached to her, and an oxygen mask covering half her face. The nurse in attendance was going back and forth between their mother and other patients; she was kindly towards them, but suggested they come back the following day during visiting hours. The ward was busy and they were apparently in the way.

Her sisters urged Joanna to stay with one of them, but she chose instead to return to her mother's flat. She wanted to be there, surrounded by her mom's things, and besides—that's where Ryan would come later. Her heart was heavy when she walked in the door and saw the bedroom where her mother had so nearly died. As she sat on the edge of the bed, she put her head in her hands and said aloud, "Why, Mom? What made you do this? I am so, so sorry. I didn't realize how unhappy you were."

It was as she wiped her eyes that she saw a piece of paper lying on the floor. A suicide note, she wondered? Would it explain why her mother had been desperate enough to try and end her life? But when she grabbed it and read the words, her blood began to boil. So, this was what had pushed her mother over the edge.

Grabbing her phone, even though it was 4:30 a.m., she texted her father: *My mom is in ICU. I need to speak to you.*

He texted back immediately: *Come over right away.*

When she strode through his door, Joanna was clenching her fists and grinding her teeth. Tom was quick to ask, "How is your mother? What happened? Is she OK?"

"No, she's not. It's touch and go whether she makes it. She's in ICU at Groote Schuur because she OD'd on sleeping pills."

"Oh Jesus. I was afraid something like that might happen."

Joanna turned on him and blurted out, "So why in God's name did you send her that letter? No, don't answer me, listen to me. I read the letter you sent her—it was lying next to her bed. It was probably the last thing she saw before trying to end her life. It was bloody cruel. What the hell were you thinking? This is all your fault.

"You have no idea what sort of life she endured, trying to protect the people she loved from an abusive husband. He was vicious. I'm sorry if you weren't first on that list, but she didn't feel responsible for you when she left you. She felt entirely responsible for her mother and children, and she knew what August Nel was capable of if she tried to leave him. I could understand that. God, if I could forgive her, why the hell couldn't you?"

Tom opened his mouth to speak, but she cut him off. "I'll tell you why. Because you're in love with yourself and that bloody photograph over there, hanging on the wall. That's what matters most to you. I thought you had it in your study because you loved my mother. I was wrong. You resurrected it and have it hanging here in your flat because of your ego; because you won first fucking prize with this bloody masterpiece of yours. But the woman in the photograph—you have no idea about her. You don't care about her. All you care about is yourself."

"Joanna, stop it," Tom said. "That's enough. I don't want to hear any more of this. You're distraught because of what's happened. You're saying things you'll regret later."

"No, I'm not. I mean every word I've said and if my mom doesn't recover, I'll blame you for her death. The injury you caused was worse than when August stabbed her. He went ballistic after seeing that wretched photograph of yours. But I'm telling you, the way you attacked her in that note was just as bad. It was cruel. You should be ashamed of yourself.

"My mother always believed in you—she said nothing but good things about you, and what a fine father I had. I thought so too when I met you—but not anymore. I thought you loved me, but you couldn't do this to my mother if you did; you know how much she means to me. My mom has always known what love is; she loves her family with every fiber of her being. But you...you're in love with yourself."

Joanna stopped a moment to draw breath, glancing at the photograph hanging on the wall. "I hate that fucking thing. I wish I'd never taken a picture of it and sent it to you. I hate it. It's a lie. It's all lies. What freedom did my mother ever know? None whatsoever." With that she burst into tears.

Tom was shaken. Nothing in the world mattered more to him than his daughter. He'd only just found her and he couldn't bear to lose her now. To hear these words coming from her was like a dagger to his heart—and her words pained him. Was she right? Why could he not forgive Petra when Joanna had found it in her heart to do so? She had been equally wronged. It had even been worse for her because she had to grow up with that monster.

With a heavy heart, he walked over to his daughter and murmured, "I'm so sorry, Joanna, sorry for everything. I've been a fool. I let anger consume me so much that I failed to see reason. I love you more than anything in this world and I can't bear to think that I've caused this much pain to you and your mother. I'm so sorry."

Joanna shrugged and looked away; she couldn't speak to him anymore. Walking out onto the balcony, her knuckles were white as she gripped the railing and stared up at the stars, trying to control her emotions. And then she felt her anger giving way to unbearable disappointment, which was almost worse; she'd so badly wanted to believe in her father. Suddenly she was aware of him standing next to her and she tensed.

"I'm really sorry, Joanna," he said once again.

"You're apologizing to the wrong person," she snapped, without looking at him. With that, she turned and left in a hurry, desperate to get away from him.

# CHAPTER 34

Still in his pajamas, Tom raced after his daughter into the corridor. He caught sight of her as she waited for the lift, but when she saw him coming, she pressed the call button with urgency and turned her back on him. "Wait, Joanna," he shouted, but it was too late. Before he could reach her, the door opened and she climbed into the lift. The doors shut—and she was gone. He ran and tried to stop her by pressing the button, but the lift had already left—and as he watched the numbers above the door indicate how fast the thing was descending, despair overcame him. He would never be able to catch up with her—and she had made it clear that she didn't want to speak to him.

Just then, he heard a neighbor's door open and a man's face peeped out behind the security chain. "What's going on? Are you alright, mate?"

Tom shrugged. By way of explanation, he said, "A bit of a disagreement with my daughter. Sorry to disturb you."

"No worries. I just wasn't sure what was happening out here. Kids these days have no regard for time, do they? Their body clocks are different from ours. I mean look at the time now! But if that's all it is and you're sure you're OK, go back to bed and forget about it. You can sort it out in the morning." With that, the man closed his door.

When Tom turned around and looked again at the

numbers, he realized that the lift had reached the ground floor. His daughter was gone and he had no idea where she was staying, nor where her mother was currently living. All he knew was that Petra was in ICU at Groote Schuur Hospital, and she might die. But Joanna would be going there at some point; that's where he would find her.

He made his way back into his flat and stopped to look at the photograph that his daughter had recently scorned. Her words stung, but instead of causing anger or indignation in him, he felt enormous sorrow—and tears began to stream down his face. If only it was as easy as going back to bed and sorting it out in the morning, but that wasn't going to happen without some action on his part.

He stood weeping in front of the photograph of Petra, but deep in thought. Joanna was wrong. It wasn't vanity that made him love this work of art. No, he had loved Petra. The photograph captured their love, and it was there forever for him to remember. When he looked at it, he was able to feel again the joy she had brought into his life, the tenderness. *That* was why he loved the photograph. It took him back to a moment in time when the world had been full of promise—because he was in love with a wonderful woman, and she loved him in return. Life was good and he had lived in hope that she would agree to leave her husband and marry him.

Which made his thoughts turn to something he had long tried to suppress—that he should've gone ahead and divorced Cynthia way back then. He should have been honest with himself and taken the lead. He should've made it clear to Petra that he meant what he said—that he would protect her and her daughters, as well as her mother. He'd had the means to do it. Would that have made a difference? Would she have married him then?

Why didn't he do that? Everything could've been so different. The more he allowed himself to think about this, the more he was overcome with remorse—and regret that he hadn't been man enough to take the lead. It hadn't been fair to Petra—or Cynthia, for that matter.

When he'd discovered the truth about Petra leaving him, he hadn't considered that he was to blame in any way for what she had done. He saw it as her fault entirely; she had lied to him, and cheated him out of his daughter. But now, Joanna had opened his eyes, making him recognize his shortcomings—and igniting his long-suppressed doubts about himself. He saw all too clearly that he'd played a major part in Petra's predicament all those years ago. His words of love had not been enough to assure her—he should have acted on them. He should've left Cynthia.

Finally, he was able to understand how difficult it had been for Petra, the woman he loved—the woman he still loved. He had got her pregnant—and his inaction had left her in a terrible position. She had good reason to hate him. He hoped that she didn't.

His head dropped into his hands as he squeezed his eyes tightly shut. "Please don't die, Petra," he groaned. "Don't die." His fingers were shaking as he called Groote Schuur Hospital and his voice trembled when he finally reached a nurse in the ICU Department. "Please can you tell me how Petra Nel is doing?" he asked.

"Who is this? Are you a family member? I only see her daughters' names listed as family members."

He swallowed hard and said, "I'm Joanna's father."

"I see. Well, just a moment—let me check."

He could hear footsteps, and then papers rustling—and all the while he held his breath. Finally, the nurse said, "I'm happy to tell you, sir, she's out of danger."

Tom could hardly utter his thanks before he fell to his knees, sobbing.

# CHAPTER 35

Exhaustion overcame Joanna and she fell into a deep sleep on Petra's bed, clutching the pillow where she could smell the sweet scent of her mom's hair. She awoke with a start when the doorbell rang and for a few moments, she was disoriented. When it rang again, she ran to answer it and discovered Ryan standing there, holding their bags.

"What time is it?" she gasped.

"11:30. It's almost lunchtime."

"Oh geez, I need to call the hospital right now."

Ryan came in and put the backpacks down. "What happened with your mom?"

It was hard for Joanna to say the words; she couldn't bring herself to say that her mother had tried to commit suicide. She whitewashed it instead and said, "She took too many sleeping pills. They had to do a stomach pump. I really need to call the nurse and see how she is this morning."

As Joanna grabbed her phone, he saw how pained she looked and felt his heart constrict. Joanna and her mom were so close, which begged the question why Petra Nel would try to take her own life. When tears started to roll down Joanna's cheeks, he feared the worst. The euphoria of the previous night was gone and he felt himself go cold as he watched her listening to the nurse. When Joanna began to cry, he rushed to console her, but she ended the call and turned to him, sobbing and laughing at the same time. "My mom has pulled through. She's going to be OK," she said. They were tears of relief.

They raced to Groote Schuur, making it there in time for visiting hours. Sitting up in bed, Petra had color in her cheeks and looked much improved since the previous night. Her face lit up when she saw her daughter and she put her arms out to Joanna, who fell into them, whispering, "Oh Mom, I'm so glad you're..." The sentence was left unfinished as the two women hugged each another.

Ryan felt himself choking up as he watched mother and daughter embracing. Feeling like an intruder, he turned to walk away—but Petra pulled away from Joanna and called him back. "Don't go, Ryan." Her voice was hoarse, although her gaze was steady. "I'm very glad Joanna has you by her side for support. I'm sorry I've caused so much..." She choked on her words and swallowed hard, grasping her throat.

"It's OK, Mom. Don't try to talk now," Joanna said.

Petra shook her head, vehemently. "No, I want you to know something. It's important." Her voice was raspy and she reached for a sip of water to soothe her throat. When she was able to speak again, she said, "It was a terrible mistake, Joanna. I wasn't trying to kill myself, I just wanted to sleep. I promise you."

Joanna nodded, wanting to believe her mother. Not to do so was unbearable.

Petra knew her daughter well though, and saw the uncertainty in her face. "It's the truth, I promise you, my liefling. It was a mistake. One pill didn't work and I was desperate to sleep, so I took some more. You see, they were beyond their expiration date and I didn't realize they still had so much strength in them. I thought I needed more because just one pill didn't work." She stared into Joanna's eyes, beseeching her daughter to believe her. "I'm so sorry this happened. I wasn't trying to kill myself; I would never do that. I just wanted to sleep. Please believe me."

Her mom looked so contrite that Joanna's doubts were dispelled. She buried her face in her mother's hair and whispered, "I do. I believe you, Mom. I just couldn't bear it if anything happened to you."

"Don't worry, liefling, I'm better now. I'm so happy that I'm still alive and I'm sorry I gave you such a fright. It was a terrible mistake. I'll never do that again. If I can't sleep, I'll get up and read a book. I'll never take another sleeping pill. I promise you. I won't..."

She was interrupted by the noise of the door opening. Petra stopped talking and they all turned to see a pair of legs appear, topped by two arms. The arms were laden with so many flowers that they obscured the face of the person holding them. The flowers were proteas.

Joanna did a double-take. "Oh, my gosh," she said. "Who's sending you such an enormous bouquet?"

Petra knew. She didn't need to see a face. She said just one word: "Tom?"

As Tom walked towards her mother, Joanna and Ryan glanced at each other and stood aside to make room for him. When he reached Petra's bedside, he laid the flowers on a nightstand and stood looking at her for a few moments, before swallowing hard. In a soft voice, he said, "I'm so sorry Petra... Can you ever forgive me?"

Joanna held her breath. She saw her mother's bottom lip quivering, but her mom didn't respond.

"I lost you once, I can't lose you again. You and our daughter are everything to me. I'm so sorry for all the pain I've caused you, both of you. I hope you don't hate me for it. I've been a fool, a selfish bloody fool."

Joanna stood absolutely still, waiting for her mother's response.

Petra still didn't speak.

"Please forgive me. I love you, I always have. My anger and stubborn pride got in the way, though. I'm so sorry, Petra. I've been pig-headed and unreasonable; I never let myself see things from your point of view. I was a lucky man to have your love once. Perhaps I don't deserve your forgiveness, but if you can find it in your heart to do so—and love me once more—I promise I'll never make that mistake again. I love you with all my heart. Please trust me."

Petra remained silent. Her eyes narrowed as she stared at him, and a frown creased her forehead. She shook her head and murmured, "I don't know, Tom. There's been a lot of water under the bridge. So many things have been said and done..."

"I know that, Petra. I know it. We were so happy once, and then we lost it. We both made mistakes and we lost each other. But let's try again. Come home with me; we'll make it our home. We've wasted so much time...let's put the past behind us. Can we start again, please?"

Tears started to roll down her cheeks and her frown slowly disappeared. There was just a moment's hesitation before Petra nodded and put her arms out to him.

Observing their embrace, Joanna's eyes welled with tears. She watched them for a moment, and then, with a faint smile, signaled to Ryan that they should leave the room. Much as she wanted to hear what was said between her parents, it didn't seem right to listen.

Once out in the hallway, she took Ryan's hands and held them tightly. It was a few moments before she was able to speak without choking on her words. When she finally collected herself, she shook her head and said softly, "I'm finding it hard to believe that my parents might finally be together after all this time. I've longed for it to happen but I never thought it would. It makes me really happy—but I'm also really nervous they'll mess things up again. God, my dad's been such a fool. I'm thankful he's come to his senses at last—and I respect him for that. It takes a lot to admit you were wrong." She hesitated before blurting out a troubling thought. "I have this feeling that I should stick around to make sure everything works out with them; I want them to be happy together. Maybe my plans will have to wait; I can't go climbing Kilimanjaro now. This is too important. It means much more than any job."

"No, no, no. You can't do that, Joanna. They're the ones who have to make it work. They're responsible for their own happiness; it's not up to you."

She wiped tears from her eyes. "I know that, but I'm afraid they'll screw it all up."

Ryan shook his head. "It's over to them. You shouldn't put your life on hold because of your concerns about them. I can see why you're worried—they've spent more than twenty years apart, and it's not like this is a fairy tale where someone can just wave a magic wand and make everyone live happily ever after. That would be unrealistic. But they both want it to work, and they've each known enough unhappiness to know that they don't want to go back to that unhappy place."

"I suppose you're right—if they want it badly enough, they'll make it work. I want to believe that. Maybe they'll treasure what they have even more, because they lost it once. You're very wise, you know." She dried her eyes with her sleeve and looked up at him. "You know, if there's something I've learned from all this, Ryan—it's that you shouldn't be so full of fear that you deny love. I guess that's what I've been doing, isn't it? I've also been a fool, just like my parents." She squeezed his hands and added, "Thank you for loving me—and being so patient."

He smiled, too filled with emotion to speak, but Joanna wasn't finished; she wanted to say what was in her heart, with no holds barred. "How lucky we were to find each other in Mkuze that day. What were the chances of it happening? A guy from San Francisco and a woman from Cape Town, coming together in the same place at the same time, somewhere in a remote game reserve in Africa—and now we're going to be married there. I think I fell in love with you next to the fire that first day we met, but I've been dancing around ever since, too afraid to admit it." Still holding his hands, in an unwavering voice she said, "I don't just *think* it, I *know* that I love you more than anything in the world—and I won't let what we have slip away. This is for keeps."

# GLOSSARY

Ag ................................ *an expression of frustration or disgust*

Bakkie ........................ *a small truck*

Biltong ....................... *dried meat, similar to jerky*

Cape Coloureds...... *a South African ethnic group comprised of persons of multiple mixed races (European, San, African, S.E. Asian), it is one of the predominant population groups of the Western Cape. The spelling 'Coloured' (rather than the American form 'colored') is the way it is used in South Africa for this group of people.*

Doos ........................... *a box, or a womb, but also a term used derogatively to describe someone*

Dorp ........................... *a small town (Afrikaans)*

Fokken........................ *a curse word, similar in sound and meaning to one used in English*

Hamba........................ *go away (Zulu)*

Ja ................................ *Yes*

Jislaaik....................... *an expression of shock, pronounced yislike (Afrikaans)*

Jussus ........................ *an exclamation emphasizing shock or disbelief, meaning Jesus or Jeepers (Afrikaans)*

Liefling ...................... *darling (Afrikaans)*

Load Shedding ........ *scheduled power outages occurring daily in South Africa. When the demand for electricity exceeds the available supply, planned supply interruptions are carried out. It is a controlled way of rotating the available electricity between all customers.*

Ma ............................... *mom*

Pa ................................. *dad*

San .............................. *The San people are the oldest inhabitants of Southern Africa, where they have lived for at least 20,000 years.*

Sisi .............................. *sister*

# ACKNOWLEDGEMENTS

While writing might be a solitary activity, it takes a team to complete a book. I am grateful to my husband for listening as I discussed, at length, the characters and plot of A LABYRINTH OF SECRETS. His comments were always insightful and his patience commendable! My thanks also to Terry Hayward for his help describing court procedures to me. Thanks too to my editors, Jessica Powers and Carol Peske, whose recommendations were invaluable in shaping the novel. Thank you also to Lindsay and Luke Rothwell for their input regarding the cover, as well as to Karen Vermeulen for the cover design, and to Kathy McInnis for putting it all together.

**Other books by Glynnis Hayward:**

*A TELLING TIME*

*A SIGNIFICANT TEST OF BLOOD*

*FOUR SIDES TO A STORY*

*ROADS AND BRIDGES*
(You can read more about Mandy, David, Jabulani and Father Dlamini in *Roads and Bridges*.)

Printed in the USA
CPSIA information can be obtained
at www.ICGtesting.com
CBHW020044261223
2930CB00005B/114